THE ATTACK

Catherine Jinks has published more than forty books for adults and children. She has won many awards including the Victorian Premier's Literary Award, the Aurealis Award for science fiction, the Adelaide Festival Award and the Davitt Award for crime fiction. Catherine is a four-time winner of the Children's Book Council of Australia Book of the Year Award and in 2001 was presented with a Centenary Medal for her contribution to Australian children's literature. She lives in the Blue Mountains of New South Wales.

THE
ATTACK
CATHERINE JINKS

TEXT PUBLISHING MELBOURNE AUSTRALIA

textpublishing.com.au

The Text Publishing Company
Swann House, 22 William Street, Melbourne Victoria 3000, Australia

The Text Publishing Company (UK) Ltd
130 Wood Street, London EC2V 6DL, United Kingdom

Published by The Text Publishing Company, 2021

Book design by Text
Cover image by Austockphoto
Typeset in Adobe Garamond Pro 13/18pt by J&M Typesetting

Printed and bound in Australia by Griffin Press, part of Ovato, an accredited ISO/NZS 14001:2004 Environmental Management System printer.

ISBN: 9781922458117 (paperback)
ISBN: 9781922459442 (ebook)

A catalogue record for this book is available from the National Library of Australia.

This book is printed on paper certified against the Forest Stewardship Council® Standards. Griffin Press holds FSC chain-of-custody certification SGSHK-COC-005088. FSC promotes environmentally responsible, socially beneficial and economically viable management of the world's forests.

To Brian Jinks

2019

I RECOGNISED HIM at once. He was ten years older and three times bigger, but his eyes were the same—wideset and ice-green, with thick, dark lashes. He was still skinny. Still scabby. Still at odds with the world.

I took one look at him and it all came flooding back. Otford. Joyce. The lies. The police.

I'd fled to a deserted island, but I couldn't seem to escape Aaron Rooney.

He arrived on a Sunday with twelve other boys. Their ferry was late. I'd been waiting on the jetty for a good twenty minutes when MV *Kooringal* chugged to a halt in front of me, nudging the piles and churning up water. From the bow I was thrown a mooring line, which I looped around the nearest bollard. The throb of the engine was almost drowned by a buzz of excited voices.

Something was wrong. The ferry master wore a flinty expression. I could sense the deckhand's disquiet. Scanning the gaggle of teenage boys near the stern, I realised one of them was wrapped in a towel. His hair looked wet—or was it just greasy? Beside him, Shaun Steiger was grim-faced.

'Get back!' Shaun barked. 'Give the deckhand some room!'

He was dressed for combat. The boys were in hoodies and ripped jeans. They shouldered their lumpy backpacks, staggering as the deck bobbed beneath them. I spotted Joe Malouf helping one of the boys with his straps and buckles. Like Shaun, Joe was wearing fatigues. All four veterans were crisply turned out in spotless uniforms, neat buzzcuts and polished boots. They looked weirdly immaculate next to the teenagers.

'All right, fall in!' Shaun was using his parade-ground voice. Behind him, a dark kid with a big grin pretended to throw one leg over the bulwark. 'Fall in means line up, Mr Kollios,' Shaun continued, as if he had eyes in the back of his head. 'We don't want another accident.'

Another accident?

The deckhand shoved one end of the gangway onto the weathered boards of the jetty, then moved aside as the whooping, jostling boys spilled past her.

'Take your time!' Shaun blared. I was trying to count heads. Two. Three. Four. One of the boys started stomping towards the boathouse.

'Dean! Get back here!' Joe yelled. When the fleeing kid ignored him, he shot off in pursuit.

Six. Seven. Eight. Suddenly I saw those eyes—those familiar eyes—and my stomach clenched.

No. It couldn't be.

'Hi, Robyn.' Shaun stopped to greet me, punctilious as always. He stood at ease, feet apart, hands clasped behind him. 'You got a delivery?'

He was looking at my wheelbarrow. I nodded, my own gaze following the kid in the black Satanic Temple T-shirt. Aaron? No. Surely not.

'Do you want some help?' asked Shaun. 'Rhys could spare a minute. Eh, Rhys?'

'Roger that.' Rhys was the youngest veteran, and the tallest. I stood eye to eye with Shaun, who was six foot in his socks, but Rhys towered over us both. A gentle giant with curly blond hair, Rhys was a quiet, laid-back kind of guy because he didn't need to be anything else.

'There isn't much. Most of the stuff came yesterday.' I'd finished counting heads: thirteen. That wasn't right. There were supposed to be fourteen campers. Where was the last kid? He couldn't be on board; the deckhand was already heaving my boxes onto the jetty.

'Is that everyone?' I asked.

'Vijay did a runner on his way to Cleveland. Don't know if his poor mum's found him yet.' Shaun pivoted on his heel and pointed at the boy in the towel. 'Flynn tried to get away too. Jumped off the boat.'

I gasped.

'He's a bit of a drama queen.' Shaun's voice was dry and

reassuring. 'I said to him after we fished him out: it was gutsy, mate, but it was stupid. There's a hell of a lot of sharks in Moreton Bay.'

'Is he all right?'

'Oh, yeah. Scared himself shitless. And then he got a huge dressing-down from the skipper.' Shaun nodded at the ferry master, who was watching us from the wheelhouse window and didn't nod back. 'I hope this won't put a spanner in the works,' Shaun said. He didn't sound worried because he never sounded worried. As a commanding officer he ticked every box: he was calm but not disengaged, leathery but not ancient, greying at the temples but still dark on the crown. 'If we get banned from the ferry service, we'll have to charter a boat,' he continued thoughtfully, as the gangway was dragged back on board with a crash. 'It'll be pricey. Anyway, let's hope Flynn's got it out of his system. You right there, Rhys?'

'Yep.' Rhys had already dumped a box of iceberg lettuce into my wheelbarrow.

'Okay. Let's make a move, then.' Shaun turned back to me. 'So we'll see you in ten minutes? On the parade ground?'

He was talking about the open stretch of grass that lay between the old male and female compounds. The dirt road from the jetty ended right there, in front of the dining hall.

I nodded. 'Who's that kid in the black T-shirt? The droopy one with hair all over his face?'

Shaun glanced towards the campers, who were retreating down the jetty. I could almost hear gears clicking as he worked his way through a mental list. 'That's Darren,' he said at last.

4

'Darren King. Why? Do you know him?'

Darren? 'Maybe.' I needed another look.

'His mum'll be at the passing-out parade. Sue King? Ring a bell?' When I shook my head, Shaun started moving off. 'This won't take long,' he told me over his shoulder. 'We'll run through the usual introductions. And if there's anything you want to say...'

'One of the toilets is broken. There's a sign on the door.' I was waiting for a replacement fill valve.

Shaun raised his hand without looking back. Rhys had already flung both mooring lines at the deckhand, who was closing the starboard gate as the *Kooringal* pulled away from me. The horn sounded once, twice, three times. Shaun shouted an order.

I stood for a moment, gazing at the ferry's white wake. Darren? Aaron?

Weird.

All my deliveries came by ferry because I lived on Finch Island—or, more correctly, Buangan Pa. It had once been a lazaret. Half the old buildings had collapsed; the rest of them, lovingly restored, had been turned into a fairly basic camping and conference centre. The fences were gone. Nine lepers' huts were now fully furnished cabins. The men's dining hall was still a dining hall, but the women's had become a dormitory, as had the hospital.

Every building had been constructed in that ubiquitous

pre-war government style of white weatherboard, deep verandas and generous windows. Even the lepers' huts had their own little verandas, though not in the Aboriginal compound. If you were a black leper, you were given a hut made of corrugated iron with a concrete floor and no glass in the windows.

Those huts were pretty grim. They were at the very rear of the complex, not far from the cemetery, and shielded from the other buildings by a thicket of she-oak. I had a feeling my employer didn't want to advertise their existence. They were heritage listed so they had to be well maintained, but they were embarrassing. Shameful.

It was hard enough persuading people to book holidays in an old leper colony without that niggling reminder of Indigenous torment. Even our corporate bookings were negligible, probably because the huts didn't have bathrooms. Two former bathhouses had been nicely refitted with composting toilets and private shower cubicles, but most bankers these days probably want heated towel rails. And though the old matron's house had its own bathroom—along with three bedrooms, a kitchen and a living room, all for hire—the only other private bathroom on the island was at my place.

I lived in the back of the superintendent's quarters, behind the office and the 'museum': a large room full of photos, chamber pots, medical equipment, ledgers, samplers and cricket bats. There was also a model of the original complex, with every tiny building neatly labelled. The school groups that came to the island were always forced to shuffle past this collection, clutching their pens and project sheets. Biology classes sometimes tramped down to the mangrove swamps, where they made notes and complained about the insects. But there weren't many school visitors. My busy times were during the holidays, when the whole place was booked out by religious groups.

Otherwise, I did most of my business with Shaun's company, Vetnet.

Once a month Shaun and his staff would book the island for a six-day boot camp. They would bring over about fifteen teenage boys and give them a dose of tough love. Thanks to Shaun, I'd dealt with a lot of broken doorknobs and urine in unexpected places. But the camps must have been successful, because Shaun kept coming back. And back.

Most of the boys were sent by parents or foster carers. Some were referred by the police as part of a government diversion program. Many were problem kids. Marginal kids. Kids with learning difficulties, behavioural issues, psychological disorders. I don't know how many of them realised they'd come to an old leper colony—the word 'leper' never passed Shaun's lips. I'm not sure if most of the boys even knew what lepers were. But there was a sign near the office, and another on the door of the museum. Someone always twigged in the end.

'We're just another bunch of fucking lepers,' I heard one camper growl after he'd read the sign. 'They just want us out of sight in the middle of fucking nowhere.'

He made it sound like a bad thing. But then again, he wasn't me.

'Welcome to Finch Island. From now on you'll call me sir.'

Shaun's voice echoed across the parade ground. Thirteen boys were lined up on the grass in front of him, each standing behind a pile of clothes: a pair of army boots, some khaki socks, a boonie hat and a set of folded camo fatigues, all with name tags. I'd placed the kits in two careful rows, at arm's length from each other.

'I've done three tours of Afghanistan with the Australian Defence Force,' Shaun said, 'and I'm here to tell you I wouldn't have survived those tours without discipline, loyalty, honesty and respect.'

Some of the boys were listening. Others had let their packs slide to the ground and were flexing their sore shoulders. One had taken out his phone. One was already trying on his uniform.

The kid in the Satanic Temple T-shirt was restlessly kicking the ground. He'd lowered his head, so I couldn't see his face. But there was something ominously familiar about his inability to keep still.

'Mr Henderson!' Shaun barked at the phone kid. 'There's no signal on this island, so you might as well put that down.' He didn't even glance in my direction before adding, 'Isn't that right, Ms Ayres?'

As a matter of fact it wasn't. You could pick up a signal in a couple of spots, but you had to climb a hill to do it. I just nodded.

'Ms Ayres is the caretaker here,' Shaun explained. 'She's

employed by Queensland Parks and Wildlife. You will address her as Ms Ayres or ma'am.'

A few boys spared me a look. Most weren't interested. Darren certainly wasn't; he didn't stiffen or raise his head. He didn't seem to recognise my name.

Though Rhys's gaze flicked towards me, he maintained his poker face. So did Joe Malouf. It was Warren Doyle who winked. He was the only veteran with visible scars: a nasty divot near his jaw and another on his neck. Unlike Rhys, who was a big, placid labrador of a guy, or Joe—small and earnest and emotional—Warren had a touch of the maverick. The army had rescued him from a troubled adolescence, so maybe that had something to do with it.

'Ms Ayres is our commander-in-chief. Her rules apply here. She will always have the last word.' This was Shaun's usual spiel, but it never worked. The boys would treat me like a cross between their mother and their maid until I put my foot down. It helped that I was tall and rangy; you always have an advantage when kids need to look up at you. 'Is there anything you'd like to add, Ms Ayres?'

'Only that one of the toilets is broken.' I pointed at the men's bathroom. 'There's a sign on the door of the cubicle.'

'All right. Hear that? Stay off the broken toilet.' Shaun's brisk nod told me I could leave if I wanted. He knew I had things to do. Emails to answer. A wheelbarrow to unload.

But I couldn't drag myself away. Not until I was sure.

'On this island you gentlemen are my platoon and I am your platoon commander,' Shaun went on. 'We'll be dividing you into sections. Those in the front row will be section one. I'll be your section commander and Mr Burgin will be your 2IC.' He nodded at Rhys. 'Section two is in the back. Your commander will be Mr Doyle...' This time he aimed the nod at Warren. '...and your 2IC will be Mr Malouf over there. You will address all the officers as sir.' Raising his voice over a low mutter of protest, Shaun snapped, 'Mr King! Eyes on me, please!'

Darren looked up with a scowl—and that scowl made my heart sink.

'Mr King, we don't stare at the ground in this platoon. We look people in the eye because we have respect. Respect for ourselves and respect for each other.' Shaun studied the ragtag collection of teenagers in front of him. Then he said, 'But respect isn't a right. You have to earn it. That's why I want you to empty your bags.'

There was a stunned silence. At last the boy with the phone cried, 'You can't do that!' He had flawless skin and thick, floppy hair so beautifully cut that I decided he must have well-off parents. The only thing marring his perfection was a slightly beaky nose.

'On the contrary, Mr Henderson, we can. Your parents signed a contract to that effect.' Shaun began to pace up and down, pausing to lock eyes with every camper in the front row. 'Bags. Emptied. Now.'

'Fuck this.' It was the kid who'd stormed off the jetty. Shane?...No, Dean. His hair hung in ratty little plaits or dreadlocks—I wasn't sure exactly what they were, but they probably didn't need much maintenance. He was nearly as tall as Rhys, raw-boned, gangly and wild-looking.

He started walking away.

'Report back here, Mr Hoegel!' Shaun's voice cracked through the air like a whip, but the kid kept moving.

'There's nowhere to go, Dean,' Warren weighed in. 'We're on an island.'

Dean ignored him. So Shaun nodded at Rhys, who snapped to attention and charged off like an obedient sheepdog.

By this time several younger boys were dumping the contents of their packs onto the ground: socks, sunscreen, pyjamas, iPads, chargers, earbuds—even a comic book. Joe began to collect all the technology, which he placed in a plastic bin. *My* plastic bin.

'Wait—what?' Henderson, the kid with the fancy haircut, looked appalled. I remembered his full name: Zac Henderson. Casting my mind back to Shaun's notes, I couldn't recall much else about Zac, except that his parents had sent him.

'You can't take my phone!' he yelped, clutching his Kathmandu rucksack.

'You were told not to bring a phone,' Shaun replied. 'You were told it would be confiscated.'

'No, I wasn't!'

'Well, it was right there in the brochure. You should have read the brochure.' Before Zac could speak, Shaun addressed another kid in the front row. 'Mr Bosanko, I need you to empty your bag. Right now.'

Bosanko. I remembered *that* name. Nathan Bosanko

had been referred to Vetnet by the police. He'd already been formally cautioned for carrying a spray can in public. He also seemed to like wandering around other people's properties, though he hadn't been charged with trespassing.

He was small and slight, with little dark eyes like kalamata olives and a tattoo on his wrist that looked home-made. A slightly eerie smile was plastered across his face.

'Okay,' he said. Then he upended his backpack, which disgorged—among other things—a tape measure, a hair ribbon, a tube of icing, a mascara wand and an eraser shaped like a sushi roll.

'Do you have a phone?' asked Shaun. When Nathan produced one from his pocket, Shaun took it and said, 'Good. You'll get it back before you leave.'

Over by the women's bathrooms, Rhys was locked in a standoff with Dean Hoegel. Warren was using the sheer force of his stare to make the older kids shake out their packs. Flynn, the boy who'd jumped overboard, was wailing, 'This is so unfair! I can't do this stupid camp! I have a condition!' Zac Henderson was muttering something about human rights as Joe Malouf stooped to pick up a tattered porn magazine that had tumbled out of a bag in the front row. The owner of this bag was smirking gently; I wondered if the magazine was his way of saying 'fuck you'.

Darren King looked sullen when Shaun finally stopped in front of him. Peering at the veteran through a lank curtain of hair, the teenager offered up that familiar scowl again. But other things about him weren't familiar. His pimples. His chin-fuzz. His shoulders—wide shoulders that stood out like the wings of a coathanger. The rest of his body seemed to dangle off them in a boneless kind of way.

Was he really the same boy? It was hard to tell. Ten years can totally transform a child.

Then he emptied his rucksack. Tumbled among the clothes were a pair of cheap sunglasses, an empty chip packet and an iPhone.

There was also a brown Swiss Army knife. When I saw that, my stomach seemed to do a backflip.

Oh my God, I thought. *It's him. It really is him. It's Aaron Rooney.*

Shit.

2009

JOYCE MUST HAVE brought Aaron to school that first day. I had her name written on my drop-off schedule, though I don't remember seeing her. There were lots of parents buzzing around like flies, so she might have got lost in the crowd. I remember discussing Phoebe's eczema and Caleb's anxiety, but I didn't talk to anyone about Aaron.

Not that I wasn't braced for him. A year earlier, Aaron's parents had been told he 'wasn't ready' for a classroom. He'd just turned five then. Now he was six, and at six you have to start school. What you don't have to do is attend the hour-long transition classes that prepare little kids for their first experience of education.

Aaron hadn't gone to any transition classes. That's always a red flag because kids who miss transition often have issues. Speech problems. Developmental delays. I was new to the school—new to the town—but I'd seen nothing in my handover notes about Aaron. No transition reports. No preschool information. No medical assessments. Nothing.

'Have you met Aaron Rooney?' I'd asked Deb Olsen, who was teaching the class next door. Deb was an Otford girl, born and bred; she seemed to know everyone.

'Oh, Aaron. You can't miss him. Not when he's having a tantrum in Foodworks.' Seeing me wince, she laughed and said, 'I've heard he's a bit of a handful.'

As it turned out, Aaron wasn't the only kid in class who had trouble grasping the rules that first morning. Despite my best efforts, the kindies kept wandering around like farmyard hens. Some of them cried. Some of them yelled. It was always a bit chaotic until they learned what to do when I clapped my hands.

They would start off bewildered. Excited. Maybe a little scared. Aaron was no different—until I gave him a pencil. Day one of kindergarten was normally spent testing the children's skills. Could they point to a number? Turn a page? Follow instructions? When I asked them to draw pictures of their families, I wanted to see if they could hold a pencil.

Aaron couldn't. I watched him. He was squirming at the table closest to my desk—a skinny little boy with dark hair shorn like moleskin. Not all kindy kids are cherubs; some have Aaron's pinched look. His pale green eyes were memorable. So were the scabs on his knees, elbows, knuckles, chin. I made a mental note. Either he had bad coordination or something else was going on.

He tried to stick his pencil in his nose. His ear. His mouth. I crouched next to him and moved his stiff little fingers into the correct position. Beside me, Phoebe Canning studied him with interest. She was a sturdy redhead who claimed to be Aaron's best friend. I'd already identified her as a bit of a queen bee; she'd been telling the other kids what to do, her authority derived from an older sister in year five.

'Look, Aaron,' she said. 'You should hold it like this.'

Aaron scowled. Then he jabbed her with his pencil.

'*Ow!*' Her squeal made everyone glance up. 'You hurt me!'

'Aaron. If you're angry, use your words. Don't hurt people.' I was thinking of the form I would have to fill in.

'I'm not your friend anymore.' Phoebe grabbed her drawing. 'I'm going to sit next to Kayla.'

Aaron threw down his pencil and bolted. But he didn't leave the room. I had enough time to soothe the jangled nerves of the other kids before approaching him in the corner where he was squatting, his back to the class, his head bent over something that made my heart sink.

'What have you got there?' I said, though I could see it was a brown Swiss Army knife.

'Dad gave me it.' His voice was low and hoarse.

Great, I thought, filing that away for later. 'How does it work?'

Aaron showed me. He pulled out the corkscrew, the hook, the scissors. I nodded, keeping one eye on the rest of the class. Then I asked if I could try.

'No,' he said.

'Please? I want to see if I can do it.'

He looked confused. But he surrendered the knife, and

when I pretended to struggle with it, he helped me.

That was good.

By now the other kids were getting interested. Some of them were sliding off their chairs. I lowered my voice and told Aaron I needed to borrow his knife for a while. 'I'll give it back,' I promised. 'When school's finished.'

Aaron frowned. Something sparked in his eyes. Panic? Fury? But before I could continue, the bell rang.

'It's recess!' Phoebe announced. 'We can go play!'

The stampede nearly bowled me over. I had to jump up and wade in. Aaron was so eager to leave that he forgot about his knife. I tucked it into my pocket and made another mental note. *Lock it up.*

There was a rule about bringing favourite toys to school—especially if you could kill people with them.

~

The juniors at Otford primary were corralled into a special part of the playground. They had their own monkey bars, drinking fountains and nubbly expanse of softfall rubber. If they were scared of the bigger kids, they could always find a place to hide.

Not that any of the bigger kids were around, that first day. They weren't due back until the following week.

'I could get used to this,' Deb murmured. We were standing together in the shade, squinting at an empty swathe of bleached grass. Beyond that lay a chainlink fence, and beyond that, shimmering in the sun, the northern end of

Otford dipped gently towards Main Street.

Our school had once occupied an old wooden building on Main Street that was now Cool Beans Café. The new school was two blocks back from the shops. Six weeks earlier, on arriving in Otford, I'd been struck by the fact that the town seemed to have two of everything: butchers, supermarkets, hairdressers, pharmacies, petrol stations, pubs, primary schools. The Catholic school was on the south side, near the church; it was a two-storey Gothic pile ringed by demountables. Our school was more modest—a cluster of low brick buildings with deep verandas and lots of power points. I was impressed by the carpets, ramps, air conditioning and staff toilets.

The playground was big. Very big.

'If only we could always have just twenty-four kids rattling around in here,' said Deb. Eight of the children in front of us belonged to her class, because she'd been given a K/1 composite. The other sixteen were mine. Half of them were crawling over the equipment. Some were playing tag. But a few hung back, and they were the ones who needed watching.

Luke Mignelli was a wisp of a child with silky blond hair. I knew he was overwhelmed because he was hovering by my leg, sucking his thumb. Aaron was also standing on the sidelines. I couldn't read his expression.

'Hey, Luke.' Deb hunkered down suddenly, all smiles and dimples. She was about my age but looked more reassuring. Everything about her said 'kindy teacher'—especially her chirpy little voice.

'Do you want to play?' she asked Luke, who shook his

head. I did a quick scan of the grounds and clocked Prue Wilmott, self-described 'old boot' and learning resources teacher. With Prue as back-up, I could safely talk to Aaron.

'Are you going to play with Phoebe, mate?'

Aaron shifted uneasily. 'Dunno.'

'You could ask.'

A blank look. I realised he was going to need help. 'You could go over and say, "Can I be a bird too?" Look how Kayla and Jade are pretending to eat bread. I bet they wouldn't mind if you joined in.'

'There's no bread,' Aaron mumbled.

'No, but you can pretend there is.'

He absorbed this for a moment.

'If you go over and say, "Can I be a bird?", they might let you eat some of their invisible bread.' A sudden cry made me look around. Someone had fallen. Was it George? There were three sandy-haired boys in my class: George, Luke and Oscar. I was still trying to sort them out. This one had a very distinctive cowlick.

George, then.

As he began to cry, Prue picked him up and dusted him off. 'You're all right,' she said briskly. 'What have you done? Hurt your leg? If that starts to bleed, you'll get a special Band-aid. Let's wash it and see, okay?'

George nodded. He took Prue's hand. She was heading for retirement and as tough as nails, with a flat, scratchy voice and dyed hair cut in a jagged pageboy. Nothing seemed to faze her. 'I don't care if it's the Second Coming or the Antichrist,' she'd drawled on our last development day, 'they're bound to end up in my classroom eventually.'

A chorus of shrieks rent the air. I whipped around. Kayla had collapsed, and Aaron was standing over her.

Before I could get there, he kicked her in the ribs.

Phoebe cried, 'He punched her! Aaron punched Kayla!'

'Aaron!' I stepped in front of him. 'Aaron, stop. *Stop.*'

'Fuck you!' he spat, eyes blazing. 'Gimme back my knife! I'm gunna stab you in the guts!'

~

I already knew about the parenting order. Every week, from Monday afternoon until Friday morning, Aaron was picked up and dropped off by his father or his grandmother. But because he spent weekends with his mother, she was the one I had to ring.

'Is that…?' I checked the list. Yep; she'd dumped her married name. 'Ms McCall? Krystal McCall?'

'Uh, yeah.' She didn't sound too convinced.

'This is Robyn Ayres. From the school. I teach your son.'

'Oh, no!' Her alarm was instant. I had to yank the phone away from my ear. 'What happened?'

'Aaron's all right. He's not hurt. But there's been an incident. He hit a little girl and he's very upset.' This was a polite way of saying he'd kicked me, bitten Deb and tried to run away. 'Can you come and collect him?'

'Collect him?'

'Now. He's in sick bay. Do you know where that is?'

I was going too fast for her. 'Wait. He—he hit a little girl?'

'That's right. And kicked her.' He'd done it, I gathered, when she wouldn't play with him. 'It was quite violent. He should take a break and come back on Monday.'

She sighed. Her voice trembled when she asked, 'He's not expelled?'

'No, no. We just have to put a plan in place.' Conscious that Deb was minding my class, I said, 'Mr Bradshaw will discuss it with you when you get here. Thanks, Ms McCall.'

Then I hung up.

Beside me, Howard gave a tired nod. There were bags under his eyes and his grey suit seemed to be leaching the colour out of him. Though solidly built, he sagged a little, like a couch that had lost some stuffing.

It was too soon to know what kind of principal he was, but the early signs pointed to a plodder. So far he'd buried me in forms and spouted a lot of jargon at staff meetings.

'Okay, Aaron.' He poked his head into sick bay. 'Your mum's coming to take you home. I want you to think about what you did and why you did it. And when you see Kayla again, I want you to apologise.'

Aaron didn't answer. He was lying facedown on a narrow bed that almost filled the room. Aima Singh, the school counsellor, sat opposite him. Her schedule brought her to Otford every Friday, so she'd rushed out to help during Aaron's meltdown. With her doe eyes and comforting middle-aged spread, she seemed nice enough. But Aaron wasn't won over.

'Right.' Howard's gaze flicked from me to Aima and back

again. 'I'll see you both in my office this afternoon for a risk assessment meeting. And I'll try to bring the parents in on—'

'Howard?' A heavy-set woman was moving down the hall towards us. She was wrapped in what looked like a butcher's apron, but was otherwise well groomed in pressed polyester and nail polish. 'What did he do? Is he here?'

'Joyce.' Howard moved to intercept her. My ears pricked. This was Aaron's gran. But what was she doing at school?

'He's a good boy. He just needs a firm hand. It's his mother's fault—she lets him run riot.' Moving with unexpected speed for such a big, heavy woman, Joyce dodged the principal and barged into sick bay as if she owned it. Though she looked about fifty, she had the aggressive energy of a teenager.

'Aaron! Sit up!' she barked. 'What did you do? Eh?'

Aaron wriggled off the bed and swung around to confront her. His expression was blank.

'Did you hit someone?' she asked him. 'Is that what you did?'

'Joyce—' Howard began.

'I'll sort him out.' She jerked her chin at Aaron. 'Come on. We're going to the police station.'

'Uh—Mrs Rooney?' I felt I had to intercede, since Howard wasn't throwing his weight around. 'I'm Robyn Ayres. Aaron's teacher.'

She looked at me for the first time. Her eyes narrowed.

'Aaron's mum is scheduled to pick him up today,' I pointed out. 'So she's coming to collect him.'

Then Howard jumped in. 'But you're welcome to meet

with us on Monday afternoon, Joyce. You *and* his parents. So we can discuss intervention strategies.'

Joyce gave a snort. 'Intervention strategies?' Her voice dripped with contempt. 'I tell you what needs to be done. He needs to be taken away from his mother.'

I caught Aima's eye. She looked appalled.

'Mrs Rooney—' she began.

'This is Krystal's fault. She lets him behave like an animal. Aaron always acts up before going home with that woman. She's an unfit mother.'

'Mrs Rooney...' Aima tried to break in but her voice was too soft. And Howard was being strangely spineless.

'We can't talk now,' I said firmly. 'We should wait until Monday. This isn't the time or the place.'

I recognised Joyce's scowl. Aaron had inherited it. She was opening her mouth to give me what for when Howard said, 'Aren't you needed in the canteen, Joyce?'

Aha, I thought. *That's why she's at school.*

'There's nothing you can do here, but you're certainly needed over there,' he went on. 'If you go home at this point, how will they manage?'

When Joyce hesitated, I held my breath.

'I suppose so,' she grumbled at last. 'Wouldn't want to let the others down.' She was dominating the room, and I wondered how she did it. Perhaps it had something to do with her aggrieved air. 'This meeting of yours is on Monday?' she asked Howard, who gave a nod. 'What time?'

'Ahhh...three-thirty?' He glanced at me.

'That's fine,' I said.

'Monday at three-thirty. All right. I'll tell my son.' Joyce turned on her heel and thumped out of the room, though not before adding, 'Aaron will be okay once his mother's not involved. We've got a court date. It shouldn't be long.'

No one uttered a word until the front door had slammed behind her. Howard took off his glasses and rubbed the bridge of his nose. Aaron flung himself down again. Aima looked stunned; her hand trembled as she tucked a strand of hair behind her ear.

I finally broke the silence. 'Guess I'd better get back to class.'

'Yes. You do that.' Howard didn't even look at me.

'Bye, Aaron. See you next week.' The prospect made my heart sink, but I flashed a smile at his unresponsive back. Then I hurried down the hall and out into the harsh summer sun.

I was on the front doorstep, gulping down air, when a young woman approached me and said, 'Do you know where the sick bay is?'

I recognised her voice. 'Krystal?'

'Yes.' Unlike Joyce, Krystal McCall had an untidy, flustered look. She was very thin, with a narrow face, a wide mouth and big blue eyes.

'I'm Robyn Ayres. We spoke on the phone.'

'Oh! Yes. Hi.'

'You got here fast.'

She stared at me blankly. 'I don't work on Fridays,' she said. 'Where's Aaron?'

'If you go to Reception, you can sign in. Aaron's just down the hall from there, with the school counsellor.' I suddenly remembered his Swiss Army knife and pulled it out of my pocket. 'He brought this in today. It's not a good idea.'

Krystal gasped. Then she snatched it from me. 'That stupid knife!'

'We don't encourage students to bring any of their favourite toys from home, and this one is quite dangerous—'

'I know! I know it is. I told Scott, but he wouldn't listen.' Suddenly the words started pouring out of her. 'He's so rough with Aaron. He's always on at him to be a little man. He gets angry when he cries and hits him when he acts up—'

'Ms McCall—'

'Scott's dangerous. I'm worried he's going to hurt my son.' Krystal's eyes filled with tears. 'I don't know what to do.'

'Maybe you should go to the police.'

'Scott *is* the police. He's a senior constable.' She was gabbling at me, pressing so close I had to step back. 'Once he poured boiling water over my hand, but he said it was an accident. Nobody believed me—they thought I did it myself. They thought I was drunk.'

'Ms McCall—'

'I can't talk about it. Not to anyone. People are embarrassed. They don't want to know he used a chokehold on me. Or handcuffs. I went to the doctor but—'

'Hey!' A shout from across the playground cut her off. It was Joyce, and she was making a beeline for us. Had she been lying in wait for Krystal? 'What are you up to?' she yelled.

'Telling more lies? That's defamation! I could sue!'

Krystal shrank away. Then she plunged through the front entrance. I was standing there like a fool, my mouth hanging open, when Joyce brushed past me on her way inside.

'Just so you know, she's an alcoholic,' Joyce announced. 'And a drug addict. You can't believe a word she says.'

The door banged shut.

I took a deep breath. Everything around me looked peaceful. There was a cute koala mural on a nearby wall. Hopscotch squares had been painted on a concrete path.

I'd left Sydney to escape all the turmoil and heartbreak there. But was escape even possible?

Perhaps I was fooling myself.

2019

'RIGHT! YOU CAN put your stuff back in your bags and empty out your pockets,' Shaun Steiger told his platoon.

A rising clamour of protest was cut off by the kitchen door as I banged through it, wheeling my barrow. I spent about three minutes hastily stowing supplies: lettuce in the second fridge, bread in the pantry, bananas in a bowl.

By the time I emerged again, every kid's pocket had been emptied. Zac Henderson, now phoneless, was sitting on the grass, eyes red, arms folded.

'This is a strike,' he was saying. 'I refuse to cooperate.'

Trundling past, I cut a glance at Aaron. He was picking at a pimple, looking bored.

Then Joe Malouf intercepted me and put his plastic bin full of phones and iPads into my wheelbarrow. I knew the drill; all confiscated technology had to be locked in my safe.

I headed for the old poultry shed where I stored my garden equipment. Shaun was telling his platoon to take off their outerwear and put on their new uniforms. 'What, *here?*' someone asked. When Shaun said yes, the kids erupted. He was called a perv. A fuckwit. A faggot. I heard the thud of footsteps and turned to see another kid making a break for the jetty—Flynn, the one who'd jumped out of the boat. He didn't get far, though. Warren soon caught up with him.

After that, it was chaos. Somebody started humming stripper music. A big, chunky boy with red hair and terrible acne took off his left shoe and threw it straight at Shaun. Nathan Bosanko said, 'I'm not wearing underpants. Is that a problem?' His voice was soft and slow and weirdly glutinous, like a slug slithering into my ear.

I was relieved when my office door shut behind me at last, blocking out most of the noise.

After dumping the tech in my safe, I spun the combination lock. Then I sat down and looked at Shaun's notes: his medical forms, permission slips, emergency contact numbers. Most of this stuff had arrived several weeks earlier. But I'd also received a few documents the previous day, when I'd sat down with Shaun for our final briefing.

'You want to watch out for Tyler Metherill. He's a thief,' Shaun had warned me. 'The police think he's basically a good kid with a lot of potential. That's why they referred him. But he's constantly truanting—probably to look after his little sister. His home situation is a nightmare.'

Shaun always gave me a brief description of the more problematic campers. Then we would thrash out any billing problems and discuss his schedule. I had a lot of respect for

Shaun. He was clear, concise and well organised, unlike most of my other clients. The teachers were a mixed bunch—either scarily efficient or depressingly hopeless—but the organisers of the religious camps were a constant headache. They kept changing their minds. Neglecting to pay up. Asking for impossible things like swimming pools or medics. Sometimes they would arrive with too many kids, having enrolled a few extra at the last minute. 'Can't you just buy more food?' they would ask vaguely. I would try to explain that the ferry came three days a week, and that I couldn't just nip over to Cleveland in my tinny for an extra sack of potatoes, because I couldn't leave the island unstaffed. Not while there were visitors around.

Some of the religious camps were also a bit slapdash about medical details, but Shaun wasn't. Though I harboured some doubts about his methods, I admired his thoroughness. His notes couldn't be faulted.

I flipped through them. Ali Bashar. Nathan Bosanko. Jake Duggan. I noticed that Zac Henderson had been 'terrorising' his parents: swearing, truanting, staying out all night. Dean Hoegel, the dreadlocked kid who'd stormed off the jetty, had been sent by his grandfather. My gaze slipped down his list of behavioural problems and a familiar pattern emerged. Self-harming. Obsessive. Antisocial.

On the spectrum, I thought. Shaun's tough-love approach wouldn't do much for a kid like Dean.

Shaun had explained to me that his program was designed to imitate military basic training. He started by 'breaking down' the campers with uniforms, discipline and exercise.

Then he built them up again with positive reinforcement and stress-management techniques. 'We're using methods that embed positive behaviour,' he'd said. 'We teach 'em trust. Mutual respect. Ways of controlling their emotions. We encourage them to be the best they can be.'

Judging from the notes in front of me, he was going to have his work cut out for him.

'Mr Kollios, you are not required to make smart comments whenever you receive a command!' Shaun's voice was muffled by the walls of my office as he tried to impose his will on thirteen stroppy teenagers. Flynn was wailing in the distance. Parade drill hadn't started yet. I wondered if it ever would.

At last I reached the entry for Darren King. Darren—*Aaron*—had been sent by his mother. He'd been doing a lot of drugs. Cannabis, mostly, but his friends were getting into meth and his mother was scared. She'd flushed his stash down the toilet one day and he'd assaulted her. Then she'd told him that if he didn't go on Shaun's camp, she would call the police.

Aaron lived in Cooktown. He went to the local school. I sat staring at the sparse collection of facts in front of me, searching for more clues. He had mild asthma. He was recovering from a cold. He'd been suspended from school three times since the beginning of the year, once for being stoned, once for being violent and once for being abusive.

I felt a leaden weight settle in my stomach. This was bad. This was terrible. I'd made a massive mistake. But wasn't that the story of my life? I always trusted people who shouldn't be trusted. My mother. My ex-husband. My friend Annette.

For ten years I'd been clinging to the hope that I'd made the right call by putting my faith in Aaron's mum—and now he'd ended up in a boot camp for troubled teens.

I'd seen it coming, but I was still crushed.

The next few hours were difficult. Though the kids finally put on their uniforms, Shaun's parade drill triggered a lot of clowning. As I went about my business, he kept bellowing commands.

'Platoon—open order, march!'

'One, two, right dress!'

'Platoon will advance! Right turn—*right* turn, Jake!'

At first there was a lot of laughter. Then the punishments started. I would stroll past the parade ground with an armful of sheets and see someone doing push-ups. Or someone moving a rock. Or two kids at either end of a wooden pole, lifting it from shoulder to shoulder. 'Lower! Raise! Lower! Raise! Keep it off your head, Mr Stubbs!'

Soon the laughter gave way to a sullen silence, interspersed now and then by angry, breathless complaints. The kids grew tired. Confused. One or two of them burst into tears, but any attempts to taunt them were shut down: the veterans didn't allow bullying of any kind. 'Ten push-ups, Mr Pusnik! There will be no comments while I'm giving orders—is that clear?'

After drill, the boys were shown how to make their beds with hospital corners. I overheard howls of protest as Shaun insisted that various beds be remade over and over again. Some of the kids had probably never made a bed in their lives except by pulling up a doona. 'It's like fucking Downton Abbey,' one of them complained, his voice drifting through the dormitory window. I had to laugh.

After the bed-making came the boot-polishing, which was briefly interrupted by Dreadlock Dean's third attempt to run away. I saw him from my office, where I was returning a couple of phone messages. One message was from Zac Henderson's mother, who had a creaky little voice and who couldn't recall if she'd mentioned that Zac was allergic to seafood. Not fish: seafood. I rang and assured her the problem was duly noted. The second call was from Tyler Metherill's mother, whose message was an incoherent ramble and who didn't answer when I called back.

I scribbled a couple of entries in my daily log. Then I returned to the kitchen, where I braced myself for the next challenge. Shaun always insisted the boys help me prepare dinner every night. 'Those kids won't learn to appreciate their food unless they cook it,' he often said, and he wasn't wrong. We'd negotiated an extra fee, and I'd stipulated that no more than half his platoon could occupy the kitchen at any one time.

'You don't have to worry. We'll do it in sections, and there'll always be two officers on duty.' He seemed very confident, but I made a point of locking up all the obvious weapons: knives, skewers, meat mallets. I also drew up a risk assessment plan, assigning every kitchen activity a risk level and basing my recipes on that.

I suppose all my years of teaching hadn't been completely wasted.

'Right! This kitchen is out of bounds unless Ms Ayres says otherwise,' Shaun declared, holding open the door for seven unhappy teens. Aaron was the third to file in. He withheld eye contact and fidgeted ceaselessly, scratching his cheek, rubbing his nose, adjusting his pants.

He looked tired. They all looked tired.

'What's on the menu tonight, Ms Ayres?' Shaun's tone was jocular. Then the big redhead collapsed onto one of the chairs I'd arranged in a semi-circle. 'Marcus! Did I tell you to sit?'

'It's all right.' I didn't want them drifting around the kitchen. Nathan Bosanko had already wandered over to peer at my spice rack, licking his lips with a wet, lingering tongue. Something about that kid made my skin crawl. 'Everyone sit down. You're going to be peeling potatoes tonight.'

'Awesome,' somebody grumbled. But most of the boys seated themselves without complaint. When I handed out the vegetable peelers, Aaron didn't even look up.

'For those who've never done this before, let me show you how to peel a potato.' I began to demonstrate. 'See? It's easy.'

'Mr King!' Shaun snapped. 'Watch and learn. This is for your benefit.'

Aaron grimaced and raised his head. Our eyes locked. I felt a kind of jolt in my gut, but his expression remained blank.

'Is this all for making chips?' asked a freckled kid with a footballer's build. He had sandy hair, blue eyes and a hectoring voice. 'You can buy frozen chips, in case you don't realise.'

'Not helpful, Connor,' Rhys warned him.

Connor, I thought. *That makes sense.* Connor Pusnik was an old-fashioned bully. His parents had sent him to Vetnet after his third school expulsion. 'He's got some sort of acquired brain injury from playing sport,' Shaun had told me. 'At least, that's the excuse I was given.'

I'd seen Connor jostling some of the other campers on his way through the kitchen door. Shaun had missed it, but I've known quite a few Connors, over the years. Kids like him are responsible for a lot of homeschooling.

By this time Nathan had already plucked a potato from the pile in front of him and started peeling it, slowly and deliberately. The process seemed to fascinate him; he was almost cross-eyed as he studied each growing spiral of skin. The others joined in one by one. Aaron worked sluggishly. Connor hacked away as if he was trying to defend himself. Dean nervously dabbed at a potato with his peeler like someone trying to flick a dead fly off a table.

I soon realised the youngest boy in the group was the most experienced. 'Well done, Ali,' Shaun said, beaming down at him. Ali Bashar was short, plump and meekly acquiescent, but he managed to work his way through half-a-dozen potatoes in the time it took everybody else to peel just one. He was an experienced kitchenhand, lovingly trained. I wondered what on earth he was doing on Finch Island.

'According to his parents, he won't come out of his room,' Shaun had told me. 'Skips school. Talks back. Spends all his time on the computer. Sounds like he's a target, but that's okay. We'll send him home with a load of self-confidence and various techniques he can use against bullying. You watch— we can work wonders with kids like Ali.'

I hoped so, but I had my doubts.

'What the fuck are you doing, Marcus?' Connor's voice pricked like a needle. 'You're only meant to peel off the skin.'

'I'm getting rid of this brown spot,' said the redhead. He had a thick, muffled way of talking. 'Don't I have to?'

'Not by peeling everything off! If you keep doing that, you'll be down to a bloody pea there soon, not a potato!'

I caught a glimpse of Marcus on my way to the stove, his face reddening beneath the acne. Rhys said to him, 'You're okay, mate. We'll dig out your brown spot with a knife.'

'What a fucking idiot,' Connor scoffed—and that was when Marcus took a swing at him.

But Rhys was too quick. He blocked the punch before it landed. 'Oi,' he said. 'No.'

'He called me a fucking idiot!'

'Because he's trying to get at you.' Shaun began to lecture Marcus as I lowered my pot of water onto a hob. 'He's only doing it to make himself feel good. It's a sign of weakness.' Turning to Connor, Shaun said, 'What makes you so superior, Mr Pusnik? I don't see many potatoes in your bucket. Not like Ali's.'

Connor flushed and hit back. 'So? Ali's a food person. Look how fat he is.'

Ali winced. Rhys's face tightened.

Shaun adopted a weary tone. 'Every time I hear this kind of thing, I look at the person who said it and think: there's someone who feels worthless. Who feels so bad about himself that he needs to make other people feel even worse.'

A sudden squawk made my head snap around. Nathan was dripping blood. He held up his peeler, which had a shred of his own skin stuck to its blade.

'Look,' he said with a sickly grin. 'It works.'

There were hisses and squeals from everyone except the two veterans, who always coped beautifully in moments of high drama.

'Come on, mate.' Rhys removed the peeler from Nathan's grip. 'You'll need a dressing on that.' He began to usher Nathan out of the room.

Shaun raised his voice slightly. 'The rest of you, settle down! You've got a job to finish.' He flashed me a smile that was meant to be reassuring, but it only annoyed me. I'd already expressed my views on letting juvenile delinquents into my kitchen. Now Shaun was trying to suggest that everything was under control.

I went to get a mop to clean the blood off the floor.

'He did it deliberately,' said the smirking kid who'd brought the porn mag to camp. I looked at him, startled; he was a little shorter than me, with long, fleecy hair and hazel eyes. You could see the sculptured lines of his adult face emerging from the puppy fat. 'I was watching him. It wasn't an accident.'

'I'm sure it was.' Shaun sounded dismissive.

'It wasn't.'

'You can't possibly know that, Jake.'

Right, I thought. *Jake Duggan*. Shaun had given me the rundown on Jake, who was a suspected vandal and shoplifter, though he'd never been caught in the act. According to Shaun, there had been family violence. A schizophrenic mother. An aunt who'd agreed to house Jake, but who didn't seem to like him.

'You can't blame her,' Shaun had said. 'Since Jake showed up, all three of her kids have landed in hospital.' After hesitating for a moment, he'd fixed me with an intent look and said, 'You want to watch him. He's sneaky.'

Mopping the kitchen floor, I wondered about Jake's sneaky side. He seemed personable enough.

'There are some pretty crazy kids here,' he said with a shrug. As if to prove his point, Dean jumped up and hurled his peeler at the wall. 'Fuck this! I can't do it!' With a toss of his straggly dreads he was out the door before Shaun could move a muscle.

Connor rolled his eyes. 'Not again.'

Shaun threw me a questioning glance. When I nodded, he left. All at once I found myself with five troubled teens and no back-up.

They immediately relaxed. I could see the tension flowing out of their bodies. Half of them stopped peeling.

'I don't even like potatoes,' said Marcus.

'I do,' said Jake. 'I love potatoes. I love mashing potatoes.' His gaze slid towards me. 'I love the way they're all soft and yielding when you push them and push them…'

Oh, for fuck's sake, I thought. Sexual innuendo? Little sleazebag.

'At this rate Ali's the only one who'll be mashing any potatoes,' I said. 'If you're too slow, you'll be cutting onions.'

Connor sneered. 'Bring it on. I'm good with a knife.'

'You won't need a knife. I've got an onion chopper.' I spoke evenly, but I mentally added, *dipshit.*

'Whatever. It won't be me, anyway. It'll be Zitface, here.' Connor jerked his chin at Marcus, who scowled. 'Or Gothboy, maybe. He's so slow, I reckon he's drug-fucked.'

He was talking about Aaron, but Aaron didn't raise his head. Then Jake turned to address Marcus.

'C'mon, man,' Jake said. 'We can beat this dude. Let's do it.' He attacked his potato with dangerous enthusiasm, flicking bits of peel everywhere. Marcus grinned and copied him. As I wondered why Jake was being nice to Marcus, Connor started scraping away so competitively that his pumping elbow hit Aaron in the eye.

It might have been an accident. Aaron didn't think so. He turned and rammed his potato straight into Connor's face.

Suddenly the pair of them were rolling around on the floor.

'Hey! *Hey!* Get off!' I yelled, using my mop to separate them. Jake was laughing. Ali shrank back, terrified.

I was in despair. It was happening again. Whenever Aaron showed up, the shit hit the fan. None of the measures I'd taken all those years ago had worked—not a single one.

And here I was, still picking up the pieces.

2009

'AARON WAS TRYING to make me angry,' said Aima. 'I've seen that before when a child can only get attention from parents who are cross with them. They relax when they've managed to provoke an anger response.'

We were sitting in Howard Bradshaw's office, which was full of pastel blue chairs and anodyne photos. There were no quirky ornaments. No children's art projects. No evidence of hobbies or passions or family holidays.

Sitting behind his desk, Howard could have been a Centrelink functionary.

'Mmm. Well, we'll have to incorporate that into our risk assessment and management plan,' he said, shuffling papers.

'But we need to make a report. It's mandatory, isn't it?' I'd parked myself opposite him, between Prue Wilmott and Aima Singh.

It was still the first day of school, the kindergarten kids had all gone home, and we were discussing what to do with

Aaron Rooney. 'His mum says his dad hits him. That falls under the Care Act.'

'I'll be contacting the DHS,' said Howard.

Prue rolled her eyes.

'Why not, Prue?' asked Aima. 'There's a case to be made here.'

'Yeah, but it's been made before.' Prue's mouth twisted. 'This is a custody dispute, remember? A nasty one. The accusations keep flying.'

Aima blinked. 'And nothing's happened?'

'It's complicated.' Prue sighed when I stared at her. 'The father's a copper, the grandmother's a steamroller and the mother's an unreliable witness.'

That didn't seem right to me. 'The mother seemed scared. Genuinely scared.'

'Yeah, but she once accused her ex of knocking her out and dumping her in the middle of the road to get run over.' Before I could do more than raise my eyebrows, Prue said, 'There was CCTV from the local pub. She staggered out pissed and passed out on the median strip.' Prue's forehead creased as she searched her memory. 'I think she popped a Valium and it didn't react well to the alcohol. It was about six months ago. Right after she walked out.'

'How do you know all this?' Aima demanded.

'I live here.' Prue's tone was so flat she sounded almost bored. 'The McCalls are notorious. A bunch of them have been jailed. Drugs, mostly.'

'That doesn't mean Krystal's lying,' I pointed out.

'No, but it doesn't help that she only started talking about what Scott did to her after she filed for divorce.' Seeing me exchange looks with Aima, Prue sighed again. 'I'm not saying it didn't happen, I'm just saying it's problematic.'

'Aaron Rooney has been exposed to violent behaviour,' Aima insisted. 'I'd lay money on it.'

'And the mother doesn't look like a violent type,' I agreed.

'But we're not here to make that call.' Howard's tone was impatient. 'Obviously we'll submit a report. It will probably join a lot of other reports on the subject. Our main job is to get a risk assessment and management plan in place for this child.' He leaned towards Aima. 'The first thing you should do is make an appointment for next Friday. I'll get the parents to sign a permission slip when I see them on Monday afternoon.'

Aima nodded. She picked up her phone and tapped in some kind of diary note.

Howard flipped through his papers. 'There's no preschool letter. Did he go to preschool?'

Prue gave a snort. She was slumped in her chair, arms folded. 'Joyce Rooney thinks preschools are for lazy mothers who won't look after their kids.'

Howard continued as if she hadn't spoken. 'So we don't have any kind of behavioural diagnosis,' he said, then looked at me. 'What's your opinion? Does he need one?'

'Hard to say.' I thought for a moment. 'There's nothing wrong with his speech. His fine motor skills are okay. But he's not reading social cues and he's easily distracted. I suppose he could be on the spectrum. Or have ADHD.' It wasn't my job to make that assessment, though. 'Can we not contact Learning and Support? Maybe they'll send a caseworker.'

Howard grunted. Prue laughed. 'Good luck with that,' she said. 'They come here from Bathurst and it takes about three months.'

'If there's violence involved, a caseworker can be expedited,' Aima reminded her.

'Mmm. Well. One step at a time.' Howard's attention had returned to his papers. 'First I'll draw up an official letter. I'll give that to the parents on Monday. Then I'll need a full rundown on the domestic side of things. I'll get that on Monday too.' His shoulders sagged at the prospect.

'Have fun,' said Prue. Howard ignored her, so she turned to me. 'Word of advice—take lots of diary notes. *Lots.* Because the solicitors are bound to come calling.'

I was quick to defend myself. 'My diary notes are always thorough.'

Prue smiled crookedly. Howard picked up his pen.

'Right.' He took a deep breath. 'Let's start with the risk assessment and rating table. Duration and frequency of behaviour?'

~

I called my dad that night. I told him about Aaron, Joyce and Howard. Then I asked him what I should do with my back door.

'It's sticking,' I said. 'On the bottom.'

My new rental was a 1930s weatherboard, not in great

shape. I'd already cleared two sink traps, repaired the sash on a double-hung window and replaced six tap washers. The sliding wardrobe door in the second bedroom was giving me trouble because it was a hollow-core piece of rubbish and slightly bowed.

Dad had promised to tackle it the next time he paid me a visit. I knew it was pointless asking the landlord for help; I'd been trying for weeks to get him to install a new hot-water system. I was pretty sure the tank was leaking—and once the tank starts to leak, that's it. Game over.

'Have you tightened the hinge screws?' asked Dad.

'Of course.' It was the first thing I'd done. 'There's nothing wrong with the way it's hanging. To be honest, I think it's the doorstep. That's wood too.'

Dad grunted. He was a semi-retired builder who still did odd jobs around Kempsey—and since there was nothing he liked better than fixing things, I think he was quite pleased I'd moved into a renovator's delight. It was something for us to talk about, apart from the weather and how my divorce was going.

Being an old-fashioned country bloke, Dad didn't really know what to say about my ex, except that he was a two-timing bastard who deserved to be shot. Dad wasn't good at expressing himself. But he'd shown his support by helping me move from Sydney to Otford, where he'd stayed in my spare bedroom for a couple of days, unpacking boxes and fitting a new bathroom extractor fan.

'Try planing it,' he advised me. 'If that doesn't work, I'll replace the sill when I'm there next month.'

'Okay. Thanks.'

'No sign of a new hot-water system?'

'Nup.'

'You might have to go to the tribunal.'

'We'll see.'

Silence fell. I knew what he wanted to ask. He wanted to ask if I was all right. It was the question that hung in the air whenever we spoke. Are you all right, Rob? Are you all right, Dad? I guess we were afraid to take the lid off that sump.

'On Sunday I'm having lunch at a friend's place,' I said at last. This piece of news was guaranteed to please my dad, who'd suggested I join the Country Women's Association. 'Deb invited me. You remember her?'

'Oh, yes.' His voice warmed up. Deb had been looking after me ever since I'd arrived. She'd made me a cake, taken me shopping and introduced me to a lot of mothers with young children. Dad approved of Deb. 'That's nice of her. You've been lucky there,' he said.

'Yes. I have.' In fact I'd been so lucky I was beginning to wonder. Was there an ulterior motive for Deb's lavish welcome? Was she a church-going missionary on the trawl for sinners? 'I'll take a salad. My walnut salad. It's a barbecue.'

'Sounds good.' A distant siren wailed. 'What's that?'

'Police, maybe. Ambulance.'

'Friday night.'

'Mmm.'

'What's on for you tonight?'

'A risk-management plan.'

I had to work out the strategies I'd be using to help Aaron—though I was flying blind without a proper diagnosis. Interoception activities, perhaps? Headphones? Certainly a time-out tent.

'Shouldn't you be putting your feet up?' said Dad.

'I'm fine.'

'Okay—well, have a good evening.'

'You too.'

'I'm glad you're settling in.'

Settling in. I'd done my best to settle in. I'd bought some potted plants. Repaired things around the house. Joined the local library. I'd done everything I was supposed to do, yet I still felt as if I'd been torn out by the roots and tossed on a compost heap.

Sitting at the kitchen table, I used Aaron's risk-management plan to block out thoughts of my mangled marriage, my legal bills, and the apartment I'd loved, which was now in the process of being sold to someone else. I'd lost everything—my home, my husband, even my dog, because he wasn't really my dog. He was Troy's dog.

Strategic praise, I wrote. *Clear instructions: i.e. traffic lights—red means no talking, orange means low-level talking.*

I wasn't aware, as I laboured over my report, that across town Aaron's father Scott was becoming involved in his own traffic-light incident.

'It was that Fryer kid—Angela McCall's son. He ran a red light and when Scott Rooney pulled him over, he lost it.'

Deb's sister Sammy was holding forth to a rapt audience on Sunday when I walked out of Deb's kitchen clutching a cold drink. Sammy was a bank teller with two children and a big, bald husband named Clarke. The tiny woman next to her was a manager at Foodworks, where Deb had once introduced us. ('Peta's got four kids. Hard to believe, eh?')

I didn't recognise any of the other people in the Olsens' backyard except Deb's husband, who was stationed at the barbecue in a cloud of smoke and flies. The men gathered around him were holding stubbies. A swarm of kids shuttled between a wading pool and their mothers, who were huddled on the back patio under a shade cloth, hanging on to Sammy's every word. Water pistols were squirting. Someone was screaming. The sun beat down like a hammer because there were no trees in the garden; Deb's house was part of a new mini-development stuffed with oversized dream homes on looping cul-de-sacs—the kind of buildings my dad called 'bob-a-jobs'. The few saplings scattered around were spindly and parched-looking. The grapevine wasn't doing well.

I could feel a headache blooming behind my left eyebrow.

'Wait. *Who* lost it?' Peta asked Sammy, as I drifted towards them. 'Scott or Blaine?'

'Blaine,' Sammy replied.

'That's what the cops say, at least.' Clarke was one of two men listening to his wife. The other man was elderly and bald, with the raw, freckled skin of a redhead who'd spent too much time in the sun. I wondered if he was Deb's father.

'Yeah.' Sammy nodded. 'I mean, who knows? The police reckon Blaine attacked Scott but…' She trailed off, shrugging.

'Blaine Fryer's about forty kilos wringing wet,' said Peta. 'I don't see why Scott Rooney had to put him in hospital.'

'Concealed weapon,' the old bloke growled. When everyone looked at him, he said brusquely, 'Why not? I wouldn't be surprised. It's all about drugs, with that mob.'

'Yeah, but just think about it.' Clarke's voice held a slight edge as he addressed the man who may or may not have been his father-in-law. 'You've got two parties on opposite sides of a messy divorce. You don't think that's significant?'

The old bloke sniffed. Sammy said, 'I reckon there'll be a complaint.' She was darker than Deb and more angular.

Her husband shook his head. 'In this town? Not a chance.'

'What about the Police Integrity Commission?' someone chimed in.

Someone else laughed. 'I'd back Joyce Rooney against the Police Integrity Commission any day.'

At that point Deb emerged from the kitchen. When she asked if the meat was done, Clarke headed for the barbecue. Some of the women swooped on their offspring, telling them it was nearly time for lunch and did they need to go to the toilet? I realised one of the kids being herded past me was in my class.

'Who does Amber belong to?' I asked Deb.

'Beth. And Cam. Amber's such a sweetie.'

'I know.' Amber was one of those children who melt your heart every time they open their mouths. She was all wide-eyed wonder and boundless empathy.

'Sorry—I haven't introduced you.' Deb turned around and waved at someone. 'Beth! This is Robyn. I don't know if you've met.'

'On Friday. Briefly,' Beth said with a neat little smile.

Dammit, I thought, because I was drawing a blank. That first day of school was always a mess of new names and strange faces. It wasn't the first time I'd forgotten one.

Stalling, I said, 'Amber's such a lovely girl.'

Beth lit up. She was a small, brisk, bespectacled woman with clipped hair and a permanent crease between her eyebrows, but at the mention of her daughter everything softened: eyes, mouth, voice, posture. 'Thank you.'

'I wish I had Amber in *my* class,' Deb complained, 'though I guess poor Rob needs someone to make up for Aaron Rooney.'

Beth rolled her eyes. I was surprised at Deb. Bitching about a student to another student's mother wasn't exactly best practice.

'Joyce was on the council once,' Deb told me. 'Beth had to work with her.'

'She didn't last long.' Beth wiped her forehead with exaggerated relief. 'Burned too many bridges. Everything was always about her.' After swallowing a mouthful of lemonade, she added, 'Still got an iron grip on Rotary, though.'

'Yeah, she was throwing her weight around the CWA for a few years, but we have ways of dealing with that kind of thing. She walked out in the end.' Seeing my inquisitive glance, Deb described how Joyce's husband had owned a successful tree-lopping business, which Joyce had sold after his death. 'She used the money to buy some properties around here, so now she's living off rents. Gives her a lot of clout.'

'You should have seen her when Scott was dating Krystal.' Beth shuddered. 'She was still on the council then, and she nearly got Mitch run out of town.'

I was losing my way. Mitch? Who was Mitch?

'Mitch McCall.' Deb must have noticed my confusion, because she went on to explain, 'He's Krystal's grandfather. You must have seen his house. All that crap out front? It's not far from you. On Opal Street.'

'Lots of junk,' said Beth. 'Mirrors. Signs.'

'Oh, right.' I knew the place. It was near the edge of town and seemed to belong to a free-spirited hippy with an artistic bent. I'd noticed garden sculptures encrusted with sea-shells. Wind chimes made of Tooheys bottles. Herbs growing out of old boots. Birdbaths. Dreamcatchers. Concrete frogs.

'Joyce reckons he's a hoarder,' Beth continued. 'She got the council involved but it didn't go anywhere.'

'He's not a hoarder.' Catching her husband's eye, Deb grunted. Some silent message had passed between them. 'Sorry—I need to go and help Drew.'

'Have you seen *inside* his house?' Beth asked. But Deb was moving away, so Beth turned to me. 'The thing is, I can understand why Joyce is worried. I wouldn't want Amber visiting Aaron there. It doesn't look safe.'

'Aaron lives with Mitch?'

Beth nodded. 'Mitch took Krystal in when she left Scott,

though I hear she just applied to rent one of those townhouses in Bridge Street. Ingrid mentioned it. Do you know Ingrid? She works at P&W.'

I didn't know Ingrid. Or the townhouse on Bridge Street. I felt completely at sea, and things didn't improve as lunch was served. The conversation revolved around people I'd never met and places I'd never seen. There was also a lot of talk about children: toys, potty-training, sleep problems, runny noses.

I was the only person there who didn't have kids. It was hard. Just a few hours earlier, I'd been on Instagram stalking Annette: her baby bump, her glowing skin, her gleaming teeth. Lurking behind her in every shot, my ex looked a bit crumpled—more like her father than her fiancé.

I particularly resented her flawless skin. Three rounds of IVF had left me with a bad case of acne that hadn't quite cleared up.

'Sorry, Deb. Sorry, Robyn.' Sammy, who had been talking about anti-vaxxers, flashed me an apologetic grin. 'You're surrounded by kids all week; you probably don't want to talk about them on your day off.'

I smiled and shrugged. My personal life was none of her business. By this time it was after three, and my headache had flowered into a migraine. But some of the children were already being rounded up, and when one set of parents said their goodbyes, I felt I could safely leave too.

Driving home, I passed Mitch McCall's house. It was a standard seventies brick box, low and brown and basic, but I couldn't help admiring the garden ornaments. A totem pole made from bits of furniture. A plaque that said, *Be at peace with yourself.* A crazy mosaic sundial. None of it looked particularly dangerous, though I did notice that one of the beer-bottle wind chimes was broken. Could Aaron have done that?

Probably, I thought, and roared off.

2019

SHAUN STEIGER BELIEVED in trust. Every evening he would light a fire and his campers would sit around it, toasting marshmallows. Then he and the other veterans would talk about their experiences in Afghanistan, encouraging the boys to open up about their own fears and traumas.

I stayed on the periphery of the campfire gatherings because I didn't trust teenagers. Not in the dark. Not when it came to kitchens or fire-pits. I would wander past now and then to top up the wood or the marshmallows, counting heads and keeping an eye on the fuel load.

I would also listen to the veterans' stories. I'd heard Warren talk about driving over an improvised explosive device near Tarin Kowt. I'd heard Joe's story of coming under attack on patrol in the Mirabad Valley. Most of the boys were spellbound by this stuff; I knew how they felt, though I tried not to get carried away. I admired Shaun and Rhys and Warren and Joe, but they weren't infallible. Sometimes I saw more than they did. Shaun was good at spotting contraband. I was better at reading body language.

That first night, when I studied the group around the fire-pit, I saw that Aaron was teetering on the edge of another explosion, that sleazy, smirking Jake had formed an alliance with Marcus, that poor Ali was scared of Dreadlock Dean and that no one wanted anything to do with creepy little Nathan, who had an empty space on either side of him—probably because he was playing with a dead moth and giggling to himself. I saw that Flynn Parata, the drama queen, was deeply impressed by Joe's war stories and that Zac Henderson, wearing a brand-new Patagonia jacket to match his expensive haircut, was trying hard not to be.

'How come you didn't just lose it?' Matt Spiteri piped up. Matt was easy to identify because he wore a hearing aid. He was also the only kid who'd volunteered for camp. 'He wants to join the army when he's older,' Shaun had explained, insisting that Matt, like Ali, would gain enormous self-confidence from basic military training—self-confidence that would help him deal with bullies at school.

'I would've lost it,' Matt continued, squinting across the fire. He was the sort of kid who'd always be a target, eager, loud and opinionated. He had drifts of fuzzy hair and a mouth packed with oversized teeth.

Joe smiled at him. 'I couldn't afford to lose it, mate. None of us could. We had to stay calm.'

'How?' Before Joe could answer, Matt barrelled on. 'I always lose it. When people go for me, I'm like—*boom*!' He punched the air. 'This guy at school took my bag once and tried to run away with it and I just went off. I didn't even think about the teachers or nothing. I crash-tackled him right into a rubbish bin and then I picked up my bag and started thumping him in the head...'

At this point I wandered away. The boys were spilling their guts to the veterans, not to me. Matt Spiteri hadn't signed up to have his personal problems exposed to some middle-aged stickybeak who just happened to be walking by. This camp was all about male bonding.

I went back home, opened a bottle of beer and sat out on the front veranda with my feet up on the railing. From there I could see down the road to the jetty, where a single light burned. There were lights beyond that, too—distant lights on the water. Oddly enough, because of those lights, I felt less isolated at night than I did during the day.

Not that I was really isolated. Hemmed in, perhaps; the complex was surrounded by thick bush and mangroves, not to mention Moreton Bay itself. But I was only half an hour from Cleveland. I didn't have to deal with generators or short-wave radios; we'd had power on the island since 1954 and a submarine phone cable since 1930. And though I still had to cope with ADSL and copper lines, at least I had the internet. However slow it was, it kept me connected.

'Hey!' I'd spotted a scuttling shadow near the old matron's quarters. 'Who's that?'

The shadow froze.

'What do you think you're doing?' Hearing a muffled

giggle, I said, 'Is that you, Nathan?'

He sidled into a pool of light near my front steps. 'I was just going to the toilet.'

Oh, no you weren't. 'The toilets are back that way.' I pointed. 'As you know.'

He giggled again before heading off. I watched him until he disappeared into the men's bathroom. Christ, he was a creepy kid. All the same, I felt sorry for him. I felt sorry for anyone who ended up on Finch Island. Not the Quandamooka people—they belonged here—but the exiles. The outcasts. The rejects who were shipped over and dumped.

I thought about the lepers. They hadn't arrived by ferry; they were towed on dinghies behind the government launch. If travelling any distance by rail or sea, they were nailed into boxes. And then, at the end of their journey, they were stuck behind two-metre fences, with visitors just once every six months. No visits from children. No private bathroom. A hill to climb and fish to catch—that was all they had, in the early days.

Some of the lepers escaped on fishing boats, but most were caught. The staff went fishing too; one was found washed up among the mangroves. A boating accident, the newspapers said, though I often wondered. Who knows what kind of things went on behind those high fences? There were no police around. No unsupervised visits.

How could anyone have reported anything?

'Rob?'

I snapped to attention. Warren Doyle was standing nearby, almost lost in the darkness.

'Haven't seen Jake, have you?' he asked.

'Nope. I just saw Nathan, though. Sent him back to the bathroom.'

'Bugger.' Warren must have been tired. I hardly ever heard him swear.

'Beer?' I suggested, knowing he wasn't allowed to indulge.

'And a spliff too, if you've got one.'

'Sorry. All my mood enhancers are in the safe.' I wasn't joking. I always locked up my alcohol when the veterans came because Shaun had asked me to.

Warren snorted. 'Oh well. Better luck next time. If you see Jake, can you give him an earful?'

'Will do.'

'Sorry about this. He snuck off while Flynn was having a meltdown.'

'D'you reckon they planned it together?'

Warren shrugged. Then he began to move away.

'Five-minute showers in the morning!' I called after him.

'Yep. I know.'

'Tank water! Remind them!'

He raised his hand. Watching him, I realised that the veterans never drifted. They never wandered. They marched or bustled or forged ahead. But their body language wasn't aggressive or dominant. Not like a policeman's.

I thought about the police. I thought about calling the police. I didn't want to, because I'd had my fill of police. And Shaun definitely wouldn't approve; this was supposed to be a safe place for troubled kids. There was a duty of care. Of confidentiality. Dobbing on Aaron would be the last thing Shaun wanted.

On the other hand, the law had been broken.

I sipped my beer, pondering. The law had been broken a long time ago. Aaron was sixteen now. At sixteen, kids get to choose where they live. Why revisit the past, when Aaron ought to be looking to the future? Would calling the police help him or hurt him? Would it fix anything?

I decided it would simply cause a big, nasty mess.

That night I dreamed about Scott Rooney yelling at the top of his voice. 'What the fuck do you think you're doing?' he screamed, over and over again. 'What the *fuck* do you think you're doing?'

I still don't know what that dream was really about. Aaron? The police? The veterans?

Perhaps I was just reminding myself not to trust men in uniform.

Shaun would always rouse his campers at 6 a.m. The boys would do ten push-ups, make their beds, polish their boots and get dressed. If the beds weren't properly made, they would have to be remade—again and again—until the veterans were satisfied.

That's why I always woke early when Shaun was around. I couldn't sleep through the wails of protest from the dormitory.

By six-thirty on Monday morning I knew I would have to get up, so I did. Then I had a quick shower, threw on my clothes and shoved a bowl of instant oats into the microwave.

I was swallowing my first mouthful of coffee when someone knocked on the front door.

'Robyn?' Shaun's voice was muffled. 'Are you up?'

I wondered what had gone wrong. There had been a slight commotion just a few minutes earlier, but I'd figured it was a tantrum. Or a snake. Or a disagreement over toothbrushes.

As I trudged down the hall, I glimpsed my reflection in one of the framed photographs of former inmates and realised I hadn't dried or plaited my hair. It hung limply to my elbows like a wet towel.

'Hang on!' I had to throw the bolt one-handed because I was still holding my coffee cup. By the time I opened the door, Shaun was shouting at a knot of kids near the men's bathroom.

'Don't go in there!' he yelled. 'Stay back!'

'What's up?' I asked.

He swung around to face me. 'Sorry, Robyn. We've got a plumbing issue.'

My heart sank. 'Someone used the broken toilet?'

'No.' He began to retreat down the steps and I followed him—past the dining hall, across the parade ground, all the way to the men's bathroom. It was a beautiful morning. Gulls wheeled. Magpies warbled. There was a heavy dew.

But I didn't like the atmosphere. It seemed tense. Some of the boys stood on the grass, clutching soap and towels, looking bewildered. Others were twitchy with excitement.

A few were absent.

Rhys was stationed at the door of the men's bathroom. He stepped aside to let me in, then moved off to help Joe. I could hear rushing water as I stepped over the threshold.

'Fuck,' I said, before I could stop myself.

The bathrooms on Finch Island had once been all concrete slabs and rust stains. Now they boasted shiny chrome fittings, mosaic feature tiles and floor-to-ceiling walls between the shower cubicles. The toilets were shielded by heavy wooden doors. A bank of basins stood opposite the entrance to each building.

The men's bathroom had urinals; the women's had sanitary bins.

'There was toilet paper blocking the drain, but I moved it,' said Shaun.

The floor was awash. One of the basin supply lines—a flexi-hose—had been separated from its stop tap. And the stop tap had been separated from the wall.

'Looks to me like someone kicked the connection. Hard,' Shaun continued. 'I didn't know where to shut it off, so I thought it would be quicker if you did.'

The shut-off valve was outside, near the composting chamber. It was a ten-second trip. As I went to turn off the water, Shaun followed me, speaking in a low, urgent voice.

'I'm sorry. We'll pay for the damage. Can you fix it?'

'I can fix it.' I had plenty of spare fittings: hoses, washers, pipes, pipe clips—even stop taps. The only thing I'd run out of was fill valves. 'I just have to get my tools.'

'Right. And while you do that, we'll find out who's responsible.' Shaun's gaze swept the parade ground, jumping from face to face. 'It would've been noisy.'

'And hard. You'd need a bit of weight behind you.'

Shaun grunted. He seemed to be measuring the distance between the huts and the men's bathroom. Though the veterans slept in huts, each of them also spent two hours a night in a room off the boys' dorm. The idea was to have someone at hand in case any campers wet the bed or played up.

'Would we have heard, do you think?' Shaun asked. 'If someone was kicking a tap off a wall?'

I shrugged. 'Maybe. It's pretty quiet around here.'

'I didn't see a single kid get up during my watch. They were conked out. But the other guys might have spotted something.' Shaun rubbed his freshly shaven jaw. 'A few kids went to the toilet while we were making beds this morning. It got pretty loud, as I recall.'

'Mmm.' I was looking at the huddle of boys waiting to use the bathroom. 'Did you tell 'em about the tanks? Five-minute showers?'

Shaun nodded, his eyes narrowing.

'Well, maybe someone wants us to run out of water so you'll have to pack up and leave.' Seeing him frown, I added, 'We won't run out. We've got multiple tanks. The only thing is, you'll have to use the women's bathroom while I fix this one. And keep clear till the floor's dry. We don't want any cracked skulls.'

I hurried back home without waiting for an answer. The

veterans began to issue commands while the boys raised hell. 'We're not girls!' Connor protested. 'We can't use the girls' toilets!'

I don't know what he was afraid of. Girl germs?

My dad's old toolbox was in my laundry, along with the spare screws, clamps, fuses and wall plugs. The laundry opened off the kitchen and the kitchen lay at the rear of the house. I had to walk down the hallway from the front door to get there—and I'd just passed the bedroom when I smelled it. A rotten smell. A bad-meat smell. I thought, *That bin needs emptying*, but as I moved towards the kitchen, the smell seemed to fade.

From the kitchen threshold I saw instantly what was wrong. Back door open. Bin missing.

'Bugger.' I put down my coffee cup. Then I turned and followed the smell back into my bedroom.

I hadn't made the bed. I hadn't had time. That's why the contents of the kitchen bin had been dumped, not on my quilted bedspread, but on the tangle of sheets and blankets underneath. The bin itself lay on the floor, leaking a rancid goo.

Aaron, I thought.

2009

'DO YOU KNOW what this is?' My palms smacked together.

'Clapping!' Phoebe cried.

I cupped my ear. 'Where's your hand? I can't hear you unless you put up your hand.'

Her pudgy little arm shot into the air. 'A clap!'

'Yes. It's a clap. And what's this?' I pointed at the wall.

George yelled, 'A map!' then quickly, guiltily raised his own hand.

'That's right.' I gazed down at the sixteen restless little bodies on the floor in front of me. It was our second day together, and I was still working my way through the endless list of assessment activities. 'Can anyone think of another word that sounds like map? Or clap?'

When no one answered, I began to beat out a rhythm on my chair leg.

'*Tap*!' Amber shrieked. Then she blushed and cringed and thrust her hand over her head. There were about twelve glittering hairclips in her crisp brown curls.

'Tap. Yes.' I ticked her off my mental list, conscious that some of the kids were squirming. A few were completely at sea, eyes blank, mouths ajar. Caleb was rocking from side to side, humming to himself as he picked at a scab. Kayla was fiddling with her shoelace, her upper lip shiny with snot. She was the only child in the class with pierced ears.

Aaron was rolling around, prodding Luke with his foot. As Luke edged away, Aaron rolled closer.

'Aaron. Can you think of a word that sounds like tap?' I asked.

'Ooooh! I can!' Phoebe rose to her knees and waved at me wildly. 'Cap! Cap!'

Aaron made a farting noise. Oscar laughed.

'Maybe you're getting a bit angry?' I said to Aaron in my calmest voice, shooting Oscar a look. 'Shall we do some volcano breathing?'

Half the class immediately began to puff away, using a technique we'd already covered. I'd told them how to 'breathe out the angry bits', hoping to provide Aaron with at least one anger-management tool.

But he ignored me, climbing to his feet and trotting towards my desk.

'If you want some time out, Aaron, you can use the tent,' I suggested. Phoebe's raised hand was practically up my nose.

'Lap, miss! Lap! Lap!'

'That's good, Phoebe, but let someone else try. Aaron? Remember what I said about my stapler? My stapler has a red dot on it. That means you can't touch it without permission.'

I might as well have been talking to a wall. As Caleb began to slide under the nearest desk, Aaron picked up my stapler and opened it.

'Aaron?' I stood up. 'You could help me by putting that back in the drawer where it...ow!' The stapler bounced off my chest like a punch. I stumbled backwards.

Aaron screamed, 'Fuck off!' Then he charged straight past me, out of the room.

Luke burst into tears. Caleb started screaming. Phoebe cried, 'Aaron! Come back!' Turning to me, she added, 'He's so stupid. I'll get him.'

'No.' I was already making for the door. 'Everyone, line up. Line up, please.' By the time I reached the hallway, Aaron was already clumping across the veranda, so I stuck my head into Deb's room. 'We've got a runner,' I said breathlessly. 'Could you take mine?'

She nodded. I sped off. I could hear her raised voice as she tried to herd my kids into her classroom. They didn't really know how to line up yet—and I wasn't sure if Caleb could be prised out of his bolt hole.

'Aaron!' I yelled, swerving towards the front gate. He was metres ahead of me, moving fast. But the gate's heavy drop-bolt was wedged tightly into the footpath. He was still struggling with it when I caught up.

'Fuck off!' he screeched. 'I hate you!' He lashed out and I stepped back. Then he tackled the drop-bolt again.

'It's okay. I know you're upset. Would you like to come

and sit by yourself for a while?' Dad used to say I was born calm. I've often been complimented on the slow, measured way I talk to people. Towards the end, when Troy and I were splitting up, he used to say it drove him mad. 'Your country drawl', he called it.

Most kids seemed to respond to my country drawl, but not Aaron. He was screeching as he wrestled with the drop-bolt. When it wouldn't move, he started banging his head against the iron bars of the gate.

'Aaron!' There was a special hold I used on hysterical children. I would approach them from behind, wrap my arms around theirs (so they wouldn't hit me) then sit down and drape my legs over their legs. Sometimes I would rock them, muttering words of comfort.

I was doing this to Aaron when a pair of navy court shoes appeared beside us.

'Aaron!' a sharp voice snapped.

His grandmother was looming over us.

'Get up. Now.' For one scandalised moment I thought she was talking to me. Then Aaron mumbled, 'I can't.'

When I loosened my grip, he rolled off and lurched to his feet.

'What did I tell you?' She glared at him. '*What did I tell you?*'

'Be a good boy.' He was barely audible.

'And have you? Have you been a good boy?'

He shook his head. I opened my mouth to speak but wasn't quick enough.

'No,' Joyce told her grandson. 'You haven't been a good boy. So I guess that means I have to take you home.' She looked me in the eye as she started untying her apron. 'That's right, isn't it? You'll be wanting him off your hands again?'

Her hectoring tone made my hackles rise. But I scrambled to my feet and said, 'Um—it'll probably be detention...'

'You don't know much about kids, do you? If he gives *me* any trouble, he gets a smack.' Turning on her heel, she headed back towards the canteen, adding over her shoulder, 'We should talk about it this afternoon. You people seem to be living in la-la land. It's not my fault you're not properly trained.'

Aaron, I noticed, was biting his knuckles. Hard.

'So what exactly is this?'

Scott Rooney looked suspicious. He was peering at Howard's permission form, his thick eyebrows knotted into a frown. I could see where Aaron's colouring came from. Scott had the same olive skin and dark hair, though his eyes were hazel. And unlike Aaron, Scott was big and heavy, with hands like softball mitts and a rugby player's neck. I could easily imagine him assaulting a member of the public. Or beating up his wife.

I thought he looked like a thug.

'We just need you to sign that form so Aaron can get some counselling.' Howard spoke in a placid voice. He was safely tucked behind his desk, which was covered in a parapet of stacked files. 'Our school counsellor is available every Friday, and we think Aaron would benefit from seeing her.'

Scott sniffed.

'Aaron's all right when he's with me.' Joyce was sitting next to her son. They had the same burly shoulders and bulldog jaw. 'He's only acting up because of Krystal. She's a bad influence.'

'Which is why he may need some help dealing with her,' Howard said smoothly. He then pushed the form towards Joyce. 'Since you're his primary carer, you should probably sign that too.'

I had to admire Howard. He might have been a slave to bureaucracy, but he knew how to massage egos. The words 'primary carer' seemed to calm Joyce. She picked up a pen and signed the paper without even reading it. Then she shoved both items at Scott, who followed her lead.

'We also think he should see a paediatrician,' Howard went on. Over by the window, I tensed in my chair.

Sure enough, Scott rolled his eyes and folded his arms.

'Why? Aaron's not sick,' said Joyce.

'No, but we need to make sure he isn't disadvantaged by any learning difficulties.' Howard took a deep breath. 'Or if you'd prefer, an occupational therapist might be a good idea—'

'He's not a spastic!' Scott interrupted.

'Of course not.' Howard didn't even flinch. 'But we can't get funding for a teacher's aide without a proper diagnosis—'

'I don't understand what this crap is for.' Scott jerked his chin at all my carefully structured, painstakingly printed

Home Help worksheets, which I'd tucked into a special folder with his name on it. 'If Aaron acts up, just give him a clip on the ear. It's not rocket science.'

'It's like you can't handle a six-year-old.' Joyce was staring straight at me. 'Maybe that's because you don't have kids yourself.'

It was a low blow, but I wasn't about to let her see how much it hurt.

Howard cleared his throat. 'Aaron threw a stapler at Robyn,' he reminded Joyce. 'She could have been injured. We need to make sure it doesn't happen again.' Leaning forward, he shifted his attention to Scott. 'We should be working together for an optimal outcome. Your son has a lot going for him and we need to make sure he doesn't get left behind.'

Scott blinked. For the first time I sensed a crack in his shell.

'Then maybe *I* should be there. In the classroom,' Joyce said. 'Don't parents and grandparents come and read with the kids every morning? Maybe I should, too.'

I was horrified. 'That's a generous offer,' I said. 'Next term, perhaps. We've got enough parent helpers for kindy at the moment.'

Joyce flushed. She took a deep breath. Before she could let rip, however, Howard intervened. 'Thank you, Joyce. What a good idea. We should give that a go.' He shot me a warning look, daring me to say a word. Then he pushed my worksheet folder towards the Rooneys. 'I think the more we cooperate, the better the outcome will be. If you accept Robyn's help at home, Joyce, she'll take advantage of your help at school. It's a win-win. Especially for Aaron. I'm looking forward to seeing him blossom thanks to our combined efforts.'

I was furious, but I didn't say a word until the Rooneys had gone. Then I laid into Howard.

'Are you delusional? I don't want that woman anywhere near my classroom!'

'She's a citizen volunteer. *And* a primary carer.'

'She's nuts.'

'I don't think it helps to be confrontational, Robyn.' As I opened my mouth to tell him that Joyce was the confrontational one, he added, 'Just give it a try. It might work. And if it doesn't, we'll pull the plug. We owe it to this kid to explore every avenue.'

Suddenly his landline rang. He reached for the phone with a sigh. 'This is a scheduled call,' he told me, then picked up his handset. 'Celine! How are you? Rising to the challenge of the new year, I hope?'

Krystal came to see me late that afternoon. She'd refused to attend the meeting with Scott and Joyce. 'We can't be in the same room,' she'd said. 'And anyway, I'll be at work then.'

She was on the registers at Bretts Agricultural Supplies, which closed at five every day. We agreed to meet at school after that; I was restocking paint when she knocked on the door, very timidly, and said, 'Hello?'

She was still wearing her uniform, which was a harsh

shade of burnt orange. Her hair was a mess and she walked as if her feet hurt. Though she was probably small enough to sit on one of the kids' chairs, I offered her my own.

'Whoof!' She collapsed into it with a sigh. 'Thanks. I've been standing all day.'

'I've never been to Bretts.' It hardly needed saying, since I wasn't in the market for fence posts or bulk herbicide.

'We have great gardening stuff. Really high quality. Kent and Stowe spades.' A flicker of interest animated her features for a moment, then fled, leaving her limp and washed out. 'So what do you want me to do? Sign a paper or something?'

I handed her Howard's permission form. Then I sat on the edge of my desk and described our plan for Aaron. Counselling. A caseworker. Maybe a paediatrician? 'There are plenty of things you can do at home. That's what this program is about.' I tapped the collection of worksheets I'd printed out for her.

'Sure. I'll do that.' She started flicking through them. 'Follow the leader?' she read aloud.

'It's a body awareness exercise. You press your finger against his finger and move it around so he has to follow you. Then you swap. It's a lot of fun.'

'Scott won't do this. Even though he's got nothing else to do.' Krystal looked up at me. 'Did you hear he was suspended? On full pay? For beating up my cousin?'

'No.'

'He's home all the time now, and he's spitting chips. It's bad for Aaron. I'm really worried.'

So was I. But I didn't want to dwell on it. 'Another thing

you can do, when you go shopping with Aaron, or when you take him to a playground, is talk about things as they happen. And make sure you listen to his replies. That's very important.'

'Mmm.' Krystal's mind seemed to be on something else. 'What happened to Blaine will help me a lot. Now Scott's suspended, there'll be an inquiry. Maybe I can get Aaron away from him.'

I felt a pang of apprehension. *Please God don't let me get involved in a custody dispute.* 'Right. Okay. But legal proceedings always take a while, so in the meantime we should focus on making the current situation better for your son.' Seeing that she was still lost in some kind of revenge fantasy, I asked, 'Do you have any books at home?'

'Books?'

'Picture books.'

'Of course!' A flash of annoyance crossed her face. 'Aaron loves his books.'

I had my doubts about that. As far as I could see, he didn't even know how to turn a page. But I've lost track of how many parents have told me their children love books.

'Great!' I smiled and nodded. 'So when you're reading to him, you should ask him questions. And encourage him to ask questions too.'

'Joyce won't do that. She never lets him talk when she's reading. Not that she reads to him much. Says she's too busy.'

It was obvious Krystal couldn't stay off the topic of her ex and his mother. Every time I tried to shepherd her away from it, she would circle back. She couldn't seem to focus on anything for very long; I wondered if it was stress, fatigue or ADHD. She kept talking about her future plans: how she was going to move into a townhouse. Study part-time. Sign Aaron up for soccer.

I found it almost impossible to pin her down. At last I gave up, and told her to call me if she needed help with Aaron. 'We're in this together,' I said, knowing I sounded just like Howard Bradshaw at his smarmiest.

'You're right.' Krystal was clutching my worksheets as I walked her out of the room. 'Joyce doesn't understand that. It's always her way or the highway.'

'Mmm.' I could believe it.

'And Scott's the same. He won't let anyone tell him what to do. Except his boss.' She reached the veranda and leaned into me confidingly. 'None of those coppers believe a word I say. They all think I'm a lying bitch. But now Scott's been suspended, maybe they won't stick up for him anymore. Especially in front of a judge. Don't you think?'

I didn't know how to answer. It was none of my business. I was struggling to find the right words when an engine suddenly roared nearby. Tyres screeched. Music blared.

Krystal gasped. 'It's him!'

'What?'

'It's Scott! Shit! Look!'

I was already looking. A silver SUV was burning tracks into the road out front. I couldn't see who was inside, but Krystal seemed to have no doubt.

'He's got nothing to do all day, so he's following me.' Even as she spoke, the vehicle skidded away in a blast of exhaust fumes. If Scott was the driver, he was doing everything possible to advertise himself.

'That's stalking,' I said. 'He can't do that.'

'Yes, he can.' She clutched my arm with a cold, bony hand. 'He's seen us together. You'd better be careful,' she hissed, then hurried off to her own car.

I wondered what the hell I had got myself into. Stalking might be the least of it.

2019

'THE FRONT DOOR was unlocked. They must have come in that way and left through the back.' I stared at the puddle of tea leaves and prawn tails soaking into my bed. 'They were quick. Really quick. I ran straight outside and no one was there.'

I thought about that moment. I'd been shaking with rage. Incandescent. But I'd seen nothing from the back steps—just the distant bush, the abandoned goat yard and the old outdoor dunny. I'd even checked under the house, which was raised on low brick piers.

Nothing.

'I'm sorry. This is unacceptable.' Shaun stood beside me, gazing down at my defiled bedlinen. I'd never seen him looking so grim. 'It's a break-and-enter offence. You could call the police.'

'The police? God, no.' I tried to avoid the police. 'Can't you handle it? I'd prefer that.'

'You would?' A look of relief flitted across his face. I realised that if the police were called, and people found out...

well, let's just say that not all publicity is good publicity. The bad kind could sink a business like Vetnet. 'We'll buy you a new mattress,' he promised. 'Are there any replacements you could use in the meantime?'

I thought for a moment. The stench of two-day-old garbage was making it hard to concentrate. 'There's a double bed in the matron's quarters.'

'Then we'll bring that mattress over. The kids can do it.'

'No. I don't want them in here.' It was bad enough having Shaun in my bedroom, peering at my unmade bed and the framed photograph of my father.

'Of course. Sorry. My men will carry the mattress.' It was strange to hear Shaun sound flustered. He put out a hand as I stripped the doona off the bed. 'We'll sort this, Robyn. You fix the plumbing.'

'But my sheets need a wash—'

'We'll wash them. Please.' He obviously wasn't going to take no for an answer. 'I feel responsible. This was our fault. We weren't watching the boys.'

I took a deep breath, then coughed as the smell of bad food caught in my throat. 'Some of them were missing. When we went to check the leak.'

'I know.'

'Aaron wasn't there.'

'Aaron?' He frowned.

'Darren.' Aaron was always the first kid I looked for. Wherever I went, whatever I did, I kept my eyes peeled for Aaron. 'I didn't see him this morning.'

'Didn't you? Okay.'

'There's a good chance it was Darren.' I realised Shaun didn't have all the relevant facts. 'I know him, you see. I used to teach him.'

Shaun studied me for a moment. His eyes were like little grey theodolites, constantly measuring angles. 'And he didn't like you?'

'Not really.'

He gave a nod and a grunt. Then he began to gather up my fitted sheet, turning it into a bag of rubbish. The reek sent me stumbling backwards.

'Are you taking that to the laundry?' I asked.

'No. I'm giving the boys a life lesson. Don't worry—you fix that pipe and I'll report back when we've got a result.' Lifting his pouch full of muck, he grimaced and said, 'This is going to drip. Do you have any plastic garbage bags?'

I fetched one from the kitchen and held it open while he inserted my sheet into it. 'Those prawns have to go in the right bin,' I warned him. 'We've got a system here—'

'I'm taking them to the dormitory.' His tone was harsh. 'The boys can learn to live with them.'

Before I had a chance to say anything, he marched out of the house.

I felt as if a bomb was about to go off.

~

The bathroom repairs took about half an hour. Replacing the damaged stop tap wasn't hard, but it needed concentration. I didn't even notice my stiff joints or wet knees until I'd finished.

The whole process calmed me. I felt less shaky afterwards. There's nothing like a job well done to give you confidence in yourself. Harassment? Vandalism? Conspiracy? *Bring it on.* I surveyed my handiwork with grim satisfaction, then went outside to open the shut-off valve.

Shaun was still on the parade ground, haranguing his platoon. Everyone was fully dressed, and there wasn't a towel to be seen, but some kids looked more dishevelled than others. Aaron was there, slouched in the front row, his wet hair dripping onto his uniform. Behind him Warren was inspecting boots.

'...and if you think this kind of behaviour is going to get you sent back home, you're wrong,' Shaun was saying. 'For one thing, the next ferry doesn't come until Wednesday. And for another, I don't expel people. That's too easy. If you're misbehaving, it's a problem. And I'm here to solve problems, however long it takes.' He paused for a moment because Warren was approaching him, arms swinging, shoulders back. Warren stopped and saluted, then murmured something in Shaun's ear.

Shaun gave a nod. Warren saluted again before moving to one side.

'Mr Stubbs,' Shaun said.

Marcus was in the front row, big and rumpled, his acne inflamed by soap and hot water. He stiffened and looked around, as if for an escape hatch.

'What have you done to your boots, Mr Stubbs?' With his

hands clasped behind him, Shaun closed in on Marcus. It was like watching a cat stalk a bird.

'My boots?'

'They're a mess.' Stopping in front of him, Shaun stared down at Marcus's feet. 'The toes are all hacked up. Like you've been kicking a pipe.'

'I didn't.'

'No one else has boots like this.'

'I didn't!'

'Mr Stubbs, I don't have any respect for vandals. But I do have respect for people who own up.' Though Shaun's voice made me cringe, I couldn't drag myself away. Like everyone else on the parade ground, I was mesmerised. 'Owning up takes courage. It's the people who don't accept responsibility—'

'I didn't!'

'Yes, you did!' Shaun's bellow made me jump.

'It was Jake!' Marcus suddenly swung around and pointed. 'It was Jake's idea! He said if we used all the water, we could go home!'

Jake was invisible from where I was standing. But I could hear his tetchy voice. 'That was a joke, stupid.'

'It was not! You said we could go home! I wanna go home!'

'You're not going home, Mr Stubbs.' Shaun's tone was flat. 'You'll stay here and face the consequences of what you did.'

I didn't want to see what happened next, so I plunged back into the bathroom and spent about ten minutes testing taps and packing up my tools, making as much noise as possible. I'd had enough for one day, even though the day had barely begun. I hadn't eaten breakfast and neither had anyone else.

'Ms Ayres?' Warren's voice startled me. I looked up to see him in the doorway. 'Can we come in?' he asked.

Jake and Marcus were skulking behind him. Marcus looked upset. As I rose, Warren added, 'These two gentlemen will be cleaning the bathroom today. But they'll need the right equipment. Can you show us where it is?'

'Uh...yeah.' I stooped to pick up the toolbox.

'I'll take that.' Warren grabbed it. 'You've got enough on your plate.'

'Thanks.' If he chose to carry my tools, I was happy to let him. Jake's scornful smirk didn't worry me. I was long past being goaded or embarrassed by kids like Jake—though I did get annoyed when the salacious little shit wouldn't step aside and let me out. We did a kind of dance on the threshold; I could tell he was being deliberately obstructive. 'Oh! Sorry,' he said, but he wasn't fooling me. I knew what he wanted.

He wanted me to squeeze past.

'Back off,' I warned him.

Behind me Warren asked, 'What's up?'

'Nothing. Jake's a bit slow.' My tone was more of an insult than the actual words. Jake coloured slightly and shuffled out of my way. So did Marcus. I emerged from the bathroom onto an empty parade ground; Rhys and Joe were on the veranda of the boys' dorm, and the kids had vanished.

I quickly worked out where they were, though. I could hear Zac's shrill protest drifting through one of the dormitory windows.

'This is a health hazard! We'll all catch some nightmare disease, and then you'll be in big trouble!'

'You're right. It is a health hazard.' Shaun's voice was clear and sharp. 'And Ms Ayres had to run the risk.'

'Sir—please, sir—I think Ali's gunna puke.'

'If Ali pukes, you can clean it up.' Ignoring the howls of outrage, Shaun continued, 'Don't blame me. Blame whoever broke in.'

'Sir! Sir! It was Connor!'

'Fuck you! I did not!'

'*Mr Pusnik!*' That was Shaun again. 'Ten push-ups. Now.'

I didn't want to hear any more, so I swerved towards the kitchen. Warren followed me, with Marcus and Jake in tow. Except for butter and milk, I'd laid out everyone's breakfast the night before. The kitchen benchtops were piled high with spreads, fruit, bagged loaves and tubs of cereal. 'I'm hungry,' said Marcus, as he trudged past. No one responded.

I went into the pantry and removed a mop, a bucket, two pairs of rubber gloves, a handful of rags, some tile cleaner and a bottle of disinfectant. It didn't take long. Then Warren handed me the toolbox.

'These two boys have an apology to make,' he said. 'Marcus? You first.' There was steel in his voice.

Marcus shot him a confused glance. They were about the same height, but Warren was wiry, weathered and as hard as a rock. Marcus, with his raw skin and extra weight, seemed more brittle somehow.

'Sorry,' he mumbled.

'Do it like a man,' said Warren. 'Look her in the eye.'

'Sorry, miss.'

'Not good enough.' Warren folded his arms.

Marcus took a deep breath. His face was flushed. 'It was a dumb thing to do and I wish I never did it and I'm sorry for all the work.'

'Jake?' said Warren.

Jake tucked a lock of wavy hair behind one ear and offered me a soulful look.

'I'm really, really sorry, Miss Ayres.' He spoke softly, with an earnestness that set my teeth on edge. 'I guess I must have convinced Marcus to do this, even though I didn't really mean to because I was joking. But I was stupid not to realise that other people are stupid too.'

Marcus frowned. Warren said, 'Jake.'

'I'm partly responsible, so I deserve to be punished,' Jake went on. 'I really respect you, Miss Ayres, and I'm sorry I made your life harder. I hope you won't hold it against me and that we can be really good friends going forward.'

You had to hand it to him; the provocation was so subtle you couldn't call him on it. I was pretty sure Warren felt uneasy. I could see it in his eyes—a slight shift. A hesitation. But all he said was, 'Right. Let's go. You boys have a bathroom to clean.'

As he left, he and I exchanged the kind of glance I hadn't exchanged with anyone for a very long time. It was a glance I used to exchange with fellow teachers.

Can you believe these fucking kids?

After breakfast, I cleaned the camp kitchen. Then, while the boys were doing their PT, I cleaned my own kitchen and the rest of the house too, because it wasn't just my bedroom that felt soiled. Everything did.

I was listening to Shaun's muffled drill commands when Joe and Rhys appeared on my doorstep. They'd come for the mattress.

'While we can,' said Rhys. They both looked shame-faced—Joe especially. His big brown eyes were almost liquid with distress.

'I can't believe we dropped the ball like that,' he said. 'We owe you big time.'

'You need eyes in the back of your head with this lot,' Rhys admitted.

'We've narrowed it down, though.' Joe was so busy reas-suring me that I don't think he noticed we were moving down the hall to my bedroom. 'There's three kids we can't account for at the time of the incident—Nathan, Darren and Jake.'

'And Sam for a moment, but that would have been tight,' said Rhys, hoisting my dirty mattress up off the bed slats.

'Yeah. It would have been hard for Sam.' As Joe shoul-dered the other end of the mattress, his voice grew strained. 'Though he is a prankster. He likes his jokes.'

'It wasn't a joke,' I said.

'Hell, no! But kids—they're impulsive.' Manoeuvring his load through the door, Joe added, 'Where do you want this? Shaun said we have to bring one back from the other house…'

'Yeah, I'll unlock it for you.' But first I had to unlock the old poultry shed. Waste disposal was a big problem on Finch Island; I had an elaborate commercial composting system, and the recycling was picked up once a month, but bulky scrap defeated me. I couldn't use the dump site near the Aboriginal compound because it was heritage listed.

For the most part I just left my old bits of furniture in the poultry shed for the next caretaker to worry about.

'Stick it back there. Anywhere you can find a spot.' I pointed through the shed door. 'And lock up when you're finished.'

'Will do,' said Rhys.

I headed for the matron's quarters, where I stripped down the master bed. When Rhys and Joe finally joined me, they grabbed the mattress and shuffled straight back out again.

'So anyway,' said Joe, reverting to the subject of Shaun's investigation as if we'd never digressed, 'the boss is all set to tear those three kids a new one and see what shakes loose. Swear to God, we'll nail the bugger. But it might take the rest of the day.' Adjusting the weight that was pressing against the side of his head, he added, 'Shaun says you used to teach Darren. Is that right?'

'Yes.'

'And you think he might have done this?'

I shrugged. Over on the parade ground Shaun was bawling at his platoon. 'Advance in review order! Not funny, Mr Kollios!' The noise grated on my ears like a screen door banging.

I had to unlock my own back door because I'd decided it would be a good idea to lock absolutely everything from now on. By the time I reached the bedroom, Joe and Rhys were close behind me. 'You like puzzles?' asked Rhys, hurling my new mattress onto the bed. He'd spotted the stack of jigsaw puzzles on top of my wardrobe.

'Sometimes.' I just wanted them to leave.

'Must be good to have a few puzzles when you're here by yourself.' Rhys smiled kindly. I had a feeling he saw me as a reliable but slightly pathetic middle-aged oddball.

'Do you want us to make the bed?' Joe was eyeing the folded sheets on my dressing table.

'No, thanks.' I took a deep breath. 'You should probably get back out there.'

'Yeah. We probably should.' Then Rhys left, and the room felt bigger. Joe hesitated on the threshold, his dark eyes searching my face.

'Are you all right, Robyn?'

'Fine, thanks.' For someone who'd been an army communications specialist, he was bad at reading signals. 'There's a lot to get done is all.'

'Sure. Well…see you at lunch.'

After they'd gone, I made the bed. Then I went to answer emails in my office. But I couldn't concentrate—and it wasn't just because of Shaun's rapid-fire commands as he put the boys through their paces. Even after he'd dismissed the platoon, I found it hard to fix my attention on quotes and invoices. My thoughts kept circling back to that heap of rotting garbage.

The broken tap made sense. It was angry. Desperate. Not impulsive—the timing was too precise—but it had that genuine tang of adolescent rage.

The garbage was different. It felt wily and vicious. It felt personal.

'Robyn?' Shaun tapped on the office door. 'Have you got a moment?'

'Yeah.' A quick scan of the room told me everything was in order. There were no discarded shoes or overflowing bins. No dirty mugs on the filing cabinet.

'Warren's giving a lecture, so I figured it would be a good time to do this.' Framed in the doorway, Shaun turned his head and reached for someone who was skulking down the hall, out of sight. 'We need to settle a few things and you're an important part of the process. That's why I thought we'd start right here. Just to get the ball rolling.'

'Sure,' I said. 'Why? What's up?'

A second later, Aaron Rooney stumbled into the office.

2009

WHEN AARON WALKED into the classroom on Tuesday morning, Joyce was with him.

'He'll be a good boy today,' she said. 'He's happy because he didn't have to spend last night with his mum.'

It was five past nine. Reading was scheduled for ten o'clock. The rest of the kids, thrilled to see a new face, were swarming towards Joyce like iron filings drawn to a magnet. But before I could remind her that reading hadn't started yet, she said, 'What did Krystal tell you yesterday afternoon? Bunch of lies, I'll bet.'

I couldn't believe my ears. Her son had been stalking his ex and Joyce seemed proud of it.

'As a matter of fact,' I said coolly, 'Aaron's mum came here to sign that permission form, so he can get counselling.'

Joyce made a derisive noise. 'Krystal might be dumb, but even she wouldn't spend thirty minutes signing her name.'

Jesus. 'Now's not the time, Mrs Rooney.'

'What did she tell you? Whatever it was, it's defamation.'

I took a deep breath. 'We talked about home activities for Aaron. Reading. Role play. The same things I told you about. Are you finding them helpful?'

'Not really. I've got better things to do than your job.' She glanced around. 'Where should I sit? Over there?'

'Not yet.' I was trembling, but my voice was calm. 'First you have to sign in at the office. Then you can wait outside till we're ready.' I thrust a tip sheet into her hand. 'You should check this out while you're waiting. It tells you what to do.'

Joyce wasn't even looking at me. She was waving at Phoebe. 'I know how to read, thanks.'

'This isn't about reading. It's about teaching.' I clapped suddenly, making a noise so loud and sharp that Joyce winced. The kids began to clap along. 'Everyone on the mat!' I cried.

It was a dismissal, and Joyce knew it. She shot Aaron a warning look, then turned and left. I was much too busy to notice what she did afterwards, but at five to ten I peered out the window and saw her talking to three young mothers. I hardly recognised her; she was all bright-faced and twinkly.

I had to paste on a grin as I motioned the women inside.

'That's my mum!' Phoebe exclaimed. Some of the kids were bouncing around, shrieking with excitement. To settle them I launched into another song. Then I introduced 'all our lovely helpers' and explained what was going to happen. I spelled it out very slowly and clearly: who would be reading to whom, where everyone would sit, how long it would take. But Joyce kept interrupting. 'Why give Aaron to anyone else?' she said. And: 'You're not giving me Phoebe? I've known Phoebe all her life.'

She was a menace. When she tucked in shirts and wiped noses, she did it so abruptly that she startled the kids. Instead of asking them, 'What was that story about?' or 'What part did you enjoy the most?', she'd say, 'That was a silly book!' and 'Stop interrupting me.' She traded quips with the other women and complained about the noise coming from my end of the classroom. Once she even wandered into the supply cupboard.

The only helper who disapproved of this was Amber's mum Beth, who had once worked with Joyce at the local council. Relations between them were obviously strained. The other two mothers—Dixie and Kate—seemed smitten with Joyce. Kate Canning was crisp and glossy, with the rigidly conservative façade of someone trying to distance herself from disadvantaged roots. She and Joyce were old friends; they were constantly exchanging little eye-rolls and grimaces. Dixie, Oscar's mum, was the exact opposite. Dad would have called her 'rough as guts'. She was loud, grubby and almost as big as Joyce, with a childish enthusiasm that really appealed to the kids.

By the end of the session I'd decided that Beth and Dixie were welcome any time, that Kate was better than nothing and that Joyce was a disaster. When they finally left, I saw Joyce muttering to Dixie and Kate as they glanced in my direction. Afterwards, I spent about ten minutes comforting Luke. 'Her finger's too hard,' he said to me, over and over again. He was talking about Joyce.

Later, at lunch, I told Deb what had happened. 'It was even worse than I expected. But at least I tried.' Studying Deb's plump, freckled face, I picked up a flash of doubt. 'Or should I give her one more chance? Before I tackle Howard?'

'Maybe.' Though Deb looked like a bouncy little teenage cheerleader, she had an amazing grasp of labour relations. 'You might want to give her fair and reasonable warning before you terminate her. We're in the public service, remember. And Howard always goes by the book.'

That made sense. 'So I need to show him I tried to work it out?'

'Might be safer. Especially with someone like Joyce.'

'Okay.'

'How was Aaron during all this? How's he been today?'

'Not bad, actually.' A quick scan of the playground revealed that Aaron was squatting near the bubblers, digging in the mud with a stick. He was all by himself, but at least he wasn't strangling anyone. 'He was pretty quiet. For Aaron.'

'Quiet is good. Quiet's a start.' Deb raised her voice. '*Ivo! Get down from there!*' Dropping back to normal volume, she added, 'Howard might count that as evidence in Joyce's favour. You should make sure you've got all your bases covered before you talk to him again.'

'You think I should get it down in writing? Maybe send Joyce an email instead of calling her?'

'Yup. And watch out for Kate Canning. She might give you trouble if Joyce is around.' Seeing my raised eyebrow, Deb explained, 'Kate belongs to Joyce's gang.'

'Joyce has a gang?'

'Oh, yeah. Big time. Kate's one of her enforcers. So is Pat Haas.'

'Haas…' I knew that name.

'George's mum. She and Scott grew up together.'

Patricia Haas. My heart sank. 'She's signed up for reading too.'

'Ah.' Deb's sympathetic tone sent a chill through me. 'Well—keep an eye on her. Forewarned is forearmed.'

'Jesus.' Squinting at a blur of small bodies that seemed to shimmer in the heat, I said, 'So now I'm up against some sort of P&C mafia?'

Deb laughed. 'Yeah, but that's okay. I've got my own gang. *Stacey! Put that down!* On the subject of gangs, what are you doing this weekend? Because there's a fundraiser at the CWA hall—we make jams and preserves to raise money for rural mental health. Would you be interested? It's a lot of fun.'

I couldn't see anything fun about an afternoon spent chopping fruit and talking to people I didn't know. But as I opened my mouth to make an excuse, it occurred to me that as an outsider, I was an easy target. Deb was right: if Joyce had a gang, then I needed one too.

'Okay,' I said. 'Thanks. That would be lovely.'

After school, I spent two hours composing an email to Joyce.

Hi Joyce, it said.

Many thanks for your help and commitment. I know you want

the best possible results for Aaron and his classmates. That's why I thought I'd better touch base with you concerning the parent-helper conduct guidelines. I'm sorry we haven't discussed them before, though you'll find some of this information in the tip sheet I gave you.

At Otford Public our parent community is expected to:
- *work under the direction of the classroom teacher*
- *refer any behaviour management issues to the classroom teacher*
- *treat all students fairly and impartially*
- *promote positive attitudes and interactions*
- *refrain from discussing personal information about students with anyone other than the classroom teacher.*

You're also encouraged to bring any questions or difficulties you might have directly to the classroom teacher, rather than airing them in class. Kindy kids are so easily distracted—it's always better to keep interruptions to a minimum!

Thanks again for your assistance. Working together, we'll have Aaron reading in no time.

Best wishes

Robyn Ayres

I knew Joyce wouldn't like it, but I didn't care. The main thing was to get her off my back.

~

Joyce showed up at school the next morning with Pat Haas. I hadn't seen Pat before, though I'd talked to her on the phone. Small and solid, with a smooth, round face, she had undersized features and mousey hair pulled back in a bun.

Everything about her was bland, from her discreet ear studs to her low-heeled shoes.

She looked completely harmless, but she wasn't. I could tell that from the way she just stood there, mute and disengaged, while waves of grievance rolled off her like Chanel No.5.

Everyone tried to placate her. Even Joyce. Even the kids. 'Do you want to read a different book?' Amber asked in a worried tone, after failing to mollify Pat with *Edwina the Emu*. Poor Amber had been assigned to her because I'd decided I could risk it. Kids like Caleb couldn't have coped with Pat or Joyce or even Kate, who kept surreptitiously wiping things before she touched them.

Luckily, Dixie was also there. She didn't seem fazed by Caleb's low humming or Aaron's stubborn silence. Instead she jollied them along, doing exactly what she was meant to do. She didn't need watching and neither did Kate. Even Pat was fine because she'd snagged the easiest kids.

It was Joyce who gave me trouble.

She kept whispering to the other women and creeping over to ask me for a word. The first time she approached me, I stepped aside and listened to her complain about Kayla, who was kicking chair legs. ('That little missy needs a smack.') The second time, when I told her she should speak to me after class, she came right out and said, 'You need to remind these children it's rude to talk while someone else is talking.'

Then Caleb had a panic attack. I put him in the time-out tent, where I started showing him how to slow his breathing by blowing bubbles. I'd already spoken to Howard about a learning-and-support assessment for Caleb, because we needed funding for a teacher's aide; it wasn't easy, coping by myself, and the last thing I needed was Joyce undermining me in front of the class. But that's exactly what she did, while I was down on all fours with my head in the tent.

'Kids like that are just looking for attention,' she said, her voice loud enough to be heard over the muted buzz of children's chatter. 'The more you give them, the more they act up.'

I didn't stiffen or scowl. Knowing that any hint of tension would trigger Caleb, I smiled as he blew a bubble. 'That's it! Well done!' Then I backed out of the tent and went to help Chloe, who needed a new glue stick.

It wasn't until the mothers were leaving that I finally spoke to Joyce. She was putting away some of the craft supplies, even though I hadn't asked her to. When I saw her bustling around, ripping paintbrushes out of kids' hands, I decided enough was enough.

I picked up a basket of paddle-pop sticks and followed her into the supply cupboard, where she immediately started rearranging shelves.

'You should put these paints up where the children can't reach them,' she said.

'Mrs Rooney.' At times of high stress, I tend to flatten my country drawl—and I don't think it's ever been flatter. 'I'm sorry, but this isn't going to work. You're not following the guidelines I sent you, and I'm finding it disruptive. I understand you have your own opinions, but this is my classroom. What I say goes.' As she sucked in a lungful of air, I forestalled her. 'You're free to complain to the principal. Of course you are. But in my professional opinion, you should withdraw from our reading program, at least for a while. Maybe we can give it another go next term.'

A shriek from the classroom told me I'd been away too long. Hurrying back, I was just in time to stop Oscar from attacking Kayla's pigtail with a pair of craft scissors. Oscar was probably acting up because his mum had just left; I saw her through the window as she headed for her car. Kate was gone too, though Pat was on the veranda, waiting for Joyce.

I was getting Kayla out of her plastic smock when Joyce thrust her face into mine. She was tomato-red; her bushy hair seemed to crackle with electricity.

'I know what you're up to,' she spat. 'You want Krystal to do this instead of me.'

'Mrs Rooney—'

'I'll be lodging a complaint. I'll be complaining to the Department of Education. I'll have you sacked for unprofessional conduct.'

By this time there was no background noise. I was conscious that a lot of anxious faces had turned in our direction.

'Keep your voice down.' My tone was icy. 'We can't discuss this here.'

Joyce went on as if she hadn't heard. 'You're incompetent, you're a bully and you're colluding with his mother. I know all about you. I know why your husband left. You don't like men—that's your problem. You're a lesbian.'

I couldn't believe it. I literally could not believe my ears. I was too shocked to speak for a moment, and Joyce took advantage of that.

'I've got a right to be here. Aaron's my grandson. When it comes to his welfare, what I say goes. And I'm not happy.'

Joyce was big, but I was taller. I could have grabbed her arm and marched her out the door. I could have yelled at her. I could have called her a homophobic cow.

But I couldn't do any of those things because I was in a classroom full of tender little people who were watching us silently, wide-eyed and worried.

'I think you should go.' You could have chipped at my voice with a rock hammer. 'Patricia's waiting for you.'

Mentioning Pat was a good idea. It reminded Joyce of her social obligations. I'd seen Howard do it with some success, and now it worked again. Joyce hesitated for a moment, jaw set, eyes blazing. Then she turned and stomped across the room.

On the threshold she paused and said cheerily, 'Goodbye, children! I'll see you later!' It didn't sound like a threat, but that's how it was meant.

After she'd gone, the kids all looked at me. I smiled back. Then I noticed Aaron was missing.

Bugger.

'Aaron?' I checked again, scanning the faces in front of me. Nope. 'Where's Aaron?'

Little heads turned this way and that as I edged towards

the supply cupboard. There was no one inside. Then a squeaky voice said, 'Teacher.'

It was Chloe, a fragile elf of a girl who always looked bemused, as if the world was one big puzzle that she couldn't quite solve. She was so quiet I worried she might have a speech problem. She certainly had a lisp.

'Aaron'th in the tent,' she squeaked.

'Oh! Thanks, Chloe.' I told the kids to hang up their smocks, then hurried over to the time-out tent. Sure enough, peering inside, I saw Aaron curled up on the blanket. One whiff told me all I needed to know.

He'd wet his pants.

'Aaron?' I spoke very softly. 'Do you want to go to the bathroom?'

He didn't answer.

'You can put on some new clothes—'

'*No!*' he screeched. 'Stupid bitch!'

'Aaron—'

'Stupid bitch! Stupid bitch!' Suddenly he sprang up, arms spread. The tent came crashing down. He burst out of its crumpled folds and attacked it, stamping and screaming.

'Aaron!' I tried to put a hand on his arm; he slapped me away and lunged for the nearest chair.

I managed to dodge it just before it hit the wall behind me.

'Everyone stand up and walk out the door!' I had to shout over Aaron's cries. We had already practised our evacuation plan, but the kids still looked bewildered.

I snatched up a yellow card from my desk and gave it to Phoebe. The card said: *There is an incident in Ms Ayres' classroom.*

'Everyone stand up and walk out the door!' I repeated, as another chair went flying. Someone started to sob. Phoebe seized Kayla's hand and charged towards the exit, but I had to nudge the other kids, who were frozen in horror.

'Quick!' I said. 'Don't run!' Meanwhile Aaron had seized a third chair and was sweeping it across a table top, scattering books and pencils.

'Stupid bitch! Stupid *bitch!*' he roared.

As I closed my classroom door behind me, I saw Deb hovering in the hallway. Phoebe walked right up to her and shoved the yellow card into her hand.

'Who is it?' Deb asked me.

'Aaron.' It hardly needed saying. Aaron was the main reason we even had an evacuation plan.

Deb flinched at the sound of a thump that shook the foundations. 'Take this to the office,' she said, returning the yellow card to Phoebe. 'Do you know where the office is?'

'Yes! I know!' Phoebe was almost bursting with pride. I'd shown my whole class where the office was on their very first day.

'Take Amber with you,' Deb told her, before guiding the other kids through the door to her room. They were scared. Caleb was whining and Luke wouldn't let go of her sleeve.

I glanced back into my own room, which looked as if a cyclone had blown through it. Aaron was attacking my desk with a plastic tub. I'd left my purse under the desk, as well as my sunglasses.

Let's hope Joyce hasn't gone, I thought, watching Aaron vent. There was nothing I could do to stop him, short of a chokehold.

And that filled me with a profound sense of failure.

2019

'OKAY, DARREN.' SHAUN closed my office door. 'I brought you here because none of us remember seeing you earlier, when someone was in this house. Can you tell us where you went?'

Aaron's expression was sulky. 'I dunno.'

'Sir,' Shaun snapped.

'Sir.' Aaron made it sound like an insult.

'You weren't in the dorm. You weren't in the bathroom. You weren't outside the bathroom.' When Aaron didn't answer, Shaun leaned towards him. 'Where did you go?'

'Not in here,' said Aaron. His voice sounded strange to me—too deep and resonant. My memory was full of his six-year-old chirp.

'Where were you, then?' asked Shaun.

'Dunno.' Aaron shrugged. 'Pissing on the bricks?'

Shaun frowned. 'What's that supposed to mean?'

'We weren't allowed in the toilet, but I had to take a piss. So I went out the back and did it there.'

'On the bricks?' Shaun said.

Aaron nodded.

'What bricks?'

'Those things—you know. Those piles of bricks. They hold up the buildings.'

The brick piers, I thought, and wondered if I should start hosing them down.

'Are you a dog, Mr King?' Shaun demanded.

'No.' A pause. 'Sir.'

'Well, you're acting like one. Dogs piss on walls, not people.' Before Aaron could do more than scowl, Shaun said, 'Did you see anyone else while you were back there?'

''Course not.' Aaron's tone was contemptuous. 'I was taking a piss. I didn't want any perverts watching me.'

'Sir,' Shaun reminded him.

'Sir.'

I couldn't understand why Aaron had been brought to my office. What was the plan? That I would embarrass a confession out of him? Play good cop to Shaun's bad cop?

I had to admit, Aaron looked guilty. He couldn't meet my eye. He kept scratching and shuffling like someone tortured by regret.

I thought, *Maybe it's the drugs he was on.*

'Have you heard any other boys discussing this?' Shaun asked.

Aaron stopped moving. 'No,' he growled, omitting the 'sir'.

'So there hasn't been any talk?' Shaun's tone suggested he didn't believe a word of it.

'Maybe. I dunno. I don't listen to those losers.'

'Do you have any thoughts on who was responsible?' As Shaun moved, the floor creaked in a vaguely threatening way. 'Because this doesn't make sense. I understand why someone might dump rubbish on my bed, or Mr Doyle's. We're making your life a misery. But why target Ms Ayres? All she does is clean up after you.'

Aaron said nothing. Shaun stopped next to him, tilting his head so that Aaron couldn't turn away without looking scared. 'What I'm saying, Darren, is we think the dropkick who did this might hold some grudge against her. And you're the only one who falls into that category.'

Aaron's head jerked up. '*Me?*' He sounded genuinely perplexed.

'Because you know each other.'

'Bullshit!' There was a touch of outrage in Aaron's voice. I couldn't tell if it was the outrage of someone falsely accused or the outrage of a teenager who'd been bracketed with a lame bit of background noise like me.

'I used to be your teacher in Otford. When you were six.' I was watching him closely when I said this, and caught something deep in his pale green eyes. A twitch. A slight recoil. 'Don't you remember?'

'No.' Too quick.

'It wasn't for long, but you made an impression.' As he shook his head, I added, 'That was before you changed your name.'

Aaron blinked. So did Shaun. I hadn't told anyone about

the name-change business in case it threw doubt on my whole story. Claiming I knew Aaron was one thing. Claiming he'd changed his name was another.

Shaun suddenly looked perturbed. But I was more interested in Aaron. A pink tide was creeping across his sallow cheeks. 'I dunno what you're talking about,' he said.

'You used to be called Aaron.' I was carefully monitoring every shift. Every flicker. Every breath he took. 'I tried to help. I really did. You were probably told a lot of lies about me.'

'Fuck this.' Aaron's tension exploded into a whirlwind of movement. He spun around and flung himself at the door. 'She's crazy! I'm outta here!' Then he vanished, leaving Shaun rooted to the spot.

Silence fell. I could almost see the world realigning itself in Shaun's head.

'He does remember me,' I insisted. 'At least, he does now.'

'Robyn...' Shaun trailed off.

'I'm not sure he's the vandal, though. I couldn't tell.'

Shaun took a deep breath. 'Why would he have changed his name?'

'A lot of reasons.' Marriage. Fear. 'I think he's hiding.'

'Why?'

I didn't want to go into it. I didn't want to expose myself. 'It's a long story.'

For a few seconds Shaun was silent. I could feel him withdrawing, even though he was still in the room. At last he said, 'Well—we'll keep asking questions. See if we can get to the bottom of this. In the meantime, I'll leave you to it.'

He was out the door and clumping down the front steps before it suddenly occurred to me: what if he'd added me to his suspect list? What if he was wondering if I'd dumped garbage on my own bed? I was a middle-aged woman living alone. I had to be crazy. Neurotic. Paranoid.

Stop it. I abandoned my invoices and went to sort out lunch.

There was a hill on Finch Island. From the peak you could see all the way to the mainland, across a wide expanse of brilliant sapphire bay. But the view was splintered into little shards by a network of tree trunks because the entire hill was heavily wooded. Only one small section had been cleared: a narrow strip that led from the base of the eastern slope to a spot about two-thirds of the way up.

This was where someone had put a zipline.

I'm sure it paid for itself in bookings, but the public liability insurance must have been monstrous. There was so much risk involved; even the path up there was challenging. A wide, sandy fire trail left the lazaret at its western end, meandered for about ten minutes through clumps of she-oak and scribbly bark, then arrived at the cemetery. From there the path was just a collection of uneven steps, zigzagging up the hillside until it reached something that looked like a two-storey treehouse.

The treehouse was actually a starting platform, with the tree supporting the cable. I had to inspect this cable regularly, along with the platforms, turnbuckles, stop block, trolleys, ropes and safety harnesses. The ropes and safety harnesses were kept in the boat house, where I stopped briefly before heading up the hill just in time to avoid the lunch stampede.

It felt good to get away, even though the cemetery was my least favourite part of the island. About two hundred people had been buried there, in a scrubby clearing that contained no more than half-a-dozen rusty iron crosses and a handful of wooden headboards. I'd learnt about these graves as part of my job, and there was one in particular that I found deeply sad. It belonged to a woman who'd given birth in the lazaret. Her baby had been taken from her and she'd died a year later. Though she was buried in consecrated ground, I couldn't help wondering if she'd killed herself.

I mourned that woman every time I walked past. I also mourned the Aboriginal lepers who were buried so far from their country. Most of them lay in unmarked graves; I was probably walking over their bones as I skirted the edge of the clearing and made for the zipline.

But beyond the cemetery, things improved. The trees grew taller. The views grew better. The steep path kept me so preoccupied that I stopped fretting about dead people. When at last I reached the starting platform, I was feeling calmer than I had in days.

For a few minutes I sat on the upper platform, enjoying the view. I thought about Aaron. How much did he remember? I was pretty sure he remembered Otford, but did he remember me? And if he didn't, why would he have attacked my bed?

Mentioning his real name had touched a nerve, so he must have remembered something. But how much did he really understand? He'd been six years old back then. Whatever he knew now would be highly coloured. Broken up. Filtered through the eyes of an adult.

There was no telling what role I played in his personal mythology.

At last I got up and ran through my usual checklist. I spun the wheels on the trolley and inspected its side plates for signs of friction. I examined the cable and cable clamps. Finally I started downhill again, to where a smaller platform marked the end of the zipline. Here I checked the brake, the stop block, the emergency arrest device and the tree pads, tightening a few nuts and bolts while I was at it.

I knew the veterans could be trusted. I knew they would test the equipment and use it properly. All the same, I felt a niggling sense of dread every time the zipline was used, because I was ultimately responsible. The buck stopped with me. If anything went wrong, I would be as much to blame as Shaun Steiger.

That's why I had to suppress a wince when I reached the end of the fire trail and bumped into a loose formation of uniformed campers. The veterans, who were with them, ordered them to step aside. Most of the kids were fizzing with excitement, though some looked less than thrilled. Marcus had been given the heavy bag of ropes. Jake was toting the safety harnesses. They both wore surly expressions as they shuffled out of my way.

'How's it going?' Warren asked me. He was bringing up the rear, where Ali and Aaron, damp with sweat, were dragging their feet.

Aaron stiffened. He was more aware of me now.

'It's all good,' I said. 'Just keep an eye on those carabiners.'

'Will do.'

Leaving them, I hurried home, where everything was quiet and peaceful. No veterans were shouting commands. No boys were screeching in the dormitory. The kitchen was a mess; I soon found myself sponging down benchtops, mopping the floor and tidying the fridge. I even had to pick some recyclables out of the compost. But it was calm. Relaxing. Without visitors around, I could hear the distant sigh of surf on the shore.

I'd been on high alert for a whole day, so it was good to let down my guard for a while.

Then I went outside to empty kitchen bins and realised the silence was making my skin crawl. The wind had died down. The birds had stopped cheeping. I stood for a moment, listening hard and scanning the grounds. Nothing moved. The whole place seemed to be holding its breath.

'Hello?' My voice sounded feeble. I wasn't expecting an answer, and I didn't get one. Yet I felt as if someone was out there, watching.

By the time Shaun and his campers returned, I'd been holed up in my office for three hours, doors locked, blinds drawn.

~

That evening, section two helped make dinner. There were only six of them, but they were noisier than section one—probably because they'd just conquered the zipline. Adrenaline was still flowing; they were so pumped that they didn't even make a fuss about peeling potatoes.

'Did you see Connor?' Sam crowed as he scraped away. 'That dude was so scared!'

Sam Kollios had the kind of ADHD that left you feeling exhausted after about ten minutes. He was a class clown, forever playing practical jokes and cracking one-liners. His parents had sent him to Finch Island because he'd started street-racing and train-surfing, and they were afraid he was going to get himself killed.

He'd already dropped a handful of potato peel down Flynn's collar.

'I didn't notice *you* pushing to the front of the line, Sam.' Warren was propped against a wall, supervising his section. 'What's important is that Connor faced his fears and gave it a go. Just like the rest of you.'

'That's right,' Joe chimed in earnestly. 'You can't be brave unless you start out scared.'

'*I* was scared! I was really scared!' Matt Spiteri was making a mess of his potato, hacking ragged chunks out of it. 'But I did it anyway and now I'm not scared anymore.'

Inwardly I cringed, wondering what the other boys would make of this. After a single day at camp, Matt was already covered in Band-aids and mosquito bites. It amazed me that someone hadn't knocked out one of his prominent teeth.

But the other kids ignored Matt. He might as well have been invisible.

'Flynn was scared. He was shitting his pants.' Sam grinned at Flynn, who had returned from the zipline with a limp. Flynn was always hurting himself, and every injury seemed to trigger an explosion. His tantrums erupted whenever he was upset, according to Shaun. They had stopped traffic, injured family members and locked down schools as Flynn wailed and ranted and flung himself off absolutely anything: seats, kerbs, beds, boats, bikes.

Since he was tall and big-boned, with multiple piercings and a shock of dyed pink fuzz on his scalp, he frightened people during these outbursts. And he also attracted a lot of attention.

'I wasn't scared,' he retorted. 'I was *hurting*. I hurt my foot.'

'You were screaming. All the way down,' said Sam.

'Because it hurt me!' Before Sam could do more than snicker, Flynn added, 'Anyway, *you* were screaming. I heard you.'

'Everyone was screaming,' Warren weighed in. 'It's what you always do on a zipline. Scream your lungs out because it's such a buzz.'

'Connor didn't think it was a buzz.' Zac Henderson spoke up without taking his eyes off his potato. I could already see a difference in Zac. He was quieter. Less strident. All his smart-arse talk of human rights had stopped. 'I was at the other end of the line when Connor got there, and he was shaking. His eyes were popping out. I think he's really scared of heights but he won't admit it in case we lay into him like he lays into us.'

Startled, I shot a glance at Warren. He raised his eyebrows.

Who would have expected such insight from Zac?

'I'm gunna dare him,' Sam announced gleefully. 'I'm gunna dare him to climb up on that big old tank out there.'

'No, you're not,' said Warren.

'He's a fuckwit, sir.'

'Oi!' Warren's tone sharpened. 'Language!'

The atmosphere hardened. Silence fell. I switched on both ovens as the boys laboured over their potatoes, brows furrowed, tongues out. Bruno in particular was painfully slow. A blank-faced kid who seemed to trudge through his days, he slipped under the radar most of the time because he rarely reacted to anything. He was the most unresponsive kid I'd ever seen; Shaun and I couldn't agree on what might be wrong. Depression? Attachment disorder?

He was as quiet as Sam Kollios was noisy.

'Connor's such a dick,' Sam said at last. He couldn't shut up for long. 'I hope we go back there. I wanna see him squirm. I'll say, "Hey, Connor, let's sneak up the hill tonight. No? Why not? You scared?"'

'Leave him alone.' It was Tyler who broke in—skinny little Tyler, with his bony face and white-blond buzz cut. I hadn't heard Tyler speak before. He was always on the fringes, watching, assessing, never asking or answering questions. His voice was low and hoarse and as rough as steel wool. I remembered what Shaun had said—that Tyler was probably stealing and wagging school to take care of his little sister.

'If you mess with that fucker, he'll mess with someone else,' Tyler said. 'Like Ali or Dean. Just leave him alone.'

'Language,' Warren said half-heartedly, but I could tell he was impressed. Those cops were right about Tyler, I thought. He deserved a second chance.

Then Flynn screamed, 'Ow! Ah! I peeled myself! I peeled myself!' Dropping his potato, he jumped to his feet and hopped around the room. The other boys groaned and rolled their eyes.

'Fucking diva,' Zac growled.

Joe went for the first-aid kit. Warren had to raise his voice. In the end Flynn didn't need a Band-aid because the peeler hadn't drawn blood. But what with his over-the-top performance, and Sam's attempt to hide Matt's peeler, and Tyler's bitter denunciation of Sam's 'fucking stupid practical jokes', I was relieved to finally walk out of that kitchen. An hour of unrelieved teenage sniping was as much as I could take.

It astonished me that Warren could put up with all the noise and drama. But I suppose he'd endured much worse. 'When you've been shot at,' he'd once told me, 'teenage boys are no big deal.'

I ate dinner by myself, at home, as the sky darkened. Then I trudged back out to monitor the campfire, keeping a close eye on every trip to the toilet. Matt went, and Flynn, and Connor and Dean, but none of them interfered with the plumbing. While the boys went to brush their teeth, I cleaned the kitchen. While they put on their pyjamas, I doused the smoking campfire.

Most of them were in bed by the time I headed back to my house. I passed Rhys on the way, shepherding Marcus Stubbs into the men's bathroom. When I wished them both goodnight, Marcus surprised me by saluting.

'Good one, mate,' said Rhys. 'Nicely done.'

It was nine o'clock. Half an hour later I was tucked between clean sheets. The doors were locked and bolted. The windows were shut. The curtains were drawn. The veranda light was on.

But the mattress from the matron's house was full of lumps. I found myself rolling around in the dark, wide awake, trying to find a comfortable spot. An hour passed. Then another. I knew I needed sleep; I had to get up early.

It was close to midnight when I heard something outside— a scuffling sound, followed by a hiss and a muffled squawk.

I sat up, then leaped out of bed and padded to the front door, where I hesitated for a moment. A rifle was locked in a gun safe behind the office desk. But I'd been told not to touch firearms if there were visitors on the island, so I darted into the museum and grabbed a pre-war cricket bat before stepping onto the veranda.

There was movement over by the dining hall. A pale T-shirt was just visible in the darkness, clinging to a large, muscular torso. Warren's?

No, Shaun's. Even with his back turned, I recognised his strutting gait.

He was hustling someone away from my house—someone in a dark tank top and droopy sweat pants. Someone with wide shoulders and flapping limbs.

Aaron Rooney.

2009

AARON WAS SUSPENDED for two days after his Wednesday-morning meltdown.

I didn't have to tell Joyce the bad news. Howard did it for me. He arrived just in time to watch Aaron throw a chair at a window. Then, after Joyce had yanked her grandson out of the classroom, Howard took them both back to his office.

I saw her at recess, storming across the playground with clenched fists. Behind her, Aaron looked bloodless and lethargic, like a little ghost. The image haunted me for a long time. I even mentioned it to Howard that afternoon.

'Joyce was furious. She'll take it out on Aaron. I'm wondering if his tantrum had something to do with her—she was really angry when I told her to leave. Aaron might have been scared because he knew what she'd be like after school.'

Howard grimaced. 'That's pure speculation.'

'Yeah, but—'

'Why did you tell her to leave?'

'Because she's impossible.' I explained why, concluding with, 'She has to be in control. There's nothing she won't do, I swear to God. If Aaron comes back with a scab on his lip, I'm calling the police.'

'No. Don't.'

'I know his dad's a policeman, but—'

'Robyn, this is someone's kid. We can't go barging in because you have a hunch. Do you understand how delicate this is?' He peered at me. 'Do you?'

'Of course.'

'Then why are you behaving like a bull in a china shop?' Before I could defend myself, he said, 'I told Learning and Support about our lockdown and they're sending a caseworker next week. If Aima or the caseworker think a police report is warranted, then their recommendation will have more weight than ours. They know the difference between trauma and autism.' He sighed and leaned back in his chair, making it creak. 'I applaud your concern, but there are proper channels for this kind of thing. If you don't follow them, you can get in a real mess. Believe me, Robyn, I've been here longer than you have.'

In other words, he was covering his arse. And mine. I had to give him credit for that, but I still felt a responsibility towards Krystal. She needed to know what was going on, so I called her after work. I told her Aaron had been suspended, then mentioned the caseworker. 'Have you been able to contact a paediatrician?' I asked.

'No.' Krystal sounded vague. She couldn't seem to absorb

what I was saying; I wondered if she was in shock. 'Does that mean Aaron won't be at school on Friday?'

'Yes.'

'Which means I'll have to pick him up from Joyce's house?'

'Unless you want to make other arrangements.'

'Shit.' She was beginning to sound tearful. 'Shit, shit, shit.'

'He'll be going to school very briefly on Friday for his counsellor's appointment.'

'Oh, Joyce won't let him do that. She'll say he's sick or something.' There was a long pause. I was about to fill it when Krystal said, 'Do you think you could come with me on Friday afternoon? When I collect Aaron?'

I was aghast. 'Uh…no. Sorry.'

'Then will you write a report for me? About all this?' The words started gushing out of her. 'I'm applying to the Family Court for a revised parenting order. My lawyer says I need supporting documents. He says one of them should be a teacher's report with Aaron's missed days and stuff. His tantrums. Can you do that?'

I thought for a moment. 'When do you need it by?'

'Um—next week?'

'Okay.' Howard didn't want me to call the police, but a teacher's report might be the next best thing.

'Really?' Krystal's astonishment made me wonder how often she received help from anyone. 'Are you sure? Do you want to talk to my lawyer?'

'No. That's fine. I know the drill.'

'You do? Wow! Thanks!'

'In the meantime, you should practise those exercises I gave you for Aaron. It might help him calm down.'

'I'll do that, I promise.' Krystal's voice grew wobbly. 'It's not his fault. He's like this because of his dad. He'll settle once he's with me—I know he will.'

It was the only time I ever heard her sound exactly like her mother-in-law.

Thursday was peaceful without Aaron. Caleb seemed calmer. George was less distracted. The only parents who showed up were Beth and Dixie; Joyce didn't even come to the canteen because she was looking after her grandson.

I don't know why Scott couldn't babysit. Perhaps he was busy stalking his ex or bitching about her to his mates. On Thursday afternoon I saw him outside Foodworks, ear-bashing some heavyset bloke with a beard and a ute. When Scott caught my eye, he scowled and said something to his friend, who stared at me.

I should have stared right back, but I didn't. I finished packing my groceries into the car and drove away.

Friday wasn't quite as peaceful, thanks to the parent helpers. Pat Haas arrived with Kate Canning, making me wonder if Pat could even drive. Then Kate asked me if it was true Joyce had been banned from the classroom.

'Of course not,' I said. 'She just won't be reading with the kids for a while.'

Kate sniffed. 'I think that's a mistake,' she said, and was

crisply resentful from then on. So was Pat, who stood around oozing dissatisfaction. When they finally left, I saw them in the playground talking to Joyce, who had arrived for Aaron's appointment with the school counsellor. The three of them talked urgently for five minutes as Aaron kicked clumps of grass out of the lawn.

I didn't see him after the appointment, but I did get a chance to ask Aima how it had gone.

'Interesting,' she said.

'Useful?'

'I hope so.' She didn't sound very sure.

'Did Joyce give you hell?'

Aima smiled. 'You know I can't answer that.'

'I might need some counselling myself if I have to put up with the Rooneys for much longer.'

I was joking, but the joke quickly soured. That afternoon, on my way home from work, I passed Mitch McCall's colourful house and noticed a silver SUV parked across the road. Scott Rooney's car. Slowing, I wondered if Scott was delivering Aaron to Krystal. Then I spotted a silhouette behind the wheel.

Scott was sitting there, motionless, watching Krystal's front door.

Fucker, I thought, and leaned on my horn as I drove past.

'Which was stupid,' I told my father that night, during our weekly phone catch-up. 'It's just going to fan the flames.'

'I dunno, love.' Dad always tried to be supportive. 'He sounds like he needs a good kick in the arse.'

'Yeah, but it's not my job to do that.'

'Seems to me it's your job to do bloody everything.'

'Mmm.' I thought briefly about the report I had to write for Krystal, then changed the subject. 'I'll be making jam tomorrow with the CWA. To raise money for rural mental health services.'

'That's wonderful. Good on you.' After a brief pause, he said gruffly, 'Mental health is very important.'

It was as close as he would ever come to asking if I was all right. I'd hit a bad patch in Sydney after Troy left. For that reason—and because of my mother—Dad always worried about my mental health.

'You can have a taste when you're here next,' I promised. 'You can sample a jar of Robyn's Old-time Tangy Mental Health Marmalade.'

'Was it your friend who invited you? Deborah?'

'Yep.'

'She's a marvel, that girl.'

'She is.'

I didn't realise what a marvel she really was until I arrived at the CWA hall and saw that Deb was pretty much in charge. About twenty women were crammed into the kitchen at the rear of the building—which was a friendly old fibro with lots of fire extinguishers—and every one of those women looked to Deb for guidance about jar lifters, sterilised lids, setting points and caramelised sugar. Even some of the older women needed her help. I calculated that half the people there were as clueless as me. The rest were wiry old experts with arthritic joints and clunky false teeth who were probably good at scones, too.

Deb's sister Sammy showed up, as did Beth, Amber's mum. There was so much noise and bustle in the kitchen that I didn't really get to talk to anyone until after the sealed jars had been left to cool. We were enjoying tea and biscuits in the main hall when Beth finally approached me and said, 'I want to talk to you about Joyce.'

I smothered a sigh. That's the problem with small towns; you can never get away. 'She won't be coming back as a parent helper,' I said.

Beth blinked. 'She won't?'

'I asked her not to.'

Beth stared at me, then laughed. 'Wow. I didn't know that. Wow.' She seemed slightly alarmed. 'What did she do when you told her?'

'Nothing.'

'Are you sure?' She sat down and leaned towards me. 'There'll be something. You watch. She once spilled coffee all over my keyboard while I was away from my desk. I could never prove it; people thought I was being paranoid.' Glancing around, she lowered her voice. 'Just be careful. She does things. Weird things. You wouldn't believe some of the things she does.'

I was unnerved. Beth was such a neat, no-nonsense kind of woman, with her steel-rimmed glasses and low-maintenance hairstyle. To hear her muttering like a conspiracy theorist made me wonder if I'd underestimated Joyce. Deb and Howard had already warned me; now Beth was getting in on the act. They made Joyce sound like a cross between the Stasi and Pablo Escobar.

Later that afternoon, when I arrived back home, something happened that rattled me even more. I'd driven past Mitch McCall's place and noted with relief that Scott Rooney wasn't sitting outside. But on reaching my own house, I pulled into the driveway, turned off the engine and began to feel uneasy.

It took me a few seconds to work out why.

My house stood on a corner. The wire fence out front had been partially engulfed by a shaggy photinia hedge, which shielded half my front yard from the neighbours across the street. Behind the hedge was a large square of dusty grass, with a chipped birdbath in the middle of it. I'd found this lifeless patch so dispiriting that I'd edged it with planters full of roses, hydrangeas, gerberas and geraniums. Their riotous colour filled me with a sense of achievement whenever I came home.

But this time there were no flowers to greet me. Every single blossom had been snipped off and taken away.

~

'Did the neighbours see anyone?' asked Deb.

'No.'

'So it might not have been Joyce.' As I rolled my eyes, she added, 'People take flowers, you know. It happened to my dad. Someone stole his zinnias.'

'I know. I realise that. I can't prove it was her. But who else would bother?'

Deb sighed, then broke away to greet some of her students. It was Monday morning and we were stationed in the hallway outside our classrooms, waiting for school to start. A steady flow of new arrivals meant that I hadn't been able to thrash things out properly with Deb. And when Krystal showed up with her son, I had to abandon the subject of missing flowers.

'Hello, Aaron,' I said. His scabs weren't fresh. His face was clean. He looked good.

'Say hello to Miss Ayres,' Krystal prompted.

'Hello, Miss Ayres.'

'Aaron's got something to show you.'

'Really?' I'd already noticed he was clutching a cardboard box.

'I made it.' He spoke so softly I could barely hear him. 'It's a pig.'

'A pig! Wow!' I was genuinely delighted.

'He made it with his Poppy,' said Krystal. 'Didn't you Aaron?'

'Yis.'

'Can you show me?' I asked. When he nodded, I flipped open the box and admired the pig. It was a papier-mache ball studded with egg-carton legs, button eyes and sponge ears. Its tail was a twisted pipe cleaner, stuck on with duct tape.

'This is so good, Aaron.' Seeing him smile for the first time, I was smitten by guilt. I had to remember he was a child, not an incendiary device. 'What's it called?'

'Lilla.'

'Well, Lilla's beautiful.' I stroked the pig's back. 'Would

you like me to keep her here for the day, so everyone can see her? You can take her home after school.'

Aaron's face clouded. He shook his head. Suddenly I remembered: 'home' was going to be different that night.

'We'll give it to Poppy,' said Krystal. 'Poppy will look after it.' When she reached for the box, Aaron's bottom lip trembled. It was a danger sign. I knew that.

'What if I tell everyone in the class about Lilla, and tomorrow we'll all make a pig?' I suggested. 'We'll read *Old Pig*, which is a lovely book, and then we'll make pigs of our own. You can show us how to do it, okay?'

Aaron stared at me, transfixed. Then he nodded.

'Wow, Aaron!' Krystal gently plucked the box from her son's loosening grip. 'Soon everyone will have a pig, thanks to you!'

'But not until tomorrow.' I had to rejig the schedule. 'Can you hold on till tomorrow?'

He nodded again—and for the rest of the morning he was no trouble at all. Sometimes he even joined in when we sang. Dixie spotted the change at once. 'Aaron was really listening today,' she told me. Before I could ask her to lower her voice, she continued, 'His granny's gunna be stoked. Can't wait to tell her.'

Oh great, I thought. *So Joyce will be getting a full rundown.* I glanced at Kate, but she was on her knees shelving books and I couldn't see her expression. I couldn't see Pat, either. Where was she? Then I spotted her out in the hall, waiting. She wouldn't meet my eye.

'Joyce loves that kid,' Dixie went on. 'She'd do anything for him. I guess that's why she gets a bit stroppy, eh?' Dixie's booming laugh almost rattled the windows. She threw back her head and opened her mouth so wide I could see the fillings in her molars.

I didn't have to answer because Luke started crying and I went to comfort him. Then the parents all left, and the recess bell rang, and I found myself in the hall, wrangling children. 'Stop running, George! Kayla, don't forget your playlunch. Oscar—slow down!'

The kids' backpacks hung off labelled hooks outside the classroom door. Watching some of the little buggers pull food out of their bags was like watching them disembowel an animal. Pockets were left gaping, with hats and spare undies spilling out. There were always a lot of stuck zips and leaky juice boxes. I would keep my eyes peeled for kids who didn't have any snacks, in case I had to break out the emergency biscuits in my desk drawer. But everybody seemed to have food that day. Phoebe had enough for a three-course meal.

I was helping Caleb extract a muesli bar from his backpack when I heard a shriek and a clatter. Turning, I was relieved to see no one flat on the floor. Aaron had simply dropped his lunchbox. An apple was rolling down the hallway. A sandwich lay near a shoe.

Then Phoebe started screaming.

2019

'DARREN SAYS HE wanted to use the phone,' Warren informed me.

It was Tuesday morning and we were sitting in my office. Out on the parade ground the campers were doing PT; I could hear Shaun yelling at them. But I hadn't been near them since the previous night.

After lying awake till the early hours, wondering if Aaron was going to come back, I felt too tired to cope with a herd of teenagers.

'The *phone?*' I echoed.

'He's saying he wanted to call his mum. And he knew there had to be a landline in here somewhere, so...'

'So he decided to break in?' I thought fleetingly of the lepers, who would also have been desperate to talk to their families. Their children had been forced to wave at them from moored boats. Their wives or husbands had been allowed to visit for just thirty minutes every six months. Kissing was forbidden. Hugging. Shaking hands. Even the letters sent by inmates were disinfected with formalin.

As for the phone: official use only.

'Are you sure he's telling the truth?' I demanded. 'Maybe he just wanted to get in here and trash the place while I was asleep.'

Warren took a deep breath. 'The thing is—'

'Because his family have a history of trespass. I've dealt with them before.'

Warren studied me for a moment. His eyes were brown, like Joe's. But while Joe's were as clear as milkless tea, Warren's were almost opaque, small and wedge-shaped and so deep-set they looked almost like his scars.

'The thing is, Rob, we're pretty sure Darren didn't mess up your bed. We've been asking a lot of questions, and it turns out someone did see Darren yesterday. Pissing on the house.'

'Who?'

'Ali.'

'Ali?' If it had been anyone else, I would have suspected some kind of collusion. But Ali…

'Are you sure Aaron didn't *make* him say that?' I was clutching at straws.

Warren blinked. 'You mean Darren?'

'Darren. Yes. Darren.' I could tell he'd heard my name-change story because his eyes narrowed. But he didn't pursue it.

'No,' he said. 'We don't think so. Ali's a good kid and he thinks the sun shines out of Joe's arse. He wouldn't lie to Joe.'

I frowned. My mind was working busily. If Aaron hadn't

ruined my mattress, then who had? And why? What had Aaron been up to last night? Had he really been so desperate to call his mother?

Perhaps he'd wanted to tell her about me…

'We figure it was either Nathan or Jake,' Warren continued, 'and we think it was Jake. Because Jake probably knew what Marcus was doing to that pipe. Jake would have been primed for it. That's why he moved so fast when everyone else was distracted by the leak in the bathroom.'

It made sense. I couldn't fault the logic.

'Besides, Nathan doesn't feel right for this kind of thing.' Warren shifted uncomfortably, scratching his ear. 'He's never caused any damage, except tagging. Jake, on the other hand…' He trailed off.

'What about Jake?'

Warren sighed. 'He's got a bit of a history. With women.'

'*What?*'

'Nothing actionable. But at school, when those teachers' tyres were let down, and the phones in their bags were smashed, and everyone thought it was Jake—'

'Don't tell me.' A chill settled into my bones. 'The teachers were all women.'

'Yeah.' It was the first time I'd seen Warren look really uncomfortable. 'It's his mum, obviously. She's schizophrenic. She's been self-medicating with all kinds of shit. She almost committed suicide—'

'*My* mum committed suicide. But I never broke into anyone's house.'

Warren looked shocked. I was pretty shocked too. Normally I don't talk about my mother.

'Jesus, Robyn.' His voice was gruff. 'I'm sorry. How old were you?'

'Fifteen.'

'That's hard. I'm really sorry.' He took a deep breath. 'My mum died when I was ten.'

We looked at each other. It was a strange moment. Then he said, 'We've got a plan.'

I waited.

'The ferry's coming tomorrow. Shaun'll tell the kids we're sending your kitchen bin off to the mainland for fingerprint testing.'

Warren went on to explain that the bin would be left in Shaun's hut, covered in pepper and chilli powder. Whoever tried to sneak in and wipe the bin clean would end up red-eyed and sneezing. 'We'll keep a close eye on that hut,' he added. 'You watch—someone'll go in there.'

'You think the kids will buy it?' I was doubtful.

Warren grinned. 'Hell, yes. Shaun can make them believe anything.'

'And then what?' I was expecting to hear that the culprit would be packed off home.

'Then we'll give the little bastard something to think about.' Warren's voice held something I hadn't heard before— a flash of anger. A hint of darkness. 'Like the Steamroller.'

'Like the *what*?'

'Don't worry. It's legal.'

The whole thing sounded dodgy to me. 'Shouldn't you just send Jake home?'

'Nup.' Warren shook his head. 'Do that and they'll all try something.'

'Mmm.' I still wasn't persuaded. But when Warren asked for my kitchen bin, I gave it to him. I also gave him a plastic bag, a pepper pot and a small jar of chilli powder.

'I'll need those back,' I said. Campers in the past had borrowed all kinds of things they hadn't returned: pens, bottle openers, oven gloves, antiseptic cream.

'No worries.' Warren's smile was meant to be reassuring. 'You won't lose anything else, I swear.'

After lunch the boys went for a supervised run. They wore shorts, trainers and backpacks, and took maps and compasses with them.

There were a couple of false starts. Everyone was about to leave when Dean Hoegel dropped to the ground and curled up, his arms wrapped around his dreadlocks. Joe had to talk to him for a while. Then, when the platoon finally did set off, it had to turn around and come straight back so Flynn and Nathan could go to the toilet.

But at last the whole lot of them vanished into the bush, leaving me in full possession of the lazaret. Every building seemed to relax and expand. I threw open the dormitory windows to let the breeze carry away that teenage-boy funk. Then I cleaned up the mess in the dining hall and went to weed my vegie patch.

I'd inherited a kitchen garden from my predecessor, who had built six galvanised planters halfway between the kitchen and the poultry shed. It was a sunny spot, and the outside tap was close enough for hose-watering—though I'd recently installed a drip system. I grew herbs, legumes, brassicas, zucchini and tomatoes. I didn't raise enough to feed large groups of people; most of what I grew was for my own consumption.

I kept thinking about Aaron as I picked tufts of billygoat weed out of the broccoli bed. What if he *hadn't* been looking for a phone last night? What if he'd been coming to talk to me? I wasn't making it easy for him; I'd been avoiding the campers all day, partly because they were such a challenge and partly because I'd been keeping an eye on Shaun's hut. But no one had been near it. The boys barely had enough time to turn around, let alone go snooping.

If Aaron wanted to call his mum, I thought, it was probably so he could warn her. Maybe he was scared of what I would do. They'd both changed their names, so they were obviously in hiding. He might be scared I'd call the police.

Perhaps if I reassured him, he'd stop breaking into my house.

Or not. It was hard to tell. For all I knew, he wanted to get even. A lot had happened in Otford, most of it bad.

I was sorting through ten-year-old memories when suddenly I heard it: the sound of breathing close behind me. I spun around.

'Jake!' I clutched my chest. 'Jesus!'

'Sorry. Did I scare you?' He was grubby and scratched but wearing his usual smirk.

'What the hell…?'

'I got lost.' He didn't even try to sound convincing. 'I had to come back.'

For the bin, I thought. His eyes weren't red, though, and he wasn't sneezing. 'Well, in that case we'd better tell Mr Steiger. He'll be worried.'

'No, he won't. He'll be angry.' Jake grabbed my hand as I reached for the UHF radio on my belt. 'You've got to help me. Please. You don't know what he's like. He's a sadist.'

It was the worst performance I'd ever seen. Even the catch in his voice was fake. I shook him off, disliking the feel of his smooth, sweaty fingers.

'Nice try.' I was lifting the radio to my mouth when he snatched it away. 'Hey!'

'I've never used one of these.'

'Jake.' I lunged at him. But he skipped backwards, simpering.

'You'll have to get it off me,' he said. 'I bet you're really strong. You look strong.'

'Drop it.'

'Woof, woof!' He stuck the radio between his teeth and began to pant like a dog, prancing around, trying to make me chase him.

I wasn't about to give him the satisfaction. 'If you break it, you'll be footing the bill. For that *and* my mattress.'

He took the radio out of his mouth. 'I don't know anything about your mattress.'

'Bullshit.'

'I bet it's soft, though. Has it seen a lot of action? I bet the springs are trashed because you're so strong and athletic—'

'Oh, please.' I was losing patience. 'Grow up.'

'I'd like to grow up. I'd like to become a man. But I need help.' He leered, and I knew he was trying to make my skin crawl. 'Can you teach me, miss? We can try now. While the others are gone. I promise I'll do everything you say.'

'In that case, you can radio Mr Steiger. My bin was bait and you're the one it caught.' Dipshit. 'If I were you, I'd start grovelling.'

Jake dropped the porn-star routine and scowled. 'I got lost.'

'Yeah, right.'

'I never touched your fucking bin!'

'Doesn't matter. You're here. Which means you're the main—ow!'

The radio hit my arm as Jake launched himself at me. His shove sent me staggering. 'Bitch!'

'I'm not your mother, Jake.'

'Fuck you!'

I was backed against a planter, but when he tried to kick me, I stepped aside.

Then I picked up a rake. It was the best I could do. Suddenly he was more than just an irritation.

The gloves were off, and I was alone.

'*Now* you're scared,' he said, baring his teeth in a smile that was more like a snarl. 'Now you're really fucking scared.'

'I'm scared you're making a big mistake.'

His answer was to stamp on the radio.

At that instant I heard the buzz of distant voices. Jake heard it too. I saw him retreat a step, but I didn't let my guard down. I didn't take my eyes off him.

'They're back,' I said. 'Early. That'll be your fault.'

The radio crackled. I glanced at it—and when I looked up again, he'd bolted.

'Jake!' I didn't bother running after him. He was a lot younger than I was and had too much of a head start. 'Jake! Don't be an idiot!'

My radio spluttered a second time. I scooped it up, but the antenna was damaged. It wasn't really working. I tucked it into my pocket and went to see who'd come back.

Warren had already reached the parade ground when I got there. He'd slogged up the jetty road with Rhys and Joe and a group of tired-looking boys. Some of the boys were collapsing onto the grass. Some were bent double, hands on knees.

'Hi,' I said. 'Listen—'

'Have you seen Jake?' Warren asked.

'Yes.'

His face brightened.

'But he ran off into the bush.' I pointed. 'You might catch him if you hurry.'

Warren groaned. He cut a glance at Rhys, who nodded and reached for the radio on his belt.

'Sunray red one, this is red three, over,' Rhys said, fiddling with call buttons as he moved towards the women's bathroom. Then Warren galloped off and I didn't know what to do.

I had to tell someone about Jake, but I didn't think Joe was the right person.

The boys around me were panting and speechless. Most were flat on their backs. 'My knee,' Flynn whined. 'My knee hurts...' Beside him, Zac licked the last drops of water out of a bottle.

'Where's Shaun?' I asked.

It was Joe who answered. 'Looking for Jake,' he said, scanning the platoon. 'More to the point, where's Darren?'

I glanced around. No Aaron. I was about to ask where they'd been when I heard the distant sputter of an outboard.

Joe heard it too. We locked eyes. Connor sat up. Rhys turned. A few heads lifted.

Joe and I both moved towards the jetty.

'Stay with them!' Joe told Rhys. I was already in front, but Joe soon caught up. The motor on my tinny was still turning over, again and again.

'It's all right,' I said. 'There's no fuel.' To discourage joyriders, I only ever attached a fuel tank when I needed to go somewhere.

Joe had pulled ahead. He was closing in on Aaron, who was crouched in my boat, yanking at the starter cord.

'Darren!' Joe shouted. He hit the jetty, his footsteps

sounding hollow on the wooden planks. Aaron tugged desperately at the cord—once, twice, three times.

'There's no fuel!' I bellowed. He must have heard me because he started fumbling around for the oars. But then Joe reached him as I hit the surf.

I waded in, hoping to grab the boat and steady it.

'Darren? Mate? Leave it alone,' Joe said breathlessly, hanging off the jetty ladder. 'It won't work. You've got no petrol.'

Aaron was shaking. I knew he was scared; he looked wild. Frantic. He needed reassurance and it had to come from me.

'Aaron?' I grabbed the engine's tiller handle and looked him straight in the eye. 'I won't say anything, okay? You don't have to panic.'

He stared at me. Joe was babbling on about proper channels and dead ends, but I wasn't listening. Neither was Aaron.

'Joe?' I said. 'Can we have a minute, please?'

Joe shut up. There was a brief pause. 'All right.'

I was still watching Aaron when I heard the clomp of Joe's boots on the jetty. I waited until the hollow thuds were replaced by the crunch of dirt underfoot. Then I told Aaron, 'You're sixteen now. You can decide where you want to live. I'm not going to talk about this, so no one will get in trouble. Okay?'

Aaron seemed stunned. He didn't nod. He didn't even blink. For once he was perfectly still.

'I always liked your mum. I don't blame her for what she did, even if it was against the law. The two of you were better off in the long run.' I glanced back at Joe, but he was well out of earshot. 'She had a tough time. So did you. I just want you to know I'm not going to make things tougher. You don't have to warn her, okay? Your secret's safe with me.'

Still Aaron said nothing. His expression was unreadable. 'It's going to be fine.' I held out my hand. 'Come on. I'll tell Mr Steiger this wasn't your fault. I know you've been worried. I know you didn't break into my bedroom.' After my little run-in with Jake, I no longer had any doubts. 'Let's just go back and have a rest. You can't row this tinny to Cleveland— you're too tired.'

Aaron looked at my hand. Then he looked at my face. Then he opened his mouth as if he was about to say something. But after a moment's thought, he changed his mind and started climbing out of the boat.

2009

PHOEBE WAS SCREAMING. 'Ew, yuk! Ew, *yuk*!' On the floor near her, three large cockroaches were scurrying around Aaron's lunchbox.

Oscar darted forward and stamped on one of them.

'Shh,' I said. 'Everyone calm down.'

'Yuk, Aaron!' George couldn't keep his big mouth shut. 'Is that a bug sandwich?'

'Shut up!' Aaron shoved him hard, then rushed at Phoebe. 'Shut up! Shut up! Shut up!' Suddenly she was flat on her back.

'Aaron!' I tried to grab him, but he dodged me. He was out the door before I could stop him. 'Mrs Olsen!' I cried.

Deb stuck her head into the hallway.

'Could you finish up here?' I asked her. 'Aaron's a bit upset.'

She smiled and nodded. I hurried into the playground, which was already ringing with children's voices. Everywhere I looked, kids were crouched on the concrete or rolling around in the grass. They all wore identical blue sunhats. It was hard to tell one from the other.

'Aaron!' I couldn't see him. But I spotted Prue Wilmott, who was on recess duty. She was making a senior girl pick up an empty chip packet. 'Mrs Wilmott!' I waved at her. 'Have you seen Aaron Rooney?'

'Aaron?' Prue looked around. 'No.'

'I have,' said the senior girl, who bore a striking resemblance to Phoebe Canning. She pointed. 'He went that way. He was crying.'

Prue flicked me a sharp look but all she said was, 'Thank you, Sarah.'

Sarah Canning. Phoebe had told me about her elder sister, who was in year five and seemed to know everything. 'Did he go into the office?' I asked.

'No.' Sarah shook her head. 'He went around the back.'

I set off to look for him, circling the administration block, checking the toilets, questioning the canteen staff and peeking into every classroom. At last I found him hiding under a demountable. It was a quiet spot behind a bush, out of bounds to most students.

I hunkered down nearby. 'Hey, Aaron.'

He didn't move, but I could hear his ragged breathing. I could also see his silhouette, dark against a square of light that was framed between two brick piers.

'It's silly to make a fuss about cockroaches,' I said. 'Do you know some people keep cockroaches as pets? I used to teach a boy in Sydney called Josh who had a giant burrowing cockroach. He kept it in a fish tank and fed it gum leaves and vegetables. And it was so clean he only had to change its dirt every three months.'

Aaron's head swung towards me.

'Cockroaches are really strong too,' I told him. 'They can survive anything. And you know what? They can live for a week without a head.'

There was a shuffling noise. Aaron muttered, 'No, they can't.'

'They can. It's true.' Josh had told me all about it, and he was right. I'd looked it up. 'The reason they die is they don't have a mouth, so they can't drink or eat. But they only have to eat once a month. And they can hold their breath underwater for half an hour.'

By this time Aaron was inching towards me. 'Can they swim?' he asked.

'I don't know. They can float. And run. Cockroaches are one of the fastest insects in the world.' Josh had told me that too. We'd had a lot of conversations about cockroaches because he hadn't been interested in much else. 'If they were as big as people, they'd be faster than a car.'

I kept talking about cockroaches until I managed to lure Aaron out from under the classroom. He was so absorbed he didn't even notice when I took his hand. I led him back to where his sandwich still lay on the hallway floor, and we discussed what to do with it. In the end we decided to throw it away and order another one from the canteen.

'Do cockroaches like bread?' Aaron asked in his croaky

little voice, as we dumped his lunch in the bin.

'Absolutely.'

'Where have they gone?' He looked around.

'I don't know. Maybe they're scared.'

'I'm not scared.' He thought for a moment. 'Not like Phoebe.'

'No. Phoebe was scared. That's why you shouldn't have pushed her.'

He scowled.

'Maybe if we tell her how interesting cockroaches are, she'll stop being scared of them,' I suggested. 'Maybe we should have a lesson about cockroaches. Do you think?'

Aaron nodded. It was very encouraging. Perhaps he wasn't so difficult after all.

Then an idea struck him. 'We could catch them and put them in a tank,' he said. 'And we could chop off their heads and see if they die.'

Or perhaps there really was something wrong with him.

~

I talked to my class about headless cockroaches after recess. It seemed to go down well, though I worried about giving Luke and Chloe nightmares. Everyone laughed when I said that cockroaches have three knees on each leg.

By lunchtime half the kids wanted pet cockroaches, and no one was teasing Aaron about his sandwich. In fact he was asked to come on a roach-hunt with George and Oscar. The hunt didn't last long; it ended in a squabble that saw Aaron throwing bags around. But I sensed a difference in him. He seemed more engaged. For the rest of the afternoon he was fairly cooperative, though he hurled a book at Caleb and kept stabbing his playdough with a pencil while everyone else was making animals.

When Joyce came to pick him up after school, I was able to tell her with perfect honesty that he'd had a much better day.

'And tomorrow he'll show everyone how to make a papier-mache pig. Won't you, Aaron?' I waved at Beth as she steered Amber out of the room.

Aaron didn't answer. He was staring at the floor, his hand caught in his grandmother's strong grip.

'Well, that's good.' Joyce was in strangely high spirits. 'I have to say I'm surprised he's been behaving himself, after what happened this morning.'

I had to think for a moment. Then it clicked.

'Gail made Aaron his replacement sandwich at lunchtime. She rang me afterwards,' Joyce went on. 'It's disgusting. This poor mite is living in filth on the weekends. I'm going to call Child Protection.'

The triumph in her voice was chilling. I cut a glance at Aaron, who was hanging his full weight off her, dangling like a dead fish on a line. Joyce didn't seem to notice. She was too absorbed in Krystal's failings.

'That woman is a health hazard,' she said, then flashed a smile at Dixie, who was passing with Oscar in tow. During first term I always asked parents to collect their kindy kids from the classroom; it was safer that way. 'I'm going to need a written report from you,' Joyce added. 'I want you to say there were roaches in Aaron's lunchbox.'

Something was wrong. I could feel it. 'How did you know about the roaches?' I asked.

'Gail told me.'

'But I didn't tell Gail.' I'd been careful not to.

'Well, the kids must have been talking in the canteen. I heard Phoebe mention it a few minutes ago.' Joyce frowned. 'I hope you aren't trying to keep it a secret?'

'Of course not.' I was thinking back. Breaking things down. 'But we don't know the roaches were in the lunchbox. They could have been in the hallway.'

Joyce snorted. 'They came from the lunchbox,' she said flatly. 'Mitch McCall is a pig.'

I glanced at Aaron. He was practically on his knees, swinging back and forth like a monkey. He'd hung his head, so I couldn't see his face.

'None of the other kids had roaches in their bags,' his grandmother pointed out. 'If they had, I would have heard about it from Kate. Or Dixie. Or Pat…'

Pat Haas. I pictured her standing in the hallway, avoiding my eye. She'd been waiting out there just before the cockroach incident.

No, I thought. *Don't be crazy.*

'So? Are you going to do it or not?' Joyce sounded impatient. 'Aaron! Stand up straight!'

'Do what?' I asked.

'Write a report. About the roaches.'

My heart sank. If I was going to write a report for Krystal, I couldn't really refuse Joyce. 'Have you spoken to Pat about this?'

Her eyes narrowed. 'What?'

'Have you discussed the cockroaches with Pat Haas?'

'What do you mean?' Her voice sharpened.

'You said if any of the other kids had roaches in their bags, Pat would have told you. I was wondering when you discussed it with her.'

'Why?'

I shrugged.

'Just write that report.' Joyce gave Aaron a little shake, to make him stand on his own two feet. But she didn't look at him. She was too busy glaring at me. 'If I don't have it by Friday, I'll talk to Howard. And don't be surprised if you get a call from social services. This whole thing is going on the record.' She turned on her heel, yanking Aaron across the room as she made for the door. On the threshold she stopped for a moment. 'And if you really think the roaches are living in here, you should do something about them,' she snapped. 'Instead of sitting around with your thumb up your arse.'

She was the last parent to leave, so no one else heard her, thank God.

'I don't understand why you're in such a state,' Prue drawled later, as we sat in the Royal Hotel. It was her birthday, and some of us had decided to take her out for a drink. 'Nobody's going to forcibly spray your classroom.'

'The whole thing's weird, though,' I replied. 'Really weird. Don't you think?'

'I tell you what I think. I think it's a stroke of luck.' When I stared at her, she added: 'For Joyce.'

'Oh. Right.'

'It'll even the odds. After Scott's big stuff-up.' Prue paused to drain her glass of wine. 'I used to teach that boy, twenty years ago. He was always a little thug. And Joyce...well, don't get me started. Do you know she once accused me of ruining a student's science project just so I could blame Scott?'

'Listen.' I took a deep breath and lowered my voice, though no one else could hear. The bar was quite noisy, and my other colleagues were bitching about the Catholic school across town. 'Do you think Joyce planted those roaches?'

'No.'

I raised my eyebrows.

'She wasn't there,' said Prue. 'You told me.'

'No, but Pat was. And Kate.'

Prue grunted.

'Would they have done something like that for Joyce?' I asked.

'Oh, yeah. She used to mind Pat when Scott was little.' Prue's gaze lost focus as she thought back. 'Pat's mother was a real piece of work. She's dead now.'

'It's possible, then?'

'Sure. But don't quote me. Actually, forget it. Right now.'

'But—'

'Do you know how crazy you sound? Listen to yourself.'

She leaned towards me; I could smell the shiraz on her breath. 'Planting cockroaches? Everyone will think you're madder than Joyce.'

'In other words, I should let her get away with it.'

'Like we all do. Yes.' Prue lifted her glass to me. 'Welcome to the Honourable Society of Joyce Rooney Survivors. Our secret signal is a nervous tic.'

She gave a honk of laughter and went to get a refill.

~

I received three phone calls that night.

The first was from Linda Balodis, the learning and support caseworker. Howard had already told me she would be observing Aaron at school the next day; she was calling to arrange an eight o'clock meeting beforehand. She sounded quite nice, though it's always a strain to have some random expert scrutinising your methods.

The second call came after dinner. It was Krystal McCall, and she sounded upset. 'I heard about the cockroaches. One of the other mums told me.'

'Oh. Right.'

'Those things didn't come from here. There's no way. We don't have roaches here. We have ants in the kitchen some-times, but that's all. Have there been any roaches at school?'

'Not that I've seen.'

'Was Joyce there this morning?'

'No.' I could hear her ragged breathing and it pricked my conscience. 'But Pat Haas was.'

Silence. I didn't know what else to say. Then I heard a sniff. When Krystal spoke again, her voice was thick with tears.

'Joyce did it. She must have heard about our toilet.'

'What?'

'Our toilet backed up last night. There's stuff all over the garden and we're still waiting on a plumber.' Krystal blew her nose. 'I bet she'll call someone. I bet she's going to say our house is a dump.'

'Is it?'

'No!'

'Then don't worry. Everyone gets a blocked pipe sometimes.'

'But with the roaches too...' She seemed to want something from me. Reassurance? Gossip? Suggestions? I couldn't work it out.

'What can I tell you, Krystal? Pat Haas was at school. She was standing near the bags. That's all I know.'

The wet noises continued on the other end of the line. I couldn't just hang up on her, so I said, 'I'm still working on that report. But I'll definitely have it to you by Friday.'

She gasped. 'Oh, shit. Will it include the cockroaches?'

'Well...'

'Please don't include the cockroaches.'

'I'll be focusing on Aaron's behaviour. He ran away after the cockroach incident.' A soft whimper from Krystal made me add, 'But there's no evidence those things came from your house. I'll make that quite clear.'

'It's because of my application. About the parenting order. That's why Joyce is doing this.'

I couldn't argue: Krystal was probably right. On the other hand, it did sound nuts. 'You should get a report from the school counsellor,' I said firmly.

'Scott was at my work yesterday. He's always hanging around there, trying to freak me out.' The ragged story erupted from Krystal like steam under pressure. 'Some stock went missing but today we found it hidden behind a stack of old pallets. I think it was Scott. I think he's trying to get me sacked.'

Again, I didn't know what to say. I wasn't her mother or her best friend. What did she want from me? 'I'm sorry. You're having a rough time.'

'They're trying to drive me out of town. Him and Joyce. They've been talking to our neighbours. I don't know what to do.'

Neither did I. 'Ask your lawyer.'

'I have.'

'Then call Legal Aid. Or…is there a local women's refuge? They must see this sort of thing all the time.' I was no expert, but I figured anyone who *was* an expert must be plugged into the nearest family violence network. 'Maybe they could refer you to someone. Or give you a plan of action.'

'Really?'

'It's worth a try.'

I looked up various phone numbers for her because she seemed incapable of doing it herself. At the same time, I wondered why the hell I was counselling a woman I barely knew. Didn't she have anyone else to help her? What about Mitch, or those other McCalls?

When at last I got rid of her, I felt drained. I certainly didn't feel like tackling the report she'd asked me to write. But it wasn't going to be an easy job, and I knew that leaving it till the last minute would be a mistake, so I dragged out my diary notes.

I was surprised at the number of entries that were all about Aaron. He really dominated the narrative, eating up great chunks of time. I began to jot down the main points, sitting at my kitchen table as the clock ticked and the fridge hummed and moths gathered in the darkness outside, bumping against the windows.

The third call of the evening came at around nine o'clock, on the landline. I had to get up to answer it.

'Hello?'

Silence.

'Hello?'

Still nothing. Then a gentle click, followed by the dial tone.

Wrong number, I told myself. But I went straight to the window and drew the curtain. I also checked all the locks and turned on the porch light.

By the time I returned to my computer, I was angry. Really angry. I sat down and typed out the report Joyce had requested, starting with the date.

Today I saw three cockroaches on the floor of the hallway outside classroom 3B, I wrote.

They were in the vicinity of Aaron Rooney's fallen sandwich. The hallway had been freely accessed that morning by thirty-three lower primary children, myself, Deborah Olsen, Patricia Haas, Kate Canning and Dixie Whitaker. I have observed no other cockroaches on the premises.

I added my name, printed out the paragraph and signed at the bottom.

'Fuck you too, Joyce,' I said.

~

That night I dreamed about my mother. It wasn't the usual nightmare. Instead of being stuck behind a fence, watching the yellow freight train charge towards her, I was walking beside the track, holding her hand. She wore a filmy floral dress and my blue sandals. She was laughing. Singing. But I didn't feel resentful, the way I did when I was in my early teens. I always used to hate how she would put the rest of us through hell, then turn around and laugh. It enraged me no matter how often Dad said it wasn't her, it was her illness. It was so unfair. Why was I the one who constantly had to forgive and forget?

When I heard the screech of approaching freight cars, I tried to pull her away. She wouldn't let me. 'Come on!' she said. 'It'll be fun!' She wouldn't let go of my hand. As the train barrelled down the line towards us, she stood there grinning, waiting for it to crush her.

I did the same, closing my eyes a split second before the inevitable impact.

2019

SECTION ONE HELPED me cook dinner on Tuesday night. Jake wasn't there; he was still wandering around the island. And Shaun was out looking for him.

With only Rhys backing me up in the kitchen, I decided to unveil some gadgets. Boys love gadgets—you can get boys to do almost anything if there's a gadget involved. I gave Marcus the garlic crusher, Connor the onion chopper and Ali the electric can opener. Nathan got the salad spinner because it had no sharp edges. Dean and Aaron shared the blender. Its deafening screech didn't seem to bother the boys; Dean actively relished drowning everyone out with the flick of a switch.

If Aaron was excited about the blender, he didn't show it. He was quiet and a little distracted. He kept shooting glances at me.

Even Connor noticed. 'What's the matter, Templehead? You got the hots for our glorious leader?'

'Oi!' Rhys spoke sharply. 'That's enough!'

'I'm just saying, it's rude to stare.' Connor was getting bored; he'd run out of onions. 'Unless you're in lu-u-urve…'

I was glad when Dean turned the blender on again, silencing Connor with a high-pitched howl. All the boys were keyed up and jumpy. It was something to do with Jake, I thought—and Shaun's absence wasn't helping. I felt a bit on edge myself.

At one point, dragging a pot down from a high cupboard, I heard Connor and Marcus whispering together. '…means they'll have to call police rescue,' Connor was saying, 'and then they'll send us home.' The excitement I could sense was the tension of inmates before a jailbreak. The boys wanted to leave. They could smell a whiff of panic in the air as the hours dragged by with no news.

Then, at dusk, Shaun finally emerged from the bush with Jake. They were just in time for a late dinner. Though I didn't witness their return, I couldn't escape the commotion it caused. And at the campfire gathering, when everyone was encouraged to talk about how selfish Jake and Aaron had been, some of the kids didn't hold back. Zac was scathing. 'Fucking genius move, guys,' he said. 'This is an island. The only way out is to suck it up.'

Achievement badges were handed out, but not to the failed escapees. They weren't even allowed marshmallows.

Judging from the endless string of barked orders I heard that night, the boys took a long time getting to sleep. The noise didn't stop until half past ten. I was heading for bed myself at that point; when I heard a knock, I had to answer the door in my dressing-gown, my face gleaming with moisturiser.

Shaun and Warren were waiting on the back steps.

'Oh! Sorry, Robyn.' Shaun averted his eyes as if I was wrapped in a skimpy towel. 'Joe told me you wanted to talk, but we can do it tomorrow.'

'No. We can't.' I knew how busy he would be the next morning, and I couldn't wait until the following night. 'It's okay. Come in. I'm having chamomile tea—do you want some?'

'No, thanks,' said Shaun. To my surprise, Warren accepted. As I put the kettle on, Shaun gave me a quick rundown of his afternoon in the bush. Leaning against the fridge, arms folded, he looked immensely tired. The overhead light cast deep shadows across the crags and hollows of his face.

'Jake must have circled back,' he said. 'All his rations were gone by the time I caught up with him. I reckon he was planning to raid the kitchen.'

I wondered what else he might have been planning to do.

'Little bastard needs a good hazing.' Warren's voice was hard and dry. 'He still won't admit he came back to wipe his prints off your bin, Rob.' Frowning, he glanced down at the bin in question, which was sitting in its usual corner. 'Is that...?'

'Yes. I washed it myself.'

'Oh. Sorry.' He and Shaun exchanged a guilty look.

'It's all right. You had a lot on your plate.' It was true: Warren had been in charge while Shaun was out searching. 'But I honestly think Jake is running rings around you. If you can't make him admit to anything—'

'Don't worry. We will.' Shaun sounded confident. Warren buried his face in his mug of tea. 'We're already making progress with some of the other kids,' Shaun went on. 'I gave out badges tonight—not just to Ali and Matt, but to Marcus and Zac and Tyler as well. And Dean's finally responding. He was really making an effort with his orienteering today.'

'Probably so he could escape and find his way home,' Warren muttered.

Shaun frowned. 'No, Dean's starting to engage. Rhys saw it in the kitchen. You did too, didn't you?' He turned to me for support.

'I don't know.' Just because Dean liked sticking things in the blender didn't make him a budding chef. 'Speaking of the kitchen, I'm not comfortable having Jake there anymore. Are you sending him home tomorrow? Because you should.'

'We can't,' said Shaun. 'If we do, they'll all go bush. Don't worry. We'll sort it.'

Warren was studying me, his eyes almost hidden in their deep crevices. 'What happened, Rob?'

I told him. I described exactly what Jake had done in the vegetable garden—what he'd said, how he'd looked, why he'd run. 'That was sexual harassment. He's got a real problem. I'm a tough old boot, so it didn't bother me, but what if I'd been some poor girl his own age?'

Warren frowned. 'You're not an old boot, mate.'

'I'm sorry.' Shaun was shaking his head. 'I'm really sorry.'

'Yeah, thanks, but what are you going to *do*?' I demanded.

'We're going to sort him out.' Shaun fixed me with a level gaze. 'There's a process. It's pretty effective.'

'The Steamroller?' I asked.

'That. And other things.' If Shaun was about to elaborate, he didn't get a chance. Because Joe suddenly stuck his head into the room.

'Hey,' he said. 'Hi, Robyn. Sorry about this—'

'What?' Shaun sounded impatient. 'Has someone wet the bed?'

Joe grimaced. 'Sort of. Nathan's been jerking off.'

Warren rolled his eyes.

'He's not exactly been discreet about it,' Joe continued. 'It's freaking them out a bit.'

Shaun straightened up. 'Duty calls,' he said. 'Sorry about this.' Next thing I knew he was gone. Joe was gone too; only Warren remained, still sucking down tea.

'You don't have to worry,' he said at last. 'We won't take our eyes off Jake. He'll be under guard twenty-four seven.'

I sipped my own tea. 'The police referred him, didn't they?'

'Yeah. He's in the program.'

'And they'll see a full report when he's finished?'

'Yup. It'll all be in there. Good and bad.'

I nodded.

'What do you reckon, Rob? Is this the worst group of kids we've ever had?'

I considered the question. 'Probably.'

'We're victims of our own success.'

'Mmm.' But however successful the veterans might get, it wouldn't benefit me. My salary wouldn't go up. My employer wouldn't listen if I complained.

Warren set his empty mug down in the sink. 'Would you feel safer if I stayed here tonight? Bunked down on the couch?'

I blinked.

'Or not,' he said. 'It's up to you.'

'Oh, no. I'm fine. Thanks, though.' I was stunned. As I closed the door behind him, I considered his offer. Was this part of the Vetnet program? Was he ticking off some kind of staff-support box? Or was he actually making a pass?

He was divorced. I knew that. Shaun and Joe were married. Rhys had just broken up with his girlfriend. The veterans barely talked about their personal lives, so it was difficult to judge Warren's motives. He didn't seem like the sort of bloke who would flirt on the job.

I won't say the possibility of a date made my gorge rise, but I already had enough to worry about. The last thing I needed was someone else breathing down my neck, however fit and clean and useful he happened to be.

Anyway, I thought, *he doesn't really know who I am.* I might have looked exotic, living alone in the middle of Moreton Bay, but I was a sad case really.

Familiarity would breed contempt.

~

I slept well that night. If anyone tried to sneak into my house, I didn't hear it. And the next morning, on my way to the dining hall, I caught a glimpse of the Steamroller in action.

The boys were doing PT: squats, planks, push-ups. Some were playing a quick-reaction game along the lines of Simon Says, with Rhys yelling, 'Toes! Knees! Head! Shoulders! Toes!'

But things were different today. Each section was being drilled by only one veteran instead of two—and over in the farthest corner of the parade ground, Shaun and Joe were both shouting at Jake. 'Lower! Release! Up! Lower! Release! Up! All the way down, Jake! *All the way down!*'

After twenty minutes of that, I would have been crawling.

At breakfast Jake sat between two veterans. No one was allowed to talk to him, and he wasn't allowed to talk at all. 'Permission to speak, sir,' I heard him growl at Shaun, who promptly said, 'Permission denied.'

When Jake muttered something rude in response, he was made to do twenty push-ups right there in the dining hall. Warren and Shaun kept roaring at him until he finally buckled. It must have given the other boys indigestion; Marcus and Sam and Connor seemed to enjoy it, but Ali didn't.

As for Dean, I found him hiding in the pantry while I was cleaning up. Joe had to coax him out.

I spent more time than usual in the kitchen that morning because I had to clear some space for the ten o'clock delivery. I was expecting fresh supplies for Saturday's passing-out parade: cream, butter, strawberries, rockmelon, bread. I had to make several trips to the outside bins and kept being stopped by boys with plates to scrape. Marcus tried to throw some plastic in with the food scraps. Sam completely missed my compost tub and had to pick his toast crusts off the floor.

Aaron sidled up to me, plate in hand, and said in a low voice, 'You knew my mum.'

I looked at him sharply. His wide, pale eyes were glued to my face. 'Yes.'

'What was she like back then?'

I had to rearrange my thoughts. 'She was scared. A little disorganised. But we weren't really that close.' Sensing a weird kind of intensity in his gaze, I felt compelled to add, 'She loved you. I'm sure she still feels the same.'

Aaron pursed his lips. Then someone called to him and he loped off. I thought about our exchange as I wheeled my barrow down to the jetty. For some reason I found myself wondering if Krystal was on drugs. Or an alcoholic. *What was she like back then?* It was an odd question. It implied there was something wrong with her now.

Guilt settled over me like a blanket.

The ferry arrived two minutes late. No one got off— people hardly ever did during the week, except when school was out. A deckhand rolled my boxes down the gangway in his trolley. We exchanged a smile. Waves clopped against the keel and passengers took pictures with their phones. After the gangway was pulled back on board, a horn honked three times and the ferry slowly departed, churning up white water. I waved goodbye because I was indebted to the ferry service— without it I wouldn't have had a job.

I had to make several trips back to the kitchen with the boxes, and I was loading my last crate onto the wheelbarrow when I heard a strange noise. It was a dog barking. For a split second I thought it must be one of the boys acting up, but then I realised the noise was coming from the wrong direction.

Dogs weren't allowed on Finch Island. It was a national park. *Blow-ins*, I thought. If they hadn't used the jetty, there was only one other place they could have moored their boat: Karboora Beach. But I didn't head straight there, because I had to dump my load. I moved quickly, passing Warren and Rhys and Joe as they drilled their platoon on the parade ground. Over by the dormitory Shaun was shouting orders at Jake. 'Eyes front! Right turn! Quick march!' I couldn't get out of there fast enough.

As soon as I'd shoved all the cream in the fridge, I headed back down the jetty road, to the point where it crossed another track near the shoreline. This track skimmed the edge of the mangroves, leading straight from the jetty to the beach. It was a route that circled the whole island, though here and there it had grown almost impassable. As I hurried along it, I realised I could smell smoke.

Sure enough, when I finally emerged onto the sand I spotted a fire-pit full of burning wood—as well as a very nice fibreglass cabin cruiser, a leggy blonde woman in a batik wrap, three tanned men and a slobbering boxer. The dog was sopping wet.

'Guys! We're not alone!' One of the men had caught sight of me. He was stocky and unshaven and almost bald.

Everyone else looked around. The boxer began to yap.

'Welcome to Buangan Pa.' I pointed at a sign near the

edge of the beach. 'It's a national park, so you may want to read the conditions of use.'

'Are you a ranger?' the woman asked, removing her enormous sunglasses.

'I'm a field officer. You'll have to put that dog back on the boat.'

'What?' The woman stared at me in disbelief. Baldy frowned. The only one who looked shifty was a shorter man with a beer gut and a flashy gold watch.

Unlike his friends, he'd probably read the sign.

'Are you kidding?' said Baldy.

'Dogs aren't allowed on this island,' I told him. 'It's a nature reserve.'

'But she's not killing anything,' Baldy pointed out. 'She wouldn't hurt a fly.'

The dog was already drooling on my shoelaces. I pushed her away with one foot. 'You'll have to put her back on the boat.'

'She'll jump out again,' said Beer Gut.

'Tie her up, then.'

'We won't let her off the beach,' Baldy promised.

I'd learnt not to argue. It was a waste of time. I had to be pleasant but inexorable. 'Sorry. It's the law. I know it's hard.'

Baldy scowled. Then the third man, older and hairier than the others, said, 'For God's sake, why are you being such a bitch?'

Beer Gut flashed him a warning look.

'It's a fifteen-hundred-dollar fine,' I said in my flattest

country drawl. 'I can write it up now or you can put that dog back on the boat. Your choice.'

'For fuck's sake.' Baldy whistled at the dog. 'Here, girl! Here, Corky!'

The dog ignored him. As I watched the chase that ensued, I thought, *Good luck keeping Corky on the beach*. It took all three men to corral her and wade back to the cruiser with the animal wriggling in their arms.

'Thank you,' I said to the woman as the dog was hoisted on board. 'I appreciate this. You have a good day.'

She didn't respond. I'd barely reached the track when I heard a high-pitched keening. It was the sound of an unhappy dog trapped on a boat.

The noise followed me all the way to the jetty.

I'd had to confront quite a few visitors over the previous eighteen months, but I'd only fined two—one for ignoring a total fire ban and one for smoking in the men's bathroom. I'd also chased away a pack of drunks trying to vandalise the zipline, as well as a whispering band of teenagers who came over in a tinny late one night before creeping up the jetty road. When they saw my cocked rifle, they quickly crept back down again.

That was something I'd never reported. I was pretty sure I'd committed an offence by waving my gun around, though I didn't feel bad about it. I was all alone, miles from anywhere. The police weren't exactly a ten-minute drive away. What else could I have done?

But most visitors to the island were no trouble at all,

so when Corky's whining stopped, I naturally assumed her owners had packed up and left. It wasn't until I reached the parade ground that I heard a dog's faint, excited bark. Corky didn't sound aggrieved anymore.

'Bugger,' I said.

Warren glanced at me. He'd been watching his section march up and down. 'Everything all right?'

'Some people are here with a dog.' Sneaky bastards. Gazing over the treetops at the drifting smoke, I weighed my options.

'Do you want them to leave?' asked Warren.

I'd almost forgotten he was there. 'I want their dog to leave, that's for sure.'

'No worries. We can take care of it.' His voice boomed out: 'Platoon! Eyes front! I've got an announcement!'

~

Shaun agreed to shift Wednesday's raft-making exercise. It would be in the morning instead of the afternoon—and on the beach instead of the jetty.

His decision transformed the parade ground. Suddenly boys were running around like ants. They were sent off to fetch nails and hammers from the poultry shed. Planks and tubs from the boat-house. Rope from Shaun's hut. Paddles from Joe's. Jake was the only kid who wasn't let loose. He stayed right next to Shaun until Rhys dumped one end of a plank on his shoulder. 'I'll take the other end,' said Rhys.

I was kept busy unlocking doors. But after about fifteen minutes, the frantic activity stopped. I turned and saw all the kids lined up in their sections, toting tubs or planks or tools. Sam was wearing a bucket on his head.

'If it was me,' Warren murmured in my ear, 'and I saw a herd of screaming teenagers heading in my direction with hammers and rope, I think I'd take my picnic elsewhere, don't you?'

Then Shaun shouted a command, and everyone marched off. There was a lot of noise. I smiled when I thought about Baldy and Beer Gut and Sarong Girl. They would probably pack up as soon as they heard Flynn squealing about his latest insect bite.

'Don't pat the dog!' I yelled, though the boys couldn't hear. The last thing I wanted was for Corky to start making friends with them. We would never get rid of her if she did.

I still had supplies to put away. But I also had to make a pit stop, so instead of heading straight for the kitchen, I took a detour. And when I reached my back door, I was lucky. Lucky I'd been near a mangrove swamp. Lucky I had to clean my boots on the mat.

Lucky I looked down.

The nails were brand new and gleaming. That was why I saw them—two of them, their points rising from a crack between the floorboards. Someone had crawled under my house and pushed the nails through my chinky old wooden floor, just near the back entrance, where I was almost guaranteed to step on them.

If they'd been rusty, I don't think I would have noticed them in time.

2009

I MET WITH Linda Balodis at eight o'clock on Tuesday morning. We discussed Aaron Rooney. She was pleasant and professional, with short feathered hair and shrewd brown eyes. I was glad I'd started writing Krystal's report the previous night because it meant I had everything in my head: times, dates, strategies, absences. I didn't have to consult my diary notes when Linda asked questions.

She scribbled away as I gave her the rundown. Like most caseworkers, she'd once been a teacher herself; I felt she understood what I was talking about, though she wasn't giving anything away. There was a sense of distance.

As the kids trickled in, she watched me interact with them. I introduced her to the parents as an 'observer from the department'. Most didn't seem interested. Some assumed she was a student teacher. Only Beth asked for more details—and when I told her Linda was there to assess Aaron, she said, 'Good.'

Joyce arrived a few minutes before the bell rang. I glimpsed her out of the corner of my eye and the adrenaline immediately kicked in. My heart rate sped up. I turned to Linda. 'Here's Aaron.'

She nodded. Joyce passed Luke's dad, who was on his way out, and flashed him a brilliant smile. Then she charged straight at me, dragging Aaron with her.

'Do you have my report yet?' she asked.

'I do.' As I reached for the envelope on my desk, I said, 'This is Linda Balodis, from the Learning and Support unit in Bathurst. She's here to assess Aaron.'

Joyce turned to stare at Linda, who held out her hand.

'Nice to meet you, Mrs Rooney.'

For a split second Joyce didn't respond. Then she smiled ferociously, eyes twinkling, head bobbing.

'Well, this is great. What a relief. I'm glad *someone's* showing an interest in my grandson—he's having such a hard time, poor kid.'

Before I could intervene, she added, 'His mother lives in a pigsty. There were cockroaches in his lunchbox yesterday. No wonder he's having trouble at school. But we're working hard to solve the problem.'

Linda proffered a polite smile. Then she leaned down and said, 'Hey, Aaron. I'm Linda. Can I show you something?'

Aaron looked alarmed. He began to bite his knuckles.

'Go on, Aaron. Off you go with the nice lady.' Joyce gave him a prod and he shuffled towards Linda, who led him away as the bell rang. I was distracted for a moment, rounding up kids and collecting money, but Joyce didn't leave. She pulled my report out of its envelope and read it right there in the classroom.

It didn't take her long.

'What the hell is this?' she demanded when she'd finished. I was listening to Amber's rambling account of a sick pigeon while I fiddled with Caleb's shoe, so I couldn't really concentrate on Joyce.

'It's your report,' I said.

'Are you blaming *me* for those cockroaches?' She was hissing. Seething. Blotchy with mounting rage.

'No. I'm not blaming anyone. That's the whole point.'

'There's something wrong with you.' Her voice was too loud. 'You shouldn't be a teacher—you're unstable.'

'Enough.' I rose to my full height. 'If you want to discuss this, we can talk later. School's about to start.'

'Talk?' she spluttered. 'I'm not talking to you. I'm talking to Howard. You're not rational. You've got serious issues.' She turned on her heel and stormed out, still clutching my piece of paper.

For the rest of the morning, Aaron was loathsome.

He spat on heads. He climbed on tables. He chanted nonsense words while I was trying to talk. He wouldn't keep still, no matter what I did—and I tried everything. Blowing bubbles. Traffic lights. Time-out tent. I made my class lie on the floor, breathing in green and breathing out pink, but Aaron just rolled around making noises.

I always felt sorry for the other kids in these situations.

They had to wait. And wait. If it hadn't been for Linda, silently watching from her chair near the door, they might have started acting up too.

Things didn't improve much when the parent helpers arrived, though at least the other children managed to get some reading done while I ran around after Aaron. As I peeled his fingers off my handbag, I sensed Beth's concern and Kate's disdain. Dixie was quieter than usual. Everything seemed wrong. I was getting more and more frazzled; Linda's eyes felt like spotlights following me around.

The class were pretending to be echidnas when Aaron, who had been picking at a scab, suddenly got up and wandered over to where Beth was reading with her daughter. He snatched the book away and scurried off.

'Aaron!' said Beth. 'Give that back!'

'No.' He sat on the floor and began to rip out a page.

'Aaron.' I went to stop him. 'If you want to read, you should choose another book. You can have this book when Amber's finished.'

'Fuck you,' he said. Beth gasped.

'I'll be very sad if we can't make pigs after lunch.' I hunkered down and looked him straight in the eye, holding his gaze. 'But how can we make pigs if you're angry? You won't be able to show us what to do.' I saw his expression change, though I couldn't interpret the shift. 'Why don't you give that book back to Amber? Then you can tell me what the problem is, and we'll do some volcano breathing.'

To my surprise, he immediately stood up. Then he

marched over to where Amber was sitting and slammed the book straight into her face.

~

Chaos reigned after that. Amber shrieked. Beth jumped up, cradling her little girl. Amber's nose was bleeding. Beth was in a state. I tried to help, but she wouldn't let me. She gabbled something about the hospital. 'If that child comes anywhere near her again, I'll call the police!' she said.

She was out the door with Amber before I could apologise.

By that time Aaron was in the storeroom, pulling supplies off the shelves. I ran to intervene as crayons and paintbrushes crashed to the floor. Linda had waded in to deal with a screaming Caleb. Dixie looked bewildered. Kate had grabbed Phoebe.

I had to use my special hold on Aaron, restraining him while he thrashed and yelled and tried to headbutt me. Then all at once he went limp. 'I wanna go pee,' he mumbled.

He was holding my hand when I emerged from the storeroom. Dixie was packing up books. Kate confronted me on her way out.

'I found that very disturbing,' she said in a low voice, her handbag clamped to her ribs. 'That child needs a firm hand— you have to learn to control him. If you can't, I don't want Phoebe in this class.'

She didn't wait for my answer, storming off with a great clacking of heels. Then Dixie approached me, wearing an uncharacteristically worried expression.

'Is there anything I can do?' she asked.

I hesitated. Aaron couldn't be sent to the toilet alone, but I didn't want to put an innocent parent in the firing line.

'It's okay,' I said, glancing at the other kids. I was concerned about them.

'Do you want me to get Joyce? She's on canteen duty.'

'It's all right.' I had to talk to Linda first. If I sent Aaron home, she wouldn't be able to assess him. But I didn't want him at school. Not after what had just happened. 'Thanks anyway. I'm sorry. Better luck next time, eh?'

Dixie smiled awkwardly. She looked at Aaron for a moment, then leaned over and whispered in my ear, 'Divorced parents.'

It was Linda who finally took Aaron to the toilet. From there she hauled him off to Howard's office. I didn't see her again until recess, when she returned to the classroom for Aaron's bag.

'He's going home,' she told me, 'but he'll be back tomorrow.' She and Howard had agreed that if Aaron was suspended, she wouldn't be able to finish her evaluation.

'Is Joyce with him now?' I asked.

'She is, yes.' There was a brief pause as Linda studied my face. 'I think you're right. I think she's part of the problem.'

I felt a flutter of relief. 'Then I'll see you tomorrow?'

'I'll stay here now, if you don't mind. I'm interested in Caleb.'

'Oh. Sure.'

'He's probably on the spectrum.'

'I know.' I quickly explained where we were with Caleb. Then a bell rang, signalling the end of recess; I was about to break off when Linda cleared her throat. She looked uncomfortable.

'Is this yours?' Fishing around in the pocket of her linen dress, she pulled out a sanitary pad, partly unwrapped.

'Uh…' It was the brand I used. 'Maybe.'

'Could Aaron have taken it out of your purse?'

'Aaron?' I gaped at her. '*Aaron* had it?'

'He was trying to flush it down the toilet. I heard rustling and muttering, so I went in.' She pointed at a scratch on her arm. 'He got very upset when I stopped him.'

'God. I'm sorry.'

'And when I asked him, he said that's what you do with pads. You flush them down the toilet.'

'Only if you want a blockage,' I began, then stopped.
Shit.

'He might have seen his mother disposing of hers,' Linda said with a frown. 'I'd be interested to know if he brought this to school…'

'I'll check.' There were children heading our way, but I had just enough time to rifle through my handbag.

Sure enough, my spare pad was missing.

'Would you kindly tell me what this is?' Howard pushed a piece of paper across his desk.

I leaned forward to look. 'That's the report I wrote for Joyce.'

'Why? Why would you do that?'

'Because she asked me to.' As Howard took a deep breath, I added, 'Krystal wants a teacher's report. I was trying to be fair.'

Howard sighed. 'Jesus.'

'What's Joyce saying now?'

'You shouldn't have done this. You shouldn't be getting involved.' He shook his head and dragged a hand across his face, rearranging his eye bags. 'A teacher's report is one thing, but this is a provocation. What were you thinking?'

'She asked me to write down what happened.'

'She says you're blaming her for the cockroaches.'

'Only because she has a guilty conscience.'

'For Chrissake!' Howard slammed his palm down on the desk. 'This isn't a joke!'

'I'm not joking, Howard.' Angered by his bully-boy tactics, I told him about Pat in the hallway. I also told him about my stolen pad and Krystal's plumbing problems. Though I had no direct proof, I couldn't help wondering if Joyce had encouraged Aaron to block his mum's pipes. 'I know it sounds nuts, but people have told me to watch out for Joyce. She does crazy things. She's malevolent.'

Howard's shoulders were up around his ears. He was leaning on the desk, rubbing his forehead as if he had a migraine. 'You're going to have to let this go,' he said.

'Howard—'

'I'm telling you, this is nuts.' He was shaking his head. 'Do you know what Joyce said? She said you're biased against boys. She said you don't like boys because you don't like men.'

'*What?*' I could feel the hot blood creeping up my face. 'I hope you told her to back off!'

'Of course I did. I also told her we wouldn't be moving Aaron to Deb's class. I told her we have a policy about that.' Howard's tone was glum. 'Oh—and Beth Meyer called. She's another one who wants us to move Aaron. Or Amber. If we don't, she's going to enrol her daughter at St Killian's.'

That was a blow. We stared at each other. Outside, the only sound was the roar of a distant car engine. All the kids were long gone.

'We need to put a stop to this endless drama,' Howard said at last. 'I know Joyce is difficult, but difficult carers are part of the job. You need to disengage. If she asks you for something like this?' He tapped my report. 'Just send her to me.'

'It's hard to disengage when she picks Aaron up from school every afternoon.' I sounded grumpy. I couldn't help it.

'I told you, just send her to me.'

'All right.'

'And ease up on the conspiracy theories. You don't want Joyce suing you for slander—she's perfectly capable of it.'

Ten minutes later I was heading for my car, loaded down with folders and flash drives and exercise books. I felt bone tired; all I wanted to do was go home and soak in a hot bath. But as I popped the boot, someone called out.

'Robyn?' It was Krystal. Her beat-up blue Mazda was parked nearby, and she was standing next to it. 'Can I have a word?'

I groaned to myself. 'What's up?'

She glanced over to where someone was climbing out of her car. As soon as I saw him, I thought: *Mitch McCall.* He was short and nuggetty, with white hair and sun-baked skin. Gleaming dentures were partly concealed by a massive moustache. He was wearing a bizarre hat covered in feathers and tinsel and fluffy toys.

'This is my grandfather, Mitch,' said Krystal.

'Hello, Robyn!' Mitch's voice was as rough and warm as a woollen blanket. He bustled towards me, hand outstretched.

I shook it.

'You weren't home, so we thought you might be here.' Krystal sounded nervous. 'Mitch wanted to meet you.'

'Face to face is more polite,' Mitch said cheerfully. 'You can see what you're letting yourself in for.'

'Sorry?' I was confused.

'He wants to be a parent helper. Like Joyce,' Krystal explained. 'I can't do it because I'm working, but Mitch has plenty of time.'

My heart sank. 'Joyce isn't a parent helper anymore.'

'Pat is, though. And Kate Canning. Kayla's mum told me.'

'I've helped raise the lad. He needs someone in there looking out for him.' Mitch's pale grey eyes were full of mischief. 'I'm good with kids. Ask anyone. I do magic tricks.'

'It's about reading, Mitch, not magic.' I didn't want to come straight out and say that people would think he was a paedophile, but I had to say something. 'The point is, you're not a primary carer.'

'I bloody am. I look after him all the time.'

'You still need a working-with-children check,' I explained.

'Oh, I've got one of those.'

'You have?'

'I told you, I do magic tricks. At fetes and things.' He pointed at his head. 'This is my Mr Magic hat. I pull rabbits out of it.'

I knew what Howard would say about Mitch. He would say that Mitch was a provocation. He would ask me why I was escalating the conflict.

If Joyce heard Mitch was in my classroom, she'd go apeshit.

'I can't, Mitch. I'm sorry.' Seeing his untamed eyebrows snap together, I tried to soften the blow. 'Let me ask Mr Bradshaw. It's up to him, really.'

'Joyce was allowed to do it,' Mitch protested.

'Yeah. And we ended up with a three-ring circus.'

'But—'

'I've got to think of the kids. If you're there and Joyce hears about it—which she will—she might start throwing punches. Do you want that to happen in front of my class?'

Mitch shot a worried glance at Krystal. 'Joyce is doing crazy stuff at school. She's undermining Krys,' he said.

'I understand that.' His expression pained me. 'Honestly, I'd like to help. We could do with more men in the classroom. But my principal won't like it. He'll say we're goading Joyce. Your best bet is to talk to him—he'll have a harder time saying no if you do it yourself.'

Mitch sighed. Then he nodded. 'Fair enough. I'll give it a try. But it's a bloody disgrace, the way that woman's holding everyone hostage.'

I agreed with him, though I couldn't say so; I'd already said enough about Joyce. Turning to Krystal, I took a deep breath and told her, 'Aaron was sent home again. I was going to ring you about it.'

Mitch's whole face sagged. He squeezed Krystal's arm.

'He would have been suspended, but the caseworker has to see him tomorrow,' I continued. 'She was there today as well.'

Krystal licked her dry lips. Then she cleared her throat. 'What did he do?'

'He hit a little girl in the face. With a book.'

She covered her eyes. Mitch winced and said, 'He's seen his dad hit his mum.'

Their sorrow was genuine. I could feel it. Krystal had gone white.

'There's something else you should know. About Aaron.' I was being reckless, but I couldn't help myself. 'He tried to flush a sanitary napkin down the toilet today. Could he have seen you do that yourself, Krystal?'

'*Me?*' A red wash flooded her pale face. 'No, of course not, it blocks the—'

'Christ.' Mitch grabbed her arm, his eyes nearly popping out of his head. 'Krys, the drain! The bloody drain!'

That's when I saw it: Scott's SUV. It was parked up the road, and its brake lights suddenly flared, catching my eye.

'Jesus,' I said.

Mitch followed my gaze. 'Oh, yeah. Bastard.' He didn't sound surprised.

'Scott's always following me around.' Krystal's tone was weary. Defeated. 'I'm used to it.'

'You should take out an AVO.'

Mitch gave a snort. He tucked Krystal's arm under his, then pulled firmly at his hat brim. 'Is the headmaster—what's-his-name—is he here now?'

'Yes, but—'

'We'll go and have a word. Thanks, love. I know you've been doing your best. It must be hard.' He flashed me a plucky grin and moved off, heading straight for Howard's office. Krystal went with him, trudging along like a captive.

I toyed with the idea of following them but decided against it. Howard was likely to blame me for the visit if I did.

After climbing into my Nissan, I pulled out of the carpark. The road was lined with modest houses and a scattering of trees; it was tranquil now that all the parents had gone. But as I passed Scott, I shattered the peace by giving him a long, hard blast on the horn.

I was almost out of sight before I finally lifted my hand off the button. By that time, I felt I'd made my point. I'd put him on notice. I'd vented.

Six minutes later I arrived home, where no friendly flowers greeted me. I braked beside the mailbox and collected a couple of flyers, then parked in front of the garage. Popped the boot. Unpacked it.

I was slinging bags over my shoulder when I realised someone had been moving my planters around.

The roses and gerberas had swapped places.

2019

I PUT JARS over the vicious little nails sticking out of my kitchen floor. Then I waited.

But the campers didn't return for lunch. They were too busy building rafts on the beach. At around midday I spotted Joe leading Ali and Matt up the jetty road; they'd been sent back to assemble a picnic. I helped them make sandwiches, then stuffed some fruit, biscuits and juice boxes into four large crates. Two of the crates were loaded onto my barrow. Joe carried the third, and Matt and Ali were in charge of the fourth.

I had to push the barrow all the way to the beach—where two rafts were slowly taking shape. There was no sign of the boat or its crew.

'They left,' Warren told me with a grin. 'Couldn't get out of here fast enough.'

I nodded. Scanning the faces around me, I wondered who had stolen those nails. Not Jake; the veterans hadn't taken their eyes off him. Even now he was standing next to Rhys, winding up loose hanks of rope.

The other boys were straining and squabbling over their rafts. But the food was a major distraction. Activity slowed. Heads turned. When Shaun blew a whistle, the whole platoon scrambled across the beach and lined up in front of him. Then Joe started handing out lunch.

I moved closer, wanting the kids to look me straight in the eye. I was anxious to see how they'd react. Would they smirk? Glower? Turn away?

'Rob?' said Warren. 'You all right?'

'No.' I didn't suspect Ali or Matt or Dean. Marcus kept his focus on the food; was that greed or guilt? Nathan's wet, lingering gaze crept over me like a snail—creepy, but then Nathan was always creepy. Nothing new there.

'Why? What's up?' Warren asked.

Aaron was flicking glances in my direction. We had a shared past, though, and it was complicated. He hadn't necessarily stuck nails through my floor.

'Rob?'

Connor ignored me. So did Flynn, who was busy peeling the ham out of his sandwich. Tyler assessed me coolly, the way he assessed the whole world. Sam pulled a face at me—again, nothing new there.

'*Rob.*' Warren sounded anxious.

'Tell Shaun to come to my office.' I gave the wheelbarrow a gentle kick. 'You can put all the rubbish in there and bring it back when you're done.'

'Wait. What happened?'

'The usual.' I didn't want to talk about it—not in front of the boys. As Warren opened his mouth again, I turned and left.

I went straight home and locked all the doors, then inspected the floors in every room. No more nails. I sat at my desk and started to think.

The mischief must have happened earlier, when everyone was rushing around. There had been two boxes of nails in the poultry shed; I'd handed the first to Matt and the second to Ali. Then Matt had dropped his box, probably because someone had shoved him. I remembered seeing a knot of kids picking up the scattered nails: Matt, Flynn, Tyler, Nathan…

My only hope was that the veterans had been keeping tabs on people. One of the boys had slipped under my house and spent a couple of minutes pushing nails through the cracks between the floorboards. Had Shaun or Warren stopped to think, 'Where's so-and-so?' Had they wondered why somebody was taking so long?

A knock at the front door made my heart skip a beat. I looked around for something heavy. Picked up a desk stapler. Moved into the hallway. But it was Shaun who stood outside, peering through the glass.

He frowned when he heard me unlock the deadbolt.

'Hi.' He was all sweaty and breathless. 'What's wrong?'

I glanced down the road to the jetty. Warren and Jake were standing at the water's edge.

'Where are the others?' I asked.

'Launching their rafts.' Seeing my expression, Shaun explained, 'Joe and Rhys are with them. Don't worry—they won't be heading for Cleveland.'

'Is everyone accounted for?'

'Yes. Why? What's up?'

I ushered him into the kitchen and lifted the jars off the nails.

'Jesus.' He blanched beneath his sunburn.

I waited.

'It wasn't Jake,' he said at last. 'It couldn't have been. We were watching him the whole time.'

'I know.'

'Matt dropped a box of nails. And Zac had the other box…'

'Anyone could have picked up a nail. It's what happened afterwards that matters.' I was way ahead of him. 'Who had enough time? Did you see? Someone went missing for a couple of minutes, between about ten forty-five and eleven.'

'Not Matt,' he said. 'And not Connor. I was reaming him out for pushing Matt.'

Okay. So I could cross Connor off the list: Connor and Ali and Jake and Matt and probably Dean. That left eight. 'Think about it,' I urged Shaun. 'Ask the others. We've got to find out who did this.'

'We will.' He was staring at the nails. 'Christ, this is…I can't believe it.'

'Why was it done?' That's what I didn't get. 'Is it a prank? Is he a psychopath? Is there something he hopes to gain?'

'Could it be Darren?' Shaun asked suddenly. His eyes searched my face, as if he hoped to find an answer there.

'I don't know.' It was the obvious conclusion, but it didn't feel right. 'I don't think so.'

Without warning, Shaun hunkered down and gently touched one of the nails. 'I'll get rid of these. Have you got any pliers?'

'Don't worry. I'll sort it.'

'Rob—'

'You're busy.' I was feeling like a target again. Harassed. Persecuted. It triggered something that I could hear seeping into my voice. 'Just do your job and I'll do mine. The sooner you stop this, the sooner I'll be able to sleep.'

Shaun straightened. His look of concern annoyed me. 'I'm sorry, Robyn.'

'I'll have to report it. The department will decide what to do.' I saw something flicker across his face but couldn't pin it down. 'You need more staff. Or better screening. Or maybe you should stop taking police referrals.'

He narrowed his eyes. 'You think it was Nathan? Or Tyler?'

'I don't know. I'm just saying, something has to change.'

'Jake admitted he broke into your house.' Shaun paused for a moment, gauging my reaction. When I blinked, he continued, 'I was getting him prepped for a forced march back to the jetty, but he wanted to go on a raft. "Okay, okay, I dumped the fucking prawns!"' Shaun's imitation of Jake sounded more like a snivelling three-year-old. 'And I know he wasn't feeding me something I wanted to hear. None of the other kids saw those prawns.'

I thought about this. The Steamroller had worked—on Jake, at least. I was surprised. Impressed. It made me wonder if I should be putting more faith in Shaun's rather brutal methods.

'I didn't ask him why,' Shane went on. 'I'll do that later.' He pointed at the nearest nail. 'We'll get this bastard, Robyn.'

What could I say? I liked Shaun. And Rhys. And Warren and Joe. I didn't want to ruin their business.

'You'll have to keep an eye on the kids,' I said at last. 'All of them.'

'We will,' Shaun promised. 'From now on we'll stick to the schedule. Changing it this morning caused too much chaos.'

'And don't give them nails.'

'We can use ropes.'

'And stop calling me your commander-in-chief. Whoever did this might think I'll send you home if I get mad enough.'

Shaun nodded. 'You're right. Good point.' On his way to the door, he asked if he could bring Jake around to apologise. 'It'll be good for him. He needs to take responsibility.'

I said yes, though I wasn't keen. I'd had my fill of Jake.

On the other hand, I didn't want to look as if I was scared of him.

~

Shaun gave the boys a real bollocking that afternoon. He lined them up on the parade ground and shouted at them for ten minutes. After the thrill of the raft race, which had left them tired but exultant, Shaun cut them down to size again. 'Sneaky…stupid…betrayal…police…' From under my house I heard most of what he said; he emphasised that no one was going home. That the person responsible for trying to hurt me would be found and punished. That only someone without self-respect would do such a thing—and only honest, loyal team players would ultimately graduate from the program. Scumbags would keep returning until they 'woke up to themselves'.

Chastened, the boys were sent to the dining hall for Joe's meditation class. The other three veterans had a quick meeting on the parade ground. As soon as I joined them, they told me the kid who'd booby-trapped my floor was either Darren, Marcus, Tyler, Nathan or Zac. Flynn and Sam had been making too much noise. Dean had been having a minor meltdown.

I nodded. 'There are footprints. Under the house. You should come and see.'

I'd been smart enough to check before pulling out any nails. Though the marks weren't complete, the dirt was fine enough to bear a pretty crisp impression.

But Warren looked doubtful. 'All the boys are wearing Garmont T8s,' he pointed out. 'Can you tell us what size you're talking about?'

I couldn't. Neither could Shaun or Warren. When they came to have a look, they agreed the prints had been left by a Garmont T8 multi-terrain tactical boot, but nobody could pinpoint the size.

'It doesn't matter,' said Shaun, squatting among the cobwebs. 'We can still use these as leverage.'

'Can anyone even remember the kids' shoe sizes?' Warren was scratching his head. 'Because I can't.'

'There's a list.' I'd needed it that first day, when I was distributing uniforms. 'A lot of them were nines.'

'Good. We can use that.' Shaun followed me out of the crawl space and into my office, where he collected the list of measurements. Then he and Warren went back to their platoon, leaving me to yank the nails out of the floor. Later, on my way to the laundry, I saw Shaun sitting on the dormitory steps, talking to Aaron. Aaron was shaking his head.

Walking into the camp kitchen that evening was like walking into an ambush. Half the boys were in there with me, and any one of them could have been responsible for the nails. I found myself watching them more intently than usual. I kept thinking, *Was it you? Or you?*

Section two embraced my gadgets, just like section one. Sam almost broke the electric can opener. Matt was happy chopping onions. Tyler had problems with the garlic crusher, shooting bits of clove all over the place. I kept Flynn well away from the blender, knowing what a drama he'd make of it; he got the salad spinner instead, and complained it was giving him RSI.

The blender went to Zac and Bruno, who used it responsibly—Zac because he'd decided to obey orders, Bruno because he just stood there pushing the 'on' button when Zac told him to. I couldn't imagine Bruno shoving nails through my floor. He didn't have the energy.

Zac was also low on my list of culprits. After initially carrying on like a spoilt brat, he had become serious and cooperative, though some of the other kids got on his nerves. He had a sharp tongue and often used it on Flynn and Connor and Sam. But he didn't sass the veterans anymore, and he felt no compulsion to play games with the kitchen appliances. Looking at Zac, I could picture him as an up-and-coming lawyer or an aspiring politician. I couldn't picture him sticking nails in my floor.

'You guys don't know how lucky you are, eating like this,' Warren observed. From his post by the kitchen door he was keeping a close eye on his section. 'If you were in the army, you'd be issued with MREs. A slice of bread in a vacuum pack. Marmalade in a tube. Freeze-dried teriyaki beef.'

'Whoops!' Tyler went chasing after another garlic clove that had leaped out of the crusher and skittered across the floor into the pantry.

Sam laughed. 'Jeez, Ty, I'd hate to see you squashing a bug. There'd be guts everywhere.'

Tyler ignored him. The blender suddenly howled. I scanned the kitchen, alert for any tension or hidden rancour, but no one threw me a sideways look. No one was sulking or seething.

After dinner, while I was supervising the kitchen clean-up, I popped out to the bins and found Shaun there, with Jake.

'Uh—Miss Ayres?' Jake glanced at Shaun, who nodded.

I froze like a spotlit rabbit.

'I want to apologise,' Jake went on, 'for dumping rubbish on your bed.'

His tone was muted, his head bowed. He sounded very uncomfortable.

I waited.

'And I'm sorry for what I said yesterday,' he continued. 'It was gross.'

'It was against the law.' That made him look up. But he couldn't meet my gaze for long; his eyes quickly slid away.

'I'm not your mum,' I told him, and the colour flared in his cheeks. 'There's only one of her. You need to remember that, or you're going to wreck a lot of lives. Including your own.'

He grunted, staring at the ground. I was moving back to the kitchen when he mumbled, 'I could find out about those nails.'

I stopped. Shaun said, 'Enough.'

But Jake kept going. 'I could figure out who did it. By asking around. You'd just have to leave me alone.'

I had to admire him. He was such an operator. Shaun immediately marched him off, then came back later while I was heading across the parade ground. At that point there was a lot of traffic between the dormitory and the bathroom, so Shaun steered me towards a quieter spot near the dining hall.

'Marcus wasn't responsible for those nails. He's too slow and his feet are enormous. Size eleven,' Shaun said.

'Right.'

'I don't think it was Zac either. Gut feeling. That kid's had the smartarse knocked right out of him.' There was a pause as Shaun tracked someone's course across the grass, making sure he went straight into the bathroom. 'Nathan's my pick,' he said at last. 'I can't be certain, but there's something not right. He's too squirrelly. We'll keep him in our crosshairs—see if we can wear him down.'

'Okay.' I was tired. 'See you tomorrow, then.'

'Hang on. There's one more thing.' I saw him brace himself and wondered what was heading my way. 'We'll need that tech. The stuff in the safe. Our treasure hunt's tomorrow.'

'*Tomorrow?*' Shaun's treasure hunt involved hiding four different caches of confiscated phones and iPads across the island, then getting four teams of boys to look for them. 'You're joking.'

'It's better if we stick to the schedule. Less chance of mistakes.'

'You're sending them out on their *own?*' I couldn't believe it.

'We'll be right here, Rob. If they come back, we'll be waiting for them.' Shaun never pleaded; he laid out his arguments like artillery, blocking any escape routes. 'You know how it works. They'll do the right thing—they have to if they want to see their tech again. And we're mixing it up. Putting the smart ones in with the dopes. Zac with Connor and Flynn. Tyler with Matt and Dean—'

'Tell me you're not sending Jake out there.'

'Nope. I might have, if he hadn't pulled that stunt tonight.'

Shaun's face hardened. 'Rhys will be drilling Jake while the rest of us man the radios and patrol the perimeter. Those kids won't come anywhere near you. And if they get into strife, well...that'll be our problem. Not yours.'

I shot him a sceptical look but didn't argue. What could I have said? It was a camp; there had to be activities. And the further away the boys were, the less likely it was they'd stick nails in my floor again.

'Joe will need the tech tomorrow,' said Shaun. 'Early.'

I nodded. Then I went home, cleaned my teeth and climbed into bed. I didn't sleep well; I kept waking up and listening for the creak of floors or the rattle of windows.

If I'd known what the next day would bring, I don't think I would have slept at all.

2009

LINDA BALODIS WAS late on Wednesday morning. Aaron showed up at school before she did, trudging along behind his grandmother, her thick, blunt fingers clamped around his wrist. Joyce marched straight up to me and said, 'Mitch McCall has a drug conviction. We're applying for a no-contact order.'

'A drug conviction?' I was setting out craft supplies and paused to think. Scott must have seen me with Mitch the previous afternoon. And Joyce must have heard about it. 'When did this happen?' I asked. If Mitch had a working-with-children clearance, his conviction couldn't have been for trafficking.

'Forty-three years ago.'

'Ah.'

'It's disgraceful. Aaron shouldn't be living in the same house. We're putting a stop to that.' Joyce jabbed a finger at me. 'If Mitch comes anywhere near this school again, I'll send Aaron to St Killian's.'

It sounded tempting. But I smiled and asked, 'Did you visit my house yesterday?'

Joyce blinked. Aaron said, 'Ow.' Her grip on him must have tightened.

'What are you on about?' she snapped.

'You know what I'm on about.'

'No. I don't.' She released Aaron. 'If this is another one of your insane accusations, you'd better brace yourself. You're on thin ice, *Ms* Ayres.'

She left just as Linda arrived; they exchanged a polite greeting on the doorstep. Then Linda entertained Aaron while I managed the other kids. I was able to get through roll call without any major hiccups—though it pained me that Amber wasn't there to answer her name. Beth had left a message on my phone that morning, crisp and cold and very brief: 'This is Beth Meyer. I'm calling to let you know Amber won't be returning to school.' Click.

We sang our welcome song, then rushed through the announcements before Aaron could unleash one of his tantrums. As soon as we'd finished, I launched straight into *Old Pig*, promising we would make papier-mache pigs afterwards. Aaron, I said, would be showing us how. A papier-mache pig wasn't just busywork—we would count egg-carton cups and measure out water. And as an added benefit, it would make Aaron happy. A happy Aaron was a bearable Aaron.

Thanks to the pigs, I was hoping we might have a good day. But then the parent helpers arrived and everything fell apart.

Pat and Kate were early. I saw them through the window, chatting together. Dixie soon joined them. But as I went to wave them inside, I spotted someone else bustling across the playground. He was hard to miss in his feathered hat.

Howard had warned me the previous night. 'Mitch won't let it go,' he'd said in a voice sapped of energy. 'He kept on and on about Joyce working in the canteen. I'm tempted to ban the whole lot of them, but I think that would create more problems than it solves.' Before I could disagree, he added, 'Just give him a whirl. We can say he blew it. Use your professional opinion.'

In other words, Howard was delegating; I was the one who would have to get rid of Mitch McCall.

Kate was still sheltering under the flowering gum. When she caught sight of Mitch, her jaw dropped. Her eyebrows climbed her forehead. Then she stormed over to where I was waiting.

'You can't be serious,' she said. 'That man's a criminal. He shouldn't be allowed in here.'

'He's got a working-with-children clearance.'

'He's unhinged.' She looked genuinely horrified.

'Kate, if he's no good, he won't be coming back.'

'Tell him to leave.' Her tone was imperious.

'I can't do that.'

She promptly charged inside. Pat followed her, nearly knocking me down as she brushed past. Dixie hesitated, looking lost.

Then Mitch reached us, all gleaming false teeth and

sparkling tinsel. 'Mitch McCall, reporting for duty,' he said.

'Come in, Mitch. Hi, Dixie.' I had a bad feeling. Sure enough, I'd no sooner entered the classroom than Kate started heading back out. She was pulling Phoebe with her.

'Stand aside,' she told Mitch, who shuffled away from the door, his smile fading. Pat was untying her son's craft apron. The cheerful buzz of kids' voices was suddenly pierced by George's wail of protest. 'I don't wanna go!'

Pat seized his arm and stomped after Kate.

'Pat,' I said, but she didn't even look at me.

By now all the kids were confused. Dozens of little eyes swung in my direction. I closed the door behind Pat and announced, 'This is Mr McCall. He'll be reading with us today.'

'Hello, everyone!' Mitch doffed his hat and pulled out a squashy rubber duck that made a honking noise when he squeezed it. There was a general coo of pleasure.

Aaron beamed. 'My Poppy does magic,' he said.

I shot Mitch a warning look. He immediately shoved the duck into his pocket. 'Who wants to read a book?' he asked.

About a dozen hands went up, including Caleb's. I saw Linda making a note.

'Mr McCall will start with Aaron.' I knew there would be fireworks if I chose anyone else. A disappointed moan made me feel like the Wicked Witch of the West. I turned to Dixie and asked if she could show Mitch where to sit. 'You've got Chloe first,' I said.

Dixie nodded. She seemed uneasy, but didn't push

back. Mitch sat down with Aaron. I started distributing pipe cleaners. Things were finally settling when I heard heavy footsteps in the hallway outside.

The door banged open and I looked up. It was Joyce.

'Mrs Rooney...' I began, straightening. I could see Pat in the hallway behind her. Pat the crony. Pat the spy.

Joyce ignored me. She marched straight across the room towards Aaron. Mitch edged in front of him.

'Joyce,' he said, 'we haven't finished our book.'

That was when Aaron bolted. He darted past Mitch, ducked under Joyce's elbow and ran for the door. She whirled around and caught him just in time.

He screamed.

'You're hurting him!' Mitch cried, then shied away from her furious glare.

'Mrs Rooney.' I stepped forward. 'You can't just come in here like this.'

'I'm calling the police,' Joyce snarled. She pointed at Mitch. 'That man's a felon.'

Then she walked out, taking Aaron with her.

⁓

'...So she went off and tore Howard a new one,' I said, 'and now she's banned from the canteen.'

'Oh, love,' Dad murmured at the other end of the line.

'She must be apoplectic. God knows what she'll do to that poor kid. God knows what she'll do to me.' I'd told my dad about the planters because I felt I had to talk to someone—someone detached from the whole business. Most of my friends in Sydney were Troy's friends too. Or Annette's. I couldn't talk to them anymore.

'You should go to the police,' Dad said.

I snorted. '"Officer, I think someone moved my pot plants around."'

'It's stalking, love. It's trespass.'

'It's an absent-minded feuding lezzo. There's no proof, Dad.'

'What do you mean, lezzo?'

'Oh, didn't I tell you? Joyce has been saying I'm a lesbian and that means I hate men, which is why I've got it in for Aaron.'

There was a brief silence. At last Dad said, 'Nutter.'

'Yep.'

'I'm so sorry.'

'The reason I moved here was to get away from all the drama and stress...' I trailed off, trying not to think about that day when Annette and Troy sat down in front of me, Annette crying, Troy's voice trembling. *We feel so bad about this*, he said. *We feel so bad for you.*

'That boss of yours sounds useless,' Dad grumbled. 'He should be protecting you from this stuff.'

'He's banned Mitch as well. And now Scott has to collect Aaron at school for the next week.' The thought of Scott in my classroom made me feel sick. The thought of dealing with Aaron again filled me with a profound sense of fatigue. 'That poor caseworker. What a fiasco. I don't know if she'll have enough data to make an assessment, let alone get me a teacher's aide.'

'It's appalling. Disgraceful.' Dad was quite upset. I could hear it in his voice and was suddenly guilt-ridden. He was too old for this.

'It's all right, Dad. I'll deal with it. I always do.'

'You should write to the Education Department.'

'Mmm.' That wasn't going to happen. 'I might have a word with Prue. She's our union rep.' Prue was so jaded, though; I wasn't expecting much.

'Do that. Make sure everyone knows what's going on.'

'I will.'

'Is your house secure? Can you lock everything up?'

'I can now.' After the planter incident, I'd gone straight out and bought proper locks for the garage and backyard laundry.

'I can install some sensor lights when I'm down there next.' He hesitated for a moment. 'Do you want me to come on Saturday?'

'No, that's fine.' I liked to retreat into my burrow when I was stressed. 'We'll stick to the plan. It's only another week. By that time things may have improved.'

We kept on chatting until I told him I had to go and put my sheets in the dryer. There were other things I needed to do as well: cooking, planning, writing Krystal's report. 'I'll call you on Friday,' I said, 'as usual.'

At about half past five I banged out the back door and made for the laundry, which was a fibro hut containing a dryer, a washing machine, an old concrete tub and lots of cobwebs. I was halfway down the path when I realised something was wrong. The bare earth squelched underfoot. Tinted water was bubbling out of the drain near the laundry door.

Inside, the floor was wet. The porthole window of the front loader looked pink. My white sheets were streaked and mottled.

Someone had put something in my washing machine— and had blocked my outlet pipe as well.

'Right,' I said. 'That's it. Enough.'

It was time to make a formal complaint.

~

Otford's police station was a dumpy old building made of liver-coloured brick, low and dark and unwelcoming. The front office contained a leaflet stand, a grey couch and a wood-veneer counter. Since I couldn't see anyone, I rang a bell.

I had to ring twice before a policeman appeared.

'Can I help you?' he said. The name on his badge was Senior Constable R. Waring. He was about my age, with lots of ginger hair on his face, arms and neck.

He had to look up at me. That wasn't a good start.

'Um—yes. I want to report...' I didn't know what to call it. Trespass? Vandalism? Harassment?

He waited. He had clear blue eyes.

'Someone's harassing me,' I said.

'Who?'

'I don't know. I've got my suspicions, but...' I trailed off.

'Did you call the Police Assistance Line?'

'No. Should I have?'

He took a deep breath—the kind you take when you're thinking, *God give me strength.* 'What's your name?'

'Robyn Ayres.'

'And what seems to be the problem?'

'Someone's been at my place. While I was out.' I braced myself, knowing already that Senior Constable R. Waring wasn't going to be very receptive.

'Where do you live?'

I gave him the address. 'Yesterday I noticed my pot plants were switched around—'

'Switched around?'

'The pots. They'd been moved. So I went and bought locks for my garage and laundry.' I pulled the receipts out of my pocket to show him. 'But I was too late. Whoever moved the pots also put something in my washing machine. I only noticed when I did a load today.'

He was frowning. 'Your washing machine?'

'I washed my sheets and they turned pink. Someone put a ballpoint refill in there.'

'My wife did the same thing,' he said. 'There was a pen in my pocket and she didn't check beforehand.'

'No.' I shook my head. 'It wasn't mine. It must have been taped to the top of the drum because I didn't see it when I opened the door.' The scepticism on his face made it hard to continue, but I did. 'Anyway, another thing happened as well. My drain's blocked. Someone must have taken the cover off and shoved something down there. I don't know what because the plumber can't come until tomorrow morning.'

Waring picked up a pen and started tapping it against the desk. 'Let me get this straight. You think someone's harassing you because your drain's blocked, your pot plants seem to have moved and your washing got stained.'

My heart sank. It did sound certifiable. But now that I'd started, I had to finish. 'It's a pattern of behaviour. I'm involved in a dispute. And someone else who's fighting the same person has had the same kind of issues. A blocked drain. A cockroach infestation.'

'Hang on. Did you say cockroach?' His expression changed. Suddenly he looked interested. 'Is your dispute with Joyce Rooney?'

Here we go, I thought. 'Yes, but—'

'You're that teacher. Ayres. I remember now.' He was nodding.

Small towns. Small fucking towns. I squared my shoulders and said, 'Scott told you, did he?'

'We're not here to get involved in a custody battle, Ms Ayres.'

He put a lot of emphasis on the 'Ms'. That probably meant he'd heard I was a lesbian, in which case Scott would also have convinced him that I was in league with the McCalls.

God, I thought. *Imagine growing up here if you really were gay.*

'Was your house broken into?' he asked.

'No. But—'

'Is anything missing?'

'No. Yes.' I'd just remembered. 'My flowers. Someone came into the front yard on Saturday and picked all my flowers.'

He clicked his tongue. 'Oh, yeah. There's a low-life doing that. It happened to me a few weeks ago—they took my wife's dahlias. And our next-door neighbour's peonies, poor old bloke.' Suddenly more amenable, Waring began to rummage behind the counter. 'I can take down the details, though there's not much we can do until someone catches the bugger red-handed.'

'But what about that other stuff?' I wasn't about to get side-tracked. 'Are you going to take down those details or not?'

He didn't like my tone. Straightening, he fixed me with a flat, inscrutable look. 'I tell you what I'll do, Ms Ayres. I'll let you go and have a really good think about whether you want to get us involved. Otherwise there's a form to fill in. I'll have to ask you questions. And if you decide to formally accuse someone, I'll be checking in with them and it's going to be very unpleasant.' He leaned forward, his hairy fingers spread across the countertop. 'Are you sure you want to give people this kind of ammunition? Because from where I'm standing, that's what it looks like. Ammunition. For the other side.'

I was screwed. I knew it. No matter what I did, the Rooneys had me over a barrel.

I didn't dare ask if the police would come and dust my washing machine for fingerprints.

'I'll go and have a think about it,' I said.

'Good.'

'And then I'll talk to the plumber and find out what's in my drain. And once I've got those details, I'll write my own report—which I'll give to the police and the school and my lawyer.' My lawyer was actually a divorce lawyer, but Senior Constable Waring didn't know that. 'I just want this on the record. It's important to keep a record when you're being stalked.' Lifting my gaze, I checked the ceiling. 'No CCTV,' I said. 'Pity. But I'm guessing little country stations don't get the good stuff.'

Then I walked out before he could have the last word.

~

The plumber came at six-thirty the next morning. He was a sour, sixty-ish, shuffling character, very dark and monosyllabic. Deb had recommended him, though she'd warned me he wasn't a people person.

He used an endoscope to peer at the blockage and a water jetter to cut through it. When I asked him what the problem was, he said, 'Crap.'

'What kind of crap?'

'Bit of rag, by the look of it. Sanitary products. Dirt.'

'Could someone have put it down there? On purpose?'

He looked at me warily, as if he was afraid I might start cackling crazily and ripping my clothes off. 'It's a blockage,' he said. 'They happen.'

His water jetter was so noisy it must have woken half the neighbourhood.

2019

'HI, ROBYN.' JOE Malouf stood on the front veranda, carrying a gym bag.

'Oh! Right. The phones.' It was Thursday morning and I was still eating breakfast. 'Come in.'

I turned and led him into my office, where I unlocked the safe. Joe held open his bag so I could dump the boys' confiscated technology into it—I'd forgotten he was hiding the phones for the treasure hunt.

'You're off now, are you?' I asked.

'In a minute. Shouldn't take long, though.'

'I bet you'll be glad to get away.' The campers were making a terrible racket.

'Uh…yeah.' He zipped up his bag, then hesitated. 'There's a problem,' he said at last. 'Shaun was wondering if you could pop over to the men's.' He grimaced as I stared at him. 'Someone used the broken toilet.'

I blinked. My feelings were written all over my face.

'Who?' I said.

'Not sure. No one's fessing up. I think it's been there a while.'

'Shit.'

He nodded. 'Afraid so.'

I grabbed a bucket from the laundry and followed him out of the house. We split up on the front steps; he made for his hut while I headed for the men's bathroom. A few cheeky boys said, 'Hello, miss!' They were being herded across the parade ground, their wet hair neatly combed. Warren was with them. 'Sorry,' he mouthed as I passed.

Dean was the last kid left inside the steamy bathroom. He was brushing his teeth while Rhys supervised. They watched me fill my bucket without saying a word. By the time I returned for more water, they were gone.

I was on my fourth bucket when I heard a distant scream. *Doesn't sound good*, I thought. But I finished the last flush before leaving.

I was back on the parade ground when I saw smoke drifting from the kitchen window.

'Jesus!' I dropped my bucket and ran. The kitchen was emptying. Kids were being shooed into the dining hall. 'Out! Quick!' Warren yelled. I pushed through a pack of excited boys, coughing as the smoke grew thicker.

Shaun was alone in the kitchen. He wore oven gloves and was shaking a toaster into the sink.

'Cardboard,' he said when he saw me. 'There was cardboard in the toaster.'

I couldn't speak. I was coughing too much. A scorched cereal packet lay on the floor, soaking wet. Cornflakes crunched underfoot. There was water everywhere.

'It started when someone tried to make toast,' Shaun explained. He began to run the cold tap. I looked around. A fire extinguisher stood on the kitchen table. Thank God no one had covered the place in foam.

'It's all right. Nothing major. Just the box—and that.' Shaun jerked his head at a black mark on the ceiling.

I picked up the sodden box and rammed it into a bin. Then I went to fetch a brush and pan. All the cleaning equipment was tucked behind the freezer in the pantry. I was down on my haunches, trying to dodge clattering mop handles, when I realised the freezer wasn't humming.

It had been turned off at the wall.

'For Chrissake!' I flicked the switch and jumped up. The ice inside the freezer had melted. My chicken drumsticks were sitting in a puddle of water. 'Goddammit!'

'Robyn?'

'Someone turned the bloody freezer off!'

I rushed to check the fridges: they were still running.

'How the hell did you miss this? Weren't you watching the little bastards?' I was too furious to keep my voice down. 'Someone turned off the freezer and set fire to the kitchen! Where were *you*, Shaun?'

'Robyn—'

'I thought you were going to watch them!'

'We did.'

'The freezer must have happened last night. Do you realise that? And you're telling me none of you saw a thing?' I walked right up to him and stuck my face into his. 'This isn't bloody good enough,' I hissed.

'I know,' he said, infuriatingly calm. 'But the toilet might have been a dopey moment. Even the freezer—'

'You're saying *I* did it?'

'No.'

'You're saying I turned off the freezer and somehow... *forgot?*'

'The switch is down near all the mops and brooms. Something could have fallen against it.' His voice was slowing down as mine sped up. It was an obvious technique and it enraged me. 'I'm not saying we can rule out the boys,' he went on, 'but we can't jump to conclusions, either.'

'You think I'm plotting against you? You think this is me trying to make you look bad?'

'No!' He sounded shocked.

'Maybe you think I'm paranoid.'

'Of course not. But you need to calm down. This isn't the time or the place.'

He glanced past me. Warren was hovering at the door. Most of the kids were outside, though one or two lingered.

'You're right. I need to calm down.' I took a deep breath. 'You can clean this up. I'll take that tech into the bush.'

Shaun blinked. 'What? Oh, no. You can't—'

'I can. I know exactly what to do. You always put your caches in the same place. Half the time I have to collect the marker flags.' As Shaun opened his mouth to speak, I added, 'If all four of you can't keep these kids under control, why risk sending Joe away?' I held out my hand. 'Give me your radio. Jake stamped on mine.'

It was a tense moment. Shaun wasn't used to having his authority challenged. He looked disgruntled.

But after exchanging a glance with Warren, he passed me his walkie-talkie.

⁓

I caught Joe just in time. He'd sealed the boys' tech in water-proof containers and was heading out of his hut. There was a short argument, followed by a quick map check. Having satisfied himself that I knew where I was going, he handed over his gym bag and wished me luck.

I rushed back home for my rucksack and water bottle, then escaped into the bush. My first stop was the zipline. I left the box labelled 'number one' next to a red marker flag on the upper platform. I even paused to enjoy the view, but the dazzling sweep of water wasn't consoling. All it did was remind me how isolated I was.

The next location was a spectacular rock overhang on the western side of the hill. I sat for a while in the creamy sandstone hollow, wishing I didn't have to leave. But the silence began to niggle. I found myself listening for the rustle of leaves underfoot. Suddenly the bush seemed threatening; I realised I had no idea what was happening back at the lazaret. For all I knew, there'd been a mass breakout. Packs of boys could be roaming the island with hammers and gas guns and kitchen knives…

Oh, stop it. I dumped the second cache, planted a marker flag and moved on.

Site number three was down on the western shore—a small, roofless brick ruin near the remains of an old stone jetty. The building had once been a boat shed for the lepers but was now used only by stray tourists and seabirds. I left my third cache there, pausing to gaze at the distant line of speckled colour directly across the bay. It reassured me. Cleveland wasn't that far away. I had a phone. A boat. A gun. I had four veterans too, though they didn't fill me with confidence. They were supposed to protect me, but would they? Could I trust them?

And then, like a lightning bolt, it hit me. This wasn't about the veterans at all. This was about Otford. Seeing Aaron had brought everything back—and I was reacting so strongly because the last time something similar had happened, I almost hadn't recovered. My wounds were still tender, and another round of focused persecution was inflaming them.

'Don't follow the feelings,' I said aloud. I had to remember this wasn't Otford. I wasn't powerless. I belonged here.

Everyone else was just passing through.

My last stop was a discarded water tank in the bush. I laid the fourth box of phones on a tree stump beside the rusty remains and jammed a marker flag into the ground nearby. From there I headed straight to Karboora Beach, where I spent a peaceful half-hour skipping stones and doing some mindful breathing. Finally, when I was calm enough, I wandered back to the lazaret. It was nearly lunchtime and I had a job to do. I couldn't let the campers plunder my supplies unchecked.

As I trudged up the jetty road, I spotted a ring of teenagers sitting on the grass near the ashes of last night's campfire. Warren and Rhys were there too. Rhys was looming over Jake while Warren jabbed his finger at a topographical map and talked about contour lines. Some of the boys looked more interested than others. Aaron cut me a quick glance.

Nathan was missing. I saw that at once. And where was Shaun?

'Robyn!' It was Joe's voice; I spied him on the dormitory veranda. He beckoned to me. 'All done?' he asked when I reached him.

I nodded as I returned his bag—which had Shaun's radio in it. 'Where's Shaun?'

'In there. With Nathan.' He cocked his thumb. 'We've got a result.'

'Sorry?'

'Tyler saw Nathan slip under your house yesterday. See, we told 'em they wouldn't be getting their phones back until someone owned up—'

'Wait.' I cut him off. 'You mean Nathan's the one?'

'Looks like it.'

'Why?'

Joe shrugged. 'That's what Shaun's trying to find out.'

I decided it wasn't the right time to say sorry for losing my cool. Instead I went to the kitchen, where someone had attempted to clean up the crushed cornflakes. I mopped the floor and made a mental note: along with a new mattress, a replacement stop tap and some piping, Vetnet owed me a toaster.

After assembling the boys' lunch, I retreated to my vegie garden. While they ate, I weeded. Shaun was barking orders and calling names. At one point I saw him steering Nathan past the other kids.

I was tidying the kitchen yet again when four groups of campers marched off into the bush. One group passed the window just as Warren stuck his head through the door.

'Hey, Rob,' he said. 'You got a minute?'

I followed him. The veterans had created a command centre in the dining hall by spreading a map out on one of the tables. Shaun was there with Joe and Warren. They were all carrying radios.

Rhys was on the parade ground, drilling Nathan and Jake.

'Hi, Rob.' Like a true professional, Shaun spoke as if our run-in had never happened. 'You heard about Nathan?'

'Yes.'

'Trying to pin him down is like trying to catch a grass-hopper. He's the weirdest kid, I swear. You think he's going to own up and then he wriggles out of it.' In the brief pause that followed, we could all hear Rhys shouting commands. 'Jake says you were a soft target. That's why he did what he did. I haven't extracted a good reason from Nathan yet, but I will.'

'Okay. Thanks.' Though I didn't want to apologise in

front of the other two, I couldn't really put it off. 'Sorry about earlier. All this stuff is pushing buttons for me.'

'No sweat.' Shaun flapped his hand, dismissing the topic. 'Joe tells me all the tech's in place. Is that right?'

I nodded.

'And there aren't any other visitors on the island?'

I shook my head.

'Good. Then I suggest you enjoy the peace and quiet for a couple of hours. It won't last long.'

He was right. Exactly thirty-nine minutes later, everything went pear-shaped.

I was vacuuming the dormitory when a voice cut through the roar of the machine.

'Robyn? Robyn!'

I looked up and saw Joe. His expression alarmed me. 'What is it?' I asked, kicking the off button.

In the sudden silence he said, 'We've got a problem. Tyler's hurt.'

'What?' A jab of adrenaline shot through my veins. 'How?'

'He fell off the zipline platform.'

'Oh, shit.' That was bad.

'Matt Spiteri just called in. He says Tyler can't walk.'

'Let me warn the office. I'll tell them to stand by.'

'Warren's heading out there now—'

'I'll come too.'

'Are you sure?'

'It's my job.' There were procedures. Emergency plans. I ran back home and called the regional office, then joined Warren on the parade ground. Shaun and Joe were there too.

'What the hell's that?' Shaun demanded, squinting at the rectangular orange bag I was carrying.

'Foldable stretcher.' My first-aid kit was tucked into my backpack. 'We might need it.'

He nodded, then gave me his radio. 'Take this,' he said. 'Keep in touch.'

'Lifeflight's coming. My manager's calling them.' I gestured at the wide patch of grass surrounding us. 'They'll be landing right here. It's the designated helipad.'

Shaun frowned. 'Are you sure? What if it's just a sprain?'

'Doesn't matter. We're none of us trained medics.' Seeing his troubled expression, I asked, 'How old is Tyler? Thirteen?'

'Fourteen,' said Joe.

'He's a child. We need to cover all our bases.' I jerked my chin at Warren. 'Let's go.'

'I want a running report!' Shaun yelled after us as we beat a path to the cemetery. Then he must have grabbed Joe's radio, because I heard it sputter. 'Sunray blue two, this is red one, over,' he said.

If there was a reply, I was too far away to hear it.

Warren and I were moving at a very brisk pace when we hit the western fire trail. We didn't have much breath to spare for talking. But after about five minutes he said, 'I'll take the stretcher.'

'Thanks.' I passed it to him. 'Have you told the other kids to come back?'

'No.'

'Why not?'

'They're after their phones, remember? They won't come back till they've got what they want.' He glanced at me. 'It's better if we're not too distracted while the boys are around.'

He was right. 'But Shaun's keeping in touch?'

'We all are.' Warren unhooked his radio and raised it to his mouth. 'Sunray blue two, this is red two, over.'

A buzz of static answered him. He tried again. 'Sunray blue two, this is red two, over.'

The radio crackled to life. A distorted voice said, 'Sunray red two, this is…um…this is blue two, over.'

'Matt? It's Mr Doyle. I should be with you in about ten minutes, over.'

A wobbly: 'Okay.' Poor little Matt. He sounded so young.

'How's Tyler? Over.'

'Okay.' A brief silence. 'Over.'

'Is he conscious? Over.'

'Yeah.'

Warren waited. But apparently Matt had lost his usual urge to babble on, so Warren tried again. 'How's Dean? Over.'

There was a pause. 'Not very good,' Matt said at last.

'Can I talk to him? Over.'

Another pause—longer, this time. 'No.'

'Why? What's he doing? Over.'

'Kicking a tree.' Raucous static. 'And screaming.'

Warren grimaced. 'Roger that. Tell him we'll be there soon. Tell him there's going to be a helicopter. Does he like helicopters? Over.'

The answer was quick this time. 'How should I know?'

'Not long now, mate.' Warren's tone was sympathetic. 'Hang in there. You're a champion. Over and out.'

We'd reached the cemetery and were picking our way through the graves. 'Poor kid,' I said.

'Yeah.' Warren looked sour. I didn't blame him. This wasn't good for anyone—not for me, not for the veterans, not for Tyler. His parents wouldn't be pleased.

I wondered if I was witnessing the end of Vetnet.

Suddenly Warren's radio sprang to life again. 'Sunray red two, this is red one, over.' Shaun's voice was barely recognisable.

Warren pressed transmit. 'Sunray red one, this is red two. We're ten minutes out, over.'

'Roger that.' A spray of static. 'We just heard something from Matt. He says Tyler tried to push him down the zipline stairs. Over.'

I stopped in my tracks. 'Wait,' I stammered. 'Was that— did he—?'

Warren's pace was slowing. 'Clarify, red one—did you say Tyler tried to push Matt downstairs? Over.'

'Roger that. He says Dean intervened and there was a scuffle, during which Tyler fell. It was an accident. Over.'

Warren had halted. He turned to look at me. Then he cleared his throat. 'What was the fight about? Over.'

'Matt says there wasn't a fight. Tyler attacked him out

of the blue.' A pause, during which Warren and I began to move again, tramping through the long grass. When Shaun finally continued, his voice was halting and muffled. 'Tyler was hoping a serious injury might close the camp. He wants to get home to his sister. He says she's not safe. Over and out.'

In the silence that followed, I could hear a distant, high-pitched screech. But it was only a cockatoo.

2009

AARON DIDN'T COME to school on Thursday. Neither did Joyce or Mitch. I spoke to Howard at lunchtime.

'It's a bloody mess,' he admitted. 'Joyce says she won't send Aaron unless we ban Mitch, so I've done that now. I also told her it's against the law to keep a kid home from school.' He sighed as he checked his watch. 'At this point I just wish the whole lot of them would knock each other off, but I suppose that's why they pay me the big bucks—to put up with lunatic parents.'

Then we discussed Caleb.

After a fairly peaceful day at work, I went to the local hardware store to check out security cameras. There wasn't a big range and they were appallingly expensive, so I quickly gave up on that idea. As I drove home, I wondered if I should get a dog. But these thoughts inevitably led to Ruffles, the creaky old lab I no longer saw because she was technically Troy's. Memories of Ruffles always made me feel bad, so I filed that option away for another time.

Passing Mitch's house, I remembered Krystal's report. I'd promised it by Friday but still had to include all the latest developments: the attack on Amber, the sanitary-pad incident, the papier-mache pig. The papier-mache pig suggested to me that Aaron did better with Krystal than he did with Joyce, but I couldn't swear to it; I wasn't a judge or a psychologist. I was just the poor bugger who had to put up with him day after day.

I was jumpy when I pulled into my drive. After killing the engine, I scanned the front yard. No one had touched the pot plants. Was there dog shit on the lawn? There was. Had Joyce planted it? Maybe. But since I didn't have any gates, the culprit could just as easily have been a stray dog.

I climbed out of my car and checked the place warily, keeping an eye open for smashed windows and puddles of water. Nothing looked suspicious. The lights worked. The laundry was locked. There were no dead cats in the rubbish bin. Once I'd made sure the mailbox wasn't booby-trapped, I felt safe enough to sit down and finish Krystal's report, which kept me busy until dinnertime. I decided that if Aaron didn't come to school on Friday, I would drop the report off at Krystal's house. It seemed likely I wouldn't see Aaron before the weekend; Joyce would probably keep him home again, just to make a point.

But I was wrong. The next morning he walked into the classroom with his dad.

'Oh. Hello, Aaron.' I didn't like the look of him. He had a new scab on his knee and was biting his nails. 'Why don't you hang up your bag? Do you remember which hook belongs to you?'

'Of course he does. He's not a retard.' Scott hadn't shaved or combed his hair. His eyes were bloodshot. He was dressed in a T-shirt and baggy gym shorts.

I wondered if he'd had a big night.

'Go on. Hang up your bag,' he told his son.

Aaron dropped his backpack. Then he began to kick it across the floor.

'No!' Scott thundered. 'Not like that!'

'Aaron...' I began. But I couldn't get a word in edgeways.

'Pick it up!' Scott used his armed-suspect voice, which was loud and harsh and guaranteed to scare every kid within earshot.

'Mr Rooney—'

'Pick it up.' Scott took a menacing step towards his son. Aaron immediately scooped his bag off the floor and hurled it through the doorway, just missing Chloe.

'Little fucker,' Scott growled. 'Do that again and I'll throw *you* out the door, mate!'

But Aaron had already disappeared. I wondered if he was heading for the road.

At least Prue's on duty out there, I thought.

'Okay, listen.' Scott suddenly rounded on me, his face like a clenched fist. 'I've had enough of you. Lay off Aaron, lay off me, and lay off my mum. Okay?'

He was on the very edge of violence. I could feel it on my skin like static electricity. Luckily, there were witnesses all around us: children, parents, Deb next door.

'Moderate your tone, Mr Rooney.' I was trying to ignore my racing heart and dry mouth.

'Rick Waring's a mate of mine,' Scott continued. 'Did you really think I wouldn't find out?' He leaned towards me until I could smell him. He smelled of stale sweat. 'I don't know what the fuck your problem is. Mum thinks you're wet for Krystal. I think you're crazy. But if you don't calm down, we'll take you to court. For harassment.'

I couldn't believe what I was hearing. The sheer gall of it! I was about to tell him what he could do with himself when a piercing scream sent me bounding outside.

Aaron was in the playground, stamping on someone's Barbie doll.

The rest of the day was like an extension of the first half-hour. Aaron wasn't sent home—largely because the Barbie doll shouldn't have been at school in the first place. But he kept acting out, even after his father left. He sulked. He hid. He threw things. He made stupid noises and wiped his nose on Kayla's skirt. I was run ragged just trying to control him; teaching him was out of the question. Even the other kids grew impatient.

'Everyone's sick of you,' Phoebe told him. 'Why don't you be quiet?'

He tried to tear up her busy book after that.

Dixie had some success with him, and I thought he

seemed better after his appointment with Aima Singh; we had an outdoor lesson before lunch, and that calmed him down a bit. But by the time Krystal came to pick him up that afternoon, I was at my wits' end.

'He's not had a good day,' I said. The rest of the class hadn't had a good day either, but she didn't need to know that.

'Oh.' She looked even more distracted than usual.

'We're still waiting on his assessment. Once we have it, we'll be able to move forward.' I tucked a stray lock of hair behind my ear and tried not to look as exhausted as I felt. 'I've got your report, incidentally.'

'My report?' She sounded vague. But then something clicked in her head. 'My report! Right! Thanks!'

I shoved it at her. 'This doesn't include what happened today. But it's pretty comprehensive.'

'Thank you so much.'

'Hey, Aaron.' He was lying under a desk, kicking at the desktop above him. 'Your mum's here.'

He didn't respond. Krystal glanced around nervously, as if she was worried about eavesdroppers. But the only other child in the classroom was Kayla, whose mother often picked her up late.

'Robyn?' said Krystal. 'Can I ask you something?'

'Sure.'

'About your garage.' She began to fidget as I stared at her. 'It's pretty big, isn't it? Scott's best friend's girlfriend used to rent your house...'

I felt instantly wary. 'And?'

'Well…' The story spilled out of her. She was moving to a new townhouse on the weekend, she said. A good job and her own place would help her in court. She'd been expecting to shift all her stuff on Saturday, but now the agents were saying she wouldn't get the keys until Saturday night. 'The thing is, I bought a couch that's meant to be delivered tomorrow,' she said. 'Which is really awkward because Mitch doesn't have enough space. Especially with us there.'

I could see where this was heading, and I didn't like it. 'Why don't you change the delivery to Sunday?'

'They don't deliver on Sundays. And on Monday I'll be at work.'

'Couldn't Mitch take care of things?'

'He's volunteering.' The thump of Aaron's feet was getting louder; Krystal had to raise her voice again. 'I was wondering if you could take the delivery tomorrow and keep it for one night. You won't have to do anything—the furniture guys will dump it and we'll take it away.' Her lips peeled back in a tense, ingratiating smile. 'You live so close to Mitch. And he has a ute. He says you can always borrow it if you need anything shifted. I'm really sorry—this is so annoying. The agent wasn't clear enough.'

She almost had to shout as Aaron's feet slammed into the table. It was giving me a headache. I desperately wanted to get rid of him.

'Fine,' I said. 'When's the van due?'

'Uh…late morning. I think.'

'I'll be there.' I had nowhere else to go.

'Oh, thanks. Thank you.' Tears welled in her eyes. Suddenly she whirled around and screamed, 'Aaron! Stop it! You're annoying Miss Ayres!'

'Fuck off!' he roared back. Then he scrambled to his feet and pelted from the room.

'Sorry. I'm so sorry.' She fluttered around for a moment, like a butterfly or an injured bird, before hurrying after him. I didn't get a chance to say goodbye.

Over by the supply cupboard, Kayla stood motionless, her thumb in her mouth. I smiled at her and held out my hand.

'It's all right, Kayla. Don't worry. Your mum will be here soon.'

She took her thumb out. 'Mum says you're a died,' she announced.

I assumed she meant dyke. Unless Joyce had been threatening to kill me?

⁓

Krystal's couch arrived in a white van just before three on Saturday afternoon. I'd been waiting around for hours, cleaning the kitchen and making chicken stock. I could have left the garage open and gone shopping, I suppose, but I didn't want to encourage Scott Rooney. God knows what he could have done. Left a snake inside?

Two hefty young blokes wearing sleeveless shirts manoeuvred Krystal's couch into my garage, supervised by a leathery little woman in a fedora hat. I soon worked out they were part of the same family; the two blokes were cousins and the woman was their aunt. 'What are you moaning about?' she said to the bigger cousin when he banged his head on the garage door. 'You've got no brains to hurt.'

The couch was a three-seater, wrapped in so much plastic I could barely see what colour it was. The delivery docket attached to it had my address scribbled over the original one, which was unreadable. As soon as the van had roared away, I relocked the garage and left a message on Krystal's voicemail. She called back an hour later while I was pushing a trolley down the pasta aisle at Foodworks.

'They reckon we can pick up the keys around seven,' she told me in her hesitant, preoccupied way. 'But they've cleaned the carpets and they'll still be damp, so...'

'So you want to collect the couch tomorrow?'

'Is that all right, Robyn?'

'As long as you're not too early.' After wrangling kids all week, I liked to sleep in on Sunday mornings. 'How's Aaron?'

'Good.' She didn't sound very sure. Most children react badly to upheaval; the thought of what Aaron would be like on Monday made my blood run cold.

'Give me a call before you come,' I said, popping a can of tomatoes into my trolley. 'I don't like leaving the garage unlocked.'

'Okay.'

'That couch looks pretty heavy. Are you sure you can manage it? Just you and Mitch?'

'Oh, yeah. We've got a trolley thing.' Somehow her tone

didn't fill me with confidence. I had a feeling I would be roped in to help.

'All right.' I wondered if she'd be bringing Aaron with her. I didn't want him running around loose in my yard. There was no telling what he might do with a pair of secateurs. 'Will Aaron be coming?'

'I think so. Is that a problem?'

'Oh, no.' Yes. 'I just wondered if I should buy him something to eat. Does he like Tim Tams?'

'He loves Tim Tams.'

'Then I'll buy him a packet. In case he gets hungry.'

I hung up, not realising that I'd just spoken to Krystal for the last time.

By noon on Sunday I was growing impatient. Krystal hadn't called. No one had. I tried to call her, but she didn't pick up—and I'd left Mitch's number at school. Eventually I had to knock on his door.

He wasn't home. His ute was gone. I figured he was at Krystal's new place and cursed myself. Why hadn't I asked for the address?

I dropped by again in the early evening, on my way back from the local pool. This time Mitch's ute was parked outside his house—and Krystal's car wasn't. Neither was Scott's, I was pleased to see. There were lights on, though the blinds were closed.

When I knocked, Mitch took a long time to answer.

Finally he opened the door and peered through the crack.

'Oh. Hello,' he said. All the fizz seemed to have left him. He looked old and worn and worried.

'Hi, Mitch. I was wondering what to do about that couch.'

He stared at me blankly.

'The one Krystal left in my garage?' I prompted.

'Right. Yeah. The couch.' He rubbed his thumb across his forehead, his gaze drifting away from me.

'She said you were going to pick it up today.'

'Yeah. Sorry. I did my back in.' He winced as his hand moved from his face to his spine. 'Can it wait a bit?'

'I guess so.' It wasn't as if I actually used the garage—though I was beginning to wonder if I should lock the car up at night, to stop the Rooneys from slashing my tyres. 'But won't Krystal need somewhere to sit?'

'She's got chairs,' Mitch replied. 'Kitchen chairs.'

'Oh.'

'We'll give you a ring.' He was shutting the door in my face when something occurred to him. 'Don't take the wrappings off.'

That struck me as odd, but I didn't really think about it. I went home and ate my dinner and stalked Annette on Facebook and drank a few glasses of wine. Then I went to bed and lay there, brooding. I wasn't looking forward to work the next day. I wasn't looking forward to Aaron.

When he didn't turn up at school in the morning, I was relieved. I wondered if he was sick—or if Krystal had decided to keep him home after a weekend spent unpacking boxes.

She'd said she would be working on Monday, but that might have been a lie. She didn't leave any messages and neither did Mitch. I had no idea what was going on.

Then, at the end of the day, Scott appeared.

I was in the classroom, waving goodbye to Luke and his dad, when I spotted a looming figure in the hallway. Scott didn't look quite as threatening as usual. He was clean shaven and dressed in a pale green polo shirt. He even smiled at Pat Haas, displaying a fine set of teeth.

But I still felt a twinge of dread when I saw him. *Oh shit*, I thought. Krystal obviously hadn't told Joyce that Aaron was taking a sickie.

'Where's my son?' Scott demanded, after scoping out the classroom.

I took a deep breath. 'He's not here. He didn't come to school.'

Scott stared at me. I could see the colour creeping up his throat into his face. Then his eyes turned to slits and his brows collided.

'You gotta be joking,' he said through clenched teeth.

'No. Sorry, I haven't seen him.'

'That stupid little cunt.' He turned on his heel and stormed out, almost tripping over Phoebe on the way.

Five hours later, the police arrived at my home and told me that Krystal had abducted Aaron.

2019

WHEN WARREN AND I reached the zipline, we found Tyler lying near the bottom step. Matt was huddled a few metres away, his face wet with tears. Dean had ducked under the platform. He was pacing around like an animal in a cage.

Warren scanned the three of them, then headed straight for Dean. I hunkered down to examine Tyler. He was suet-coloured and damp with sweat, though his expression was stoic.

'It really hurts,' he muttered.

'Which leg?'

'The right,' said Matt. I tossed him a smile and shrugged off my backpack. Then I pulled out the first-aid kit.

'I think it's broken.' Tyler's voice was just a thread of sound. 'I think I felt it snap.'

'Can you move it?' I asked.

He winced. 'Hurts too much…'

I began to cut off his uniform with a pair of scissors.

Matt cried, 'Don't do that!'

'I have to, Matty. I have to see what the damage is.' I was dreading a compound fracture. But after a quick look, I decided the skin wasn't pierced—though Tyler's skinny little leg was bruised and badly swollen above the ankle. The sight of it made me feel ill. 'Warren?' I said.

'Yeah.' Warren had offered Dean a chocolate bar, which Dean was now stuffing into his gob.

Bribe, I thought. *Good one.* 'I don't think we should move him.'

Warren frowned. 'Not even with a splint?'

'No.' I wasn't a medic, but I knew enough to realise there might be internal injuries. Spinal damage. Concussion. 'We can't risk banging him around on a downhill walk. We should wait till Lifeflight gets here.'

'Roger that.' Warren sounded very calm. I caught a glimpse of what he must be like under fire. He spoke softly to Dean, then approached Matt and said, 'Listen, mate, you've done really well. But it's time you both went back.'

'Go with them,' I interrupted.

Warren raised his eyebrows.

'You can meet the medics and bring them here.' As I spoke, I heard the distant pulse of chopper blades. 'They'll be landing in a minute.'

'Okay.' He turned to the boys. 'Packs on. Let's go.'

They hesitated. Matt looked as if he was about to cry. 'Are we in trouble?' he squeaked.

'No,' Warren said firmly.

Dean started to mutter, 'Fuck this. Fuck it. *Fuck!*'

'It's okay, mate. You've done well,' Warren assured him.

Tyler said, 'Hey, Hoegel? It was my fault. They'll blame me, not you.'

Matt and Dean stared at him for a moment. Around us the tall trees danced and rustled in the wind. Then Dean emerged from beneath the platform, shouldering his backpack. He started stomping away.

'Hang on, Dean.' Warren snatched up the stretcher and followed him. 'Mr Spiteri! On the double!'

Matt stammered something as he scuttled after the other two. Seconds later they vanished into the bush.

The throbbing of the helicopter was quite loud, by this time. Even so, I felt suddenly isolated. Adrift. Abandoned by the whole world.

'Am I going to die?' Tyler's scratchy little voice trickled into my ear.

'What? No. Of course not.'

The expression on his face was hard to describe. Haunted? Sceptical? His teeth were chattering, though it was quite warm.

Shock, perhaps.

'Here.' I pulled an emergency blanket out of the first-aid kit. Ripped open the package with my teeth. Tucked the silvery sheet around him. 'It's like aluminium foil,' I joked. 'You look like a piece of fish on a barbie.'

'I'm sorry about the nails,' he said.

I froze for an instant, then pushed a corner of the blanket under his arm. 'Don't worry about that now.'

'It wasn't personal. I don't hate you or nothing. I just needed to get back to my sister.' Almost every word was separated by a gasp or a grunt. The poor kid was in a lot of pain. 'I knew I had to do something bad. Duggan did all that shit and you didn't send *him* back home. It had to be bad enough to make you chuck us all out.'

I couldn't help myself. 'You don't have to hurt people to help your sister. You just have to talk to them.'

He snorted weakly, then closed his eyes.

'Tyler?'

'You're so dumb.'

'Does it hurt?'

'I feel sick.'

'The paramedics'll be here soon.' The helicopter had fallen silent; it was probably sitting on the parade ground. *Twenty minutes,* I told myself, anxiously feeling Tyler's pulse. His skin was clammy, but I couldn't raise his legs to improve his blood flow. I couldn't move him at all. 'Looks like you'll be riding in a helicopter. Have you ever done that?'

'Once. After Dad threw me outta the car.'

If he wanted to silence me, it worked.

'At least I'm going home,' he mumbled.

I didn't say he would be going to hospital first—and would probably be staying there for a few days, if he was lucky. If he wasn't lucky...well, I refused to think about that.

Stroking his white-blond buzz cut, I offered up a silent prayer and listened for the sound of footsteps.

When the paramedics arrived, I left. There was no point staying. I paused just long enough to eavesdrop on their assessment of Tyler's condition; though they were hard to read, I picked up no hint of rising urgency in their voices, and that reassured me.

Tyler was alert enough to say goodbye.

On my way back downhill, I radioed Shaun with the news. He told me some of the boys had already returned, drawn by the noise of the helicopter—which flew directly over my head soon afterwards. Trees tossed and swayed in its rotor wash. Birds scattered. The ground seemed to shake.

By the time I reached the lazaret, a rescue stretcher was being winched aboard the chopper, which was hovering over the hill behind me. A string of campers watched from the parade ground. Rhys was there, holding binoculars. Warren raised a hand as I approached him.

'Where's Shaun?' I asked.

'On the phone.' He jabbed his thumb at my house.

'Who's he talking to? The parents?'

'The police.'

'Oh.'

'Cop called Bass sent Tyler here—Alex Bass. He'll tell the parents.' Warren hadn't taken his eyes off the dangling stretcher in the sky. 'How was Tyler when you left?'

'Still conscious.'

The boys around us erupted into a cheer as the stretcher reached the open door of the chopper. I leaned close to Warren and said, 'He apologised for the nails. Told me he thought he had to do something really bad, because you didn't send Jake home.'

Warren tore his eyes away from the mid-air rescue and fixed them on me. They glinted deep in their sockets like water at the bottom of a well.

'His dad once threw him out of a car,' I finished.

He sighed. 'Holy crap.'

'What happens now?'

'Now I guess we'll see.' As the helicopter began to rise and bank, Warren's voice boomed out. 'Right! Show's over! Platoon—atten*shun!*'

The last group of campers stumbled out of the bush soon afterwards. Ali, Bruno and Sam had gone all the way to the western side of the island, so their trip back was the longest. They seemed grateful to drop their box of phones, all of which had drained batteries—so no one made a fuss when Warren took them. 'They're probably safer with you than with us,' Zac remarked, as Ali handed over cache number three.

I was carrying the confiscated electronics to my office when I saw a police launch mooring at the jetty. The officer who disembarked was Jodie Morris. We'd spoken once before, during a search for a missing fisherman. She was a blunt object, but I found her less intimidating than most male constables. For one thing, she was quite small.

After greeting me by name, she said she'd come to collect a couple of paramedics. I told her they were due any minute and gave her a quick rundown of what had happened: a fall, a break, a rescue. I didn't mention that Tyler had been injured in a scuffle. If I ever had to testify about Tyler's attempt to push Matt downstairs, I would. But I was loath to get involved with the police. Not unless I had to.

Anyway, it was Shaun's business. Shaun's boot camp. It was his job to take the lead.

I introduced Jodie to Warren, then returned to my office and secured all the tech. After that, as I patrolled the complex, I kept a very sharp eye on the boys. Joe wasn't there; he'd flown off with Tyler in the chopper. Shaun was on the phone for at least an hour. Warren and Rhys were finding it hard to control their platoon because the kids were all tired and fractious, stirred up by the day's events. A tearful Matt had to be counselled by Rhys. Flynn kept complaining about his own 'leg injury'. Marcus punched Connor for deliberately treading on his heels.

With all this going on, none of the veterans had time to watch Jake. But I did. While everyone else goggled at Jodie as she guided the paramedics down to the launch, I kept my gaze pinned on Jake Duggan. He knew it, too. A couple of times he even winked at me.

But he didn't get the chance to skulk away and sabotage anything. I made sure of that.

Later, while Shaun addressed his troops on the parade ground, I set things up in the kitchen. Then I went and told Rhys I didn't want Jake with me that evening.

'Section one is fine. But not Jake,' I said.

'Um...'

'You can move him to section two. Tyler's gone; it shouldn't be a problem.'

Rhys glanced over at Shaun, who was trying to calm the boys. Tyler was safe, Shaun announced. Everything was under control. They'd all behaved impeccably. He was very proud of them.

'Tell Shaun it's not negotiable,' I continued. 'And tell him he needs to do something about Matt. That poor kid's a mess.'

Shaun wasn't with his section when they finally showed up to help me with dinner. Dean was also absent; I wondered if he and Shaun were discussing the day's events. As for Jake, he was out collecting firewood with section two, so Rhys and I had only five boys to wrangle: Nathan, Ali, Connor, Marcus and Aaron. Not that any of them misbehaved—they were all too tired. There was a lot of talk about Tyler's injuries, and the helicopter, and the police, but no one discussed the fight on top of the zipline platform. None of the boys in that room seemed to know about it.

'I'll tell them around the campfire,' Shaun had said to me earlier, between phone calls. 'This needs to be handled very carefully.'

I hadn't asked him what Vetnet's prospects were. I doubted he even knew. His approach so far had been business-as-usual so I followed his lead, trying to ignore the faint air of anxiety that hung over the lazaret, draining the energy out of everyone. Even the boys were affected. Flynn stopped wailing. Sam stopped clowning. They were grumpy and snappish, but they did what they were told.

I was cleaning up after dinner when Aaron approached me. He'd been quiet in the kitchen earlier, obediently peeling oranges, gaze on the floor, knee jumping uncontrollably. Presenting me with a dirty plate, he said, 'Miss? Can I talk to you for a minute?' He looked nervous.

I stiffened, then gave a nod. 'Talk away.'

'What happened when I left Otford?'

The question took me by surprise. I had to gather my thoughts for a moment. 'Well…your father and grandmother were very angry.' A memory flashed through my head like a knife. 'They blamed me for helping you run away, but I didn't. I didn't have any idea you were going anywhere.'

He waited. It still felt odd to see those familiar eyes so far off the ground.

'The police investigated,' I told him. 'But they couldn't find you—'

'Me and my mum?'

'Yes.'

'Were you her friend? Is that why you got the blame?'

I tried to remember Krystal. Her image had faded; she'd been a wispy presence at the best of times. But I recalled how she'd confided in me. How she'd appealed for my help.

'We were friendly,' I said at last. 'We weren't close.'

'Did you like her?' His voice was tense, and I wondered why. Did *he* not like her?

'I did like her, yes. Though she was a little…I don't know. Scatty?' Not too scatty to disappear, though. 'I heard she used to drink, but that was long before we met. I'm sorry if it's happening again.' I searched his face for a clue. What did he want to hear? 'All I did was store her couch in my garage. I knew nothing about her plans. Nothing.'

He absorbed all this without fidgeting or glancing away. He seemed fascinated. I remembered talking to him about cockroaches, years before. There had been no tantrums then, either. No screaming. No violence. When he was interested in something—really interested—he had the power to engage. He'd always been like that.

If only someone had built on it...

'Thanks,' he said and wandered off, leaving me with a lot of unanswered questions.

~

Joe returned to Finch Island the next morning. He came in a water taxi. The boys were practising their passing-out drill when Shaun told them to stand at ease. Then Joe announced that Tyler was in Redland Hospital, doing well.

Later, at lunch, I cornered Joe in the pantry and wrenched a few more details out of him. It was a fractured fibula, he said. Tyler would be in a cast for six to eight weeks. So far no one had turned up to visit the poor kid; his family lived near Caboolture and were 'having trouble getting in'. Sergeant Bass was expected to drop by that afternoon.

'I couldn't just hang around and wait for Bass,' Joe said with a sigh, 'though I did want to tell him how worried Tyler is about his sister. It's all he can talk about.'

'Yeah.' I felt a heaviness in my gut. 'Something bad's going on there.'

'I'll speak to Shaun. He needs to call Bass again. We can't

really help the kid if there's an emergency at home.'

After a morning spent marching up and down in formation, the boys had fun on the zipline all afternoon. It was their reward for a tough week. Despite Tyler's injury, they didn't seem put off. Only Connor looked nervous as they headed into the bush. I think I was more anxious than any of them, even though I'd checked the equipment thoroughly before lunch. I kept seeing Tyler in my mind's eye, flat on his back at the bottom of the stairs. I kept listening for the sound of screams in the distance.

I was relieved when everyone came trudging back four hours later, grimy and sweaty but all in one piece. Though tired, the boys seemed pleased with themselves. Even Flynn wasn't limping.

Dinner that night was burgers, so section two didn't have a lot to prepare. They sliced tomatoes, chopped lettuce and dumped chips onto baking trays. Jake wasn't there—he'd been moved back to section one, at my request. But Shaun had allowed him to use the zipline. 'Just to show him what he'll be missing out on if he doesn't mend his ways,' Shaun had explained to me. 'Thrills. Camaraderie. Teamwork.'

There was an air of mounting excitement around the campfire that night. Shaun talked a lot about lessons learnt and insights gained. He handed out badges to everyone except Jake. Matt and Ali and Zac were loaded down with badges. Flynn got an empathy badge because he was the only boy who ever bothered talking to Bruno—though whingeing to Bruno was probably a better way of describing it. Dean received a tidy badge. Bruno's badge was for following orders, Connor's was for trust and Nathan's was for courage (presumably because he hadn't burst into tears when wrongly accused of sticking nails through my floor).

Aaron's badge was for leadership; he'd taken charge of his team during the hunt for cache number two. He accepted the badge without even looking at it. I'd noticed how preoccupied he was. Something seemed to be weighing on him.

I wondered if he was dreading his return home.

'Tomorrow you'll be leaving Finch Island,' Shaun declared. 'It's been a pretty confronting week for all of you. There have been accidents. Punishments. You've been physically and mentally challenged. But you've also learnt a lot of things and made a lot of friends. And I'm hoping you'll take these lessons back into your everyday lives. I'm hoping you'll remember that with discipline, self-respect and trust in your mates you can achieve almost anything you set your mind to.'

Inspiring words. But just a few minutes later, Connor tripped Ali. And then Dean threw Nathan against a wall.

'For some of these kids, it's a work in progress,' Shaun admitted, once the boys were in bed. We were sitting in my office, discussing how we were going to seat, feed and control Saturday's crowd of visitors. 'We've made inroads with Connor, but he's not there yet. I might talk to his parents about our follow-up program.'

'What about Jake?' I asked. 'Is he graduating?'

'No. He won't be getting a dog-tag tomorrow.' Seeing me frown, Shaun said, 'There's no family coming, so I doubt he'll care. Bill Khatri will be collecting him. Bill's the copper who referred Jake *and* Nathan. I'll be asking Bill to send Jake back next month.'

'Do you think he will? Once he hears about Tyler?' Warren was slouched on a spindly kitchen chair, arms folded.

'It's a camp,' Shaun pointed out. 'People get hurt. That's why we have insurance.'

'Does Nathan have family coming? Or is it just the copper?' I could only imagine what it must be like, watching mums and dads and grandmothers descend on all your fellow campers when your own parents haven't shown up.

'I believe so.' Shaun checked one of his many lists. 'An aunt. Flynn has ten guests coming. Sam has eight.'

'What about Darren?'

Warren shot me a piercing look.

'Two,' said Shaun. 'Mother and brother.'

I blinked. Brother? *Krystal must have met someone*, I thought.

'You okay?' Warren asked me.

'Yeah.' I was okay. I could manage. But it was going to be interesting.

I don't think I've ever felt so nervous about meeting a parent.

2009

TWO POLICE OFFICERS paid me a visit on Monday night, after Aaron had failed to show up at school. Rick Waring was one of them. The other was a weathered, grey-haired boulder of a man who introduced himself as Sergeant Paul Ries. They hadn't come about my father, they assured me. My father was fine.

'It's Krystal McCall,' Ries said. 'I believe you know her?'

'Oh, God.' My stomach seemed to do a somersault. 'Is she hurt? Has something happened?'

'We'd prefer not to discuss it on the doorstep.'

I was stupid. I let them in. It was the shock—I'd already jumped to the worst possible conclusion, thanks to that moment twenty years earlier when two policemen had come to my father's house and told us my mother was dead.

'Did Scott do it?' I demanded, closing the door behind Rick Waring. 'Did he attack her?'

'Why would you think that, Ms Ayres?' Ries's muddy

brown eyes were almost lost in a nest of wrinkles. His teeth were large and stained. He had a military haircut and fingers like beef sausages.

'Well, he's been stalking her, hasn't he? These things often escalate.' The words spilled out before I could stop them. It wasn't until I'd finished speaking that I registered the emphasis he'd put on 'Ms'.

A warning flare went off in my head.

'So you think Krystal McCall is in danger?' Ries spoke with forced friendliness as he lowered himself into a chair. By now all my alarms were sounding.

'What's going on?' I asked.

'We were wondering if you thought Krystal might be at risk if she stayed here in town.'

'Why?'

Ries shrugged. 'Just interested.'

I looked at the two of them. Ries was practically licking his chops, like a cat on a stake-out. Waring was still on his feet, scanning the room.

'Okay.' I folded my arms. 'Tell me what's happened.'

Ries studied me for a moment. 'You don't know?'

'Of course not.'

The two cops exchanged glances. Then Ries said, 'Your friend Krystal seems to have abducted her son.'

I blinked. Stared. Tried to absorb this astonishing news.

'They drove off on Saturday night with a car full of stuff. Left a text on Mitch McCall's phone saying sorry but it was the only way.' Ries was watching me intently. 'You know

Mitch, don't you? He says you've met.'

I had to sit down. Krystal had bolted? I couldn't believe it.

'Are you sure she hasn't just…' I fumbled for the right term. 'Taken a break?'

'I don't know,' Ries said. 'You tell us.'

I frowned. What the hell…?

'We thought you might have some idea where she is,' Ries continued.

'*Me?*'

'You're friends, aren't you?'

'No.'

'Then why do you have her couch in your garage?'

My mouth dropped open. Then I remembered: they'd been talking to Mitch. 'She said it was an emergency. There was nowhere else. I felt sorry for her.'

'Why?' It was the first question Rick Waring had asked.

I glared at him. 'You should know. You're a mate of Scott's.'

'So you've discussed Scott with Krystal?' When Ries took over again, I didn't like his tone. *Enough*, I thought.

'Krystal McCall is a parent from school. We've had a few meetings. I've seen Scott Rooney following her around. That's all I know.' Then something else occurred to me. 'If she was leaving, why did she buy a new couch?'

Ries shrugged again. 'Misdirection? Or it could have been a spur-of-the-moment thing.'

I grunted. It could have been. That certainly sounded more like Krystal.

'Has she spoken to you about running away?' Ries inquired.

'No.'

'Has she talked about friends who live out of town? Or places she's always wanted to visit?'

I shook my head.

'Did she leave anything else with you?'

'No. Just the couch.'

'Are you sure?'

'Of course I'm sure.'

'So you don't have an emergency contact number? Or stuff she might want you to send her at a later date?'

I stood up. 'You can go.'

'Ms Ayres—'

'I know what this is. This is Joyce.' I was seething. 'Joyce Rooney hates my guts. Whatever she told you is a lie. I barely know Krystal.'

'That's not what we heard,' Waring interposed.

'From the Rooneys?' My voice curdled with contempt.

'There was no involvement, then? No relationship?' Ries was staying very calm.

'None.' I turned on my heel and walked to the front door, which I opened with a shaking hand.

'We're just trying to get to the bottom of this.' Ries hadn't moved. 'What's happened here is a crime. And anyone assisting in the commission of a crime can also be charged.'

'Fine. If you want to charge me, go ahead. I'll call my lawyer.' Who worked in Sydney, but they didn't know that. 'Otherwise—out.'

Ries couldn't pull off an apologetic smile. It looked more

like a snarl. 'We've only got a few more questions…'

'I've told you all I know. If I think of anything else, you'll hear from me.'

Waring's eyes narrowed. But as he opened his mouth, Ries stood up.

'We'd appreciate that,' Ries said. 'The sooner this is sorted, the better. You can imagine how the Rooneys feel right now. They're devastated.'

I didn't respond. I just waited for them to leave. It wasn't until they were thumping down my front steps that I thought to ask, 'Where were the Rooneys this weekend?'

The two of them stopped and looked back. Ries said, 'At home.' Then he followed Rick Waring back to their patrol car—which was parked on the street, in full view of my neighbours.

I wondered how long it would be before the news got out.

⁓

I dreamed about Troy that night. It was a dream that started off well, the way our marriage did; he was trying to make me wear tiny shorts because of my 'amazing giraffe legs'. And I was saying no, no, I was pregnant, couldn't he see? I would look like a balloon with two strings.

Then I was on the couch—Krystal's couch—feeling sick, lifeless, devastated, and he was talking about the baby: how great it would look with his hair and my legs. I kept saying there is no baby. *There is no baby.* But he wouldn't listen. He went on and on about how wonderful it would be, how fabulous I looked, and it all rang so hollow. I could smell decay under the words, the way I did those last few months, when I felt as if I was treading on rotten boards that might collapse at any moment. I could sense the lies, but I couldn't see them. Not until I walked into the apartment that day and there they were. Annette and Troy. Facing each other across the living room, waiting for me.

It was a shock, but not a surprise. Not really. For weeks I'd been wrestling with a creeping awareness of doom. Of desolation. Of things going wrong.

I was highly attuned to the signals.

None of my parent helpers showed up the next morning, though they all sent their kids. Oscar and George were more rambunctious than usual. Phoebe chided me at roll call.

'Aaron's not here,' she announced. 'Mum says it's your fault. Mum says you should tell the police where he's gone before something bad happens.'

'I don't know where he's gone, Phoebe, but if I did I would tell the police.' Seeing Luke's face crumple, I quickly reassured him. 'Anyway, nothing bad is going to happen. Aaron will be fine.'

Phoebe wasn't persuaded. I noticed her judgmental frown as we worked our way through my lesson plan; she corrected me a couple of times and flounced around like a little diva. She would point things out as if I couldn't see them for myself. 'Oscar's under the desk, miss.' 'George won't give Chloe the scissors.' 'Miss, this is too hard for Caleb.' It was like having a very vocal caseworker in the room.

At recess, staff kept sidling up to me and asking about Krystal.

'I hear she's done a runner,' Prue said. 'I don't blame her. Do you know where she is?'

Deb told me that Joyce had been parading around town, bombarding various shopkeepers with tales of how Krystal had packed up her battered blue car and driven away. How Mitch had received a text after she'd gone. How he'd kept it a secret until confronted by the police on Monday afternoon.

'Joyce is saying you're involved,' Deb went on. 'She's saying you have some of Krystal's stuff.'

'One couch. That's all.' I was beginning to wonder if I'd been manipulated—if Krystal's vague, tormented persona had been a façade, designed to take advantage of me. Had she planned everything, right down to the moving-house ploy that had allowed her to pack up all her household goods without causing suspicion? Or had her flight been a last-minute impulse—possibly sparked by a legal setback?

Perhaps Scott's latest attempt to freak her out had worked too well.

'You'd better be careful. If the Rooneys are on the warpath, they can do a lot of damage.' Lowering her voice, Deb asked, 'Your ex ran off with another woman, right?'

'Right.' Because I couldn't have kids. I'd mentioned this to Deb over our first round of drinks together.

'Well, Joyce told Petra that *you* were the one who ran

off with another woman. And you've been helping Krystal because...well. You know.'

'For God's sake.'

'You might want to stamp on that.'

Even Howard approached me after school. In the middle of a discussion about Caleb's progress, he suddenly said, 'Aaron's management plan is on hold for now, of course. I don't suppose you know when he'll be back?'

I flushed. 'No.'

'I've heard of cases where children have vanished for a year or more.' Howard sighed and shook his head. 'Parental abduction is very bad for the child. There have been studies.'

'I know,' I said through clenched teeth.

'The longer he's away, the worse he'll be when he shows up again. We'll all find ourselves back at square one, which is very annoying—though I imagine you're not sorry he's gone.'

'Howard.' I looked him straight in the eye. 'This had nothing to do with me.'

'Of course not,' he said, without much conviction.

It was a relief to get home at last, but even there I wasn't safe. I'd hardly had time to make a cup of tea before Mitch McCall was knocking on my door, begging for a quick word. I almost didn't recognise him; he seemed to have shrunk and his colour was dreadful. His jaunty air had completely disappeared.

'I just want to warn you, I'll be picking up that couch tomorrow,' he began. Then his whole body sagged. 'I don't know if I can return it to the store. Or if I should keep it in case...in case...' He trailed off.

I had to ask him in. I couldn't just leave him on the doorstep.

'Oh, no. Thanks, love. I'm good,' he said, though he didn't look good. 'It's the shock, you know? She didn't tell me. I had no idea. But I don't blame her; it was getting too hard. She was at the end of her rope—you could see that, eh?' Without waiting for a reply, he squared his shoulders and said, 'I don't care if they charge me. What did they expect—that I was going to dob her in? She was smart not to tell me anything. It means I have nothing to say.' Then he lowered his voice and gazed at me with desperate eyes. 'Did she tell *you* anything?'

This, I realised, was the question he'd really come to ask.

'No, Mitch. I'm sorry.'

'They found her car this morning.'

I frowned. 'Where?'

'In Coffs Harbour. Near a supermarket.'

'*Coffs Harbour?*'

'Scott had a two-year posting in Coffs right after they married. Krystal's got friends there.' He offered me a shaky smile that looked like a wound carved into his face. 'I felt better when I heard. The Rooneys couldn't have driven that car to Coffs and back. They were in town on Sunday morning. I saw 'em myself.'

'Right.' I understood his misgivings.

'Anyway, thanks for your help. And I'm sorry about the couch. I'll get rid of it as soon as I can.'

'Please, Mitch, don't worry.' My heart went out to him. 'Take your time. I don't use that garage.'

'She's got so much stuff. I don't know what to do with it…' He stared off into space for a moment, then turned and stumbled back towards his car. Worried he was going to fall, I watched him until he climbed into the driver's seat. Then I returned to the kitchen.

Three hours later, the Rooneys arrived.

I was eating a plate of thawed-out chicken stew when a thundering knock made me bite my tongue. The pain was so bad I had to sit there, taking deep breaths, while the hammering continued.

'We know you're home!' A loud voice: Scott Rooney's. I wasn't about to let him in. Instead I went to the bathroom and rinsed out my mouth. Bloodstained water swirled down the plughole.

'You have to tell us where she is!' Scott roared. 'We know you know! You've got her fucking couch in your garage!'

I wondered if I should call the police. This was harassment, pure and simple. But would the local cops even care? After all, one of them was Rick Waring.

'She's blown it, you moron,' Scott continued. 'She just lost her kid. Do you realise that?'

'We've put in a contravention application. Which means we'll get a recovery order.' That was Joyce; she must have come along with him. Though she wasn't yelling, her voice was high and abrasive. 'When they find her, they'll take Aaron away for good.'

'And then you'll be in deep shit,' Scott warned me. 'If she admits you helped her, you'll be arrested too. Your only chance is to come forward now with any information you have.' A pause, followed by more pounding. 'Hey! I'm talking to you, bitch!'

By then I was recording him on my phone. I didn't know how good the sound quality would be; I was standing at the other end of the house and there was a closed door between us. But it was worth a try.

'If you're not hiding anything, why didn't you let the police search your house?' Joyce demanded.

Search my house? The police had never even asked to search my house. I wanted to tell her that but decided not to risk it. *Don't engage*, I thought.

'For Chrissake!' Another barrage of thumps made the walls shake. Was Scott trying to break down the door? 'That's my boy out there, you cunt! And I don't even know where he is!'

'Except that he's been to Coffs Harbour,' Joyce interrupted. 'Probably because Krystal has junkie friends there.'

'He might be in a crack house right now and it's *all your fault*!'

Scott emphasised the last words with three huge bangs that sent me running to the kitchen. There I grabbed a carving knife and dialled triple zero. After one ring, a recording said, 'You have called emergency triple zero. Your call is being connected.'

Meanwhile, out on the front steps, Joyce was roaring,

'This isn't over! Don't think you can wriggle out of it! I'm going to lodge a complaint with the Department of Education!'

Then a voice in my ear asked, 'Do you require police, fire and rescue, or ambulance?'

'Police,' I whispered, as Joyce told her son, 'Come on. This is pointless. She's too scared to show her miserable face.'

'Which state are you in?' the operator wanted to know.

There was a massive thud. Scott must have punched the door again.

'Ah—New South Wales,' I said.

A click at the other end of the line was followed by a crisp, 'Where is your emergency?'

I recited my address, edging back into the living room. Scott and Joyce were silent. Had they left? I could see movement behind the grubby gauze curtain hanging across the front window.

'What is your emergency?'

'Uh—hang on...' I hurried over to the window and peered through it. Yes: there they were. Trudging down the drive towards their car.

'It's all right,' I told the operator. 'They're leaving.'

'I beg your pardon?'

'Someone was trying to break in, but they're leaving now. Thanks. I'm sorry.'

For the next few hours my dinner slowly congealed on the kitchen table as I waited to see if the Rooneys would come back. It didn't matter about the food—I'd lost my appetite. I sat up until half past eleven with my phone in my lap, ears pricked, eyes peeled. But I heard no one creeping around the garden. No one whispering in the dark.

Before finally going to bed, I turned on the outside lights and stuck chairs under the doorhandles. I put my phone and my knife on the bedside cabinet. I arranged empty beer cans where they were sure to be kicked by an intruder.

Then I hardly slept a wink for the rest of the night.

2019

IT WAS TEN o'clock on Saturday morning.

The boys' beds were stripped. Their bags were packed. They were washed, dressed and ready for the passing-out parade. Shaun had been drilling them since seven-thirty. 'Don't let your mates down,' he'd pleaded. 'Don't ruin their efforts. You're all in this together and it isn't a joke. Your families will be watching. Show 'em what you're made of. Show 'em what you can accomplish.'

I'd been even busier than the boys—cleaning toilets, washing sheets, baking scones, arranging chairs on the parade ground. Ali and Marcus had lent a hand with the chairs, but no one helped me with the food. I was still frantically slicing melons when I heard three familiar blasts from a horn. I glanced at the kitchen clock. The ferry was bang on time.

But that was okay. The parade was scheduled for ten-thirty. The fruit and cakes and sandwiches wouldn't be served till eleven. I still had an hour before the hordes descended on my morning tea.

I could hear a babble of voices as I moved crockery into the dining hall. Shaun and Joe had met the ferry and were bringing a crowd of visitors up the jetty road. Warren and Rhys were with the boys in the dormitory, where they would stay until the first bars of 'Waltzing Matilda' blasted from a pair of speakers flanking the parade ground. It was slightly overcast, thank God; people often didn't come prepared to sit out in the blazing sun. But most of our visitors were wearing hats. I saw them when I peered through the window.

I also saw Shaun huddled with Clive Creswell, the reviewing officer. Clive was a retired colonel who came to every passing-out parade. A solid bloke in his sixties with thinning white hair, he wore a wide-brimmed Akubra and all his medals. As the other visitors slowly settled into the chairs laid out for them, Clive remained standing, straight-backed and sharp-eyed. His stern gaze always had a quietening effect on the assembly.

I wasn't surprised to hear the chatter and clatter slowly fade, though once or twice a fractious voice rang out. 'Not much for the money,' someone said. Someone else loudly complained, 'There's no bloody phone reception!' A third voice hissed, 'They told us that, remember? No screens…'

Then, after a burst of static from the speakers, Shaun welcomed everyone to Buangan Pa's fifteenth Vetnet Passing-Out Parade. I'd heard his speech many times, so I went back to pulling scones from the oven while he explained his philosophy and introduced Colonel Clive Creswell, CSC. '…Conspicuous Service Cross…Army Command and Staff College…East Timor…Meritorious Unit Citation…' The list of honours was as lengthy as it was tedious. Shaun also mentioned me, and I tried to ignore that as well; it was embarrassing. 'Thanks to the Buangan Pa caretaker…responsible for this beautiful spread… she'll be relieved to see the back of us and have the island to herself again…'

I only pricked up my ears when Tyler was mentioned. Shaun revealed that Vetnet's first and only medical evacuation had occurred the day before. 'Tyler Metherill suffered a fractured fibula and is recovering in hospital,' he announced. I was interested to see how the audience reacted to this, so I slipped out onto the dining-hall veranda, which overlooked a sea of heads.

The first row of chairs was almost empty, as usual. The only person brave enough to sit there was a uniformed police officer who may or may not have been Bill Khatri, the man responsible for referring Jake. He didn't seem disturbed by Shaun's news, though it was hard to see his face under the brim of his cap. Behind him the second row was full of large, lively people who were probably related to Flynn; there was a strong family resemblance. They bobbed and swayed and muttered as Shaun emphasised how swiftly Tyler had been rescued. Behind them sat a stiff, elegant middle-aged couple dressed for an English garden party. As soon as I laid eyes on them, I thought: *Hendersons*. The man had Zac's narrow face and beaky nose. The woman looked constipated.

A few seats away sat another extended family passing around home-made snacks: a beautifully dressed matriarch, a bunch of fidgety kids and two sets of parents who seemed to be enjoying themselves hugely. With their colourful clothes and stuffed vine leaves, they were like people on a picnic. Then came someone who was probably Ali's dad, followed by a small cluster of redheads, a weary woman in Ugg boots, a glossy, well-groomed family like something off a yoghurt ad, and behind them, in the second-last row…

My heart skipped a beat.

Joyce Rooney.

Outside the dormitory, Warren barked an order. Recorded drumrolls greeted the boys as they marched down the veranda steps, advancing in sections, two by two. 'Waltzing Matilda' began to play. The audience cheered. People took pictures. A little girl jumped to her feet, clapping.

Joyce didn't move. Her bushy hair was grey now and her shoulders were hunched, but her aggrieved air hadn't changed. Sitting next to her was Scott, wearing sunglasses and a baseball cap. Even with a beard he was unmistakable. It had something to do with his size, his frown and the angle of his neck.

When the boys reached Shaun, they stopped. The music stopped too. 'Advance in review order!' he blared. There was a flurry of boots. 'On two, right dress! One! Two!' Every boy stuck out an arm and shuffled sideways. 'Eyes front! At ease!'

Joyce suddenly caught my eye. She gave a start. I wanted

to run screaming, but I held my ground. For a moment we stared at each other.

Then she leaned over and whispered to Scott, who turned his head.

By that time I was sweating and shaking. My legs felt weak. Overcome by nausea, I ducked back inside. Then I leaned against a wall and tried to collect my scattered thoughts.

Joyce and Scott. They were right here. Had they tagged along? Were they gatecrashers? Had they come in Krystal's place because she was sick or drunk or stoned? They certainly weren't Aaron's mother or brother. And Krystal...I couldn't remember seeing her, but I hadn't really looked. Not after spotting Joyce.

I craned my neck to peer through the doorway again. Outside, Clive Cresswell was inspecting the troops. He'd stopped in front of Ali, who was smiling. Shaun stood nearby with a box of dog tags. He handed one of the tags to Clive, who gave it to Ali. Clive saluted. Ali saluted. Then Clive moved on to Connor while Ali slung the dog tag around his neck.

My gaze drifted away from the boys as I scanned the people watching them. Who had I missed last time? Not the copper in front. Not Flynn's enthusiastic cheer squad. I noticed another police officer down the back—a woman—and a toothy couple whose toddler looked just like a miniature Matt Spiteri. There was also a very tall, balding man with a crumpled face, and a girl wearing a leather jacket and cornrows.

But I couldn't see Krystal. Or Scott. The chair beside Joyce was empty now.

Clive was talking to Aaron. Head cocked, eyes darting, Aaron mumbled something as he received his dog tag, then returned Clive's salute in a twitchy kind of way, shifting from foot to foot. When Clive proceeded down the row, Aaron flicked a glance at Joyce.

I followed his gaze and saw that she wasn't looking at him. She was looking at me.

Jake was the last boy in section one—and he didn't receive a dog tag. I wondered if he was going to throw a wobbly. But all he did was salute Clive with an exaggerated flourish that seemed to take the piss out of everyone.

Clive kept moving. I scoured the audience again. Had Scott switched seats? Nope. He really had vanished. The restless group down the front cheered as Flynn Parata received his dog tag. He held it up and a big, shiny teenage girl who could have been his twin sister jumped to her feet, whooping and dancing. The Kollios family laughed and clapped. Zac's father frowned.

Warren's mouth twitched. Like Joe and Rhys, he was standing at ease near his section, blank-faced. But as soon as our eyes met, his brows snapped together.

I must have been as white as a sheet.

A quick check of the parade ground told me Scott wasn't anywhere in it. Had he gone to the toilet? Was he trying to make a phone call? With a sick lurch I realised he could be coming around the back of the dining hall to accost me from behind.

That thought sent me skittering across the room, between

tables loaded with tea cups and fruit platters, until I reached the western door.

No Scott. He wasn't heading for the rear veranda.

I stood there, trembling, until another cheer from the parade ground reminded me I had cakes to slice. Strawberries to wash.

I was peeling the cling wrap off a bowl of whipped cream when the opening chords of 'Waltzing Matilda' signalled that the parade was at an end. The boys were marching back into the dormitory, where they would collect their bags before rushing to greet the people who'd come for them. Then everyone would descend on the food, and I would be kept very busy clearing things away.

I could probably avoid the Rooneys if I tried hard.

Retreating into the kitchen, I stacked the dishwasher and tried to work out what was going on. Somehow Joyce and Scott must have found Aaron. Had Krystal gone to jail? It was possible. Had Scott won sole custody? He must have. But why were Aaron's 'mother and brother' listed as his only guests? And who had sent Aaron to Finch Island in the first place? Shaun's notes had nominated Sue King, Aaron's mother. Was that Krystal? Had she been worried about her son's drug use?

And if so, why wasn't she here now?

Maybe they've all patched things up, I thought. It seemed unlikely, but it was the only explanation. Maybe Aaron's little brother was sick. Maybe Krystal—alias Sue King—had asked Joyce to fill in for her.

'Robyn.' Shaun's voice made me jump. He was standing

in the kitchen doorway. Behind him, the dining hall was filling up fast.

'Oh. Hi.' I straightened.

'Someone wants to say hello.' Shaun jerked his head at Clive, who beamed at me over a plate of scones, jam, cream and sandwiches.

'Wonderful spread. You're a marvel,' Clive declared. 'I was just telling Shaun—I only come here every month because of your delicious scones.'

He'd said the same thing the month before and the month before that. I smiled and thanked him, as usual.

'Been in the wars, I hear,' he went on, eyeing me shrewdly. 'Bit of a tough crew this time, eh?'

I glanced at Shaun. How was I supposed to answer? But Shaun's attention was elsewhere; Zac's parents had approached him. All the veterans were in high demand. Looking past Shaun, I could see Warren talking to Connor's picture-perfect family and Joe talking to the woman in the Ugg boots, who was obviously Nathan's aunt because Nathan was with her.

'The medical evacuation must have been bad enough. And I believe the lad who didn't graduate made you a target,' Clive said. I didn't know what he needed from me and was grateful when Flynn's father (or uncle or cousin) suddenly grabbed his arm and cried, 'Hey, colonel! You're a great man to come all this way for our boys!'

Next thing Clive was surrounded by Paratas, and I was able to return to my chores. Tucked away in the kitchen, I managed to keep a low profile. Zac's mother came in to ask if there was any soy or almond milk. Matt dragged his family over to thank me for 'the food and everything'. I was able to tell them, with perfect honesty, that Matt had been a real asset.

'Is it true the injured boy tried to attack him?' asked Mr Spiteri. He wore rimless spectacles and had the bleached, retiring look of an accountant or IT professional.

I nodded. 'It must have been very frightening for Matt. He may need to talk it over with someone.' Seeing the whole family exchange anxious looks, I quickly added, 'But he handled himself so well afterwards. He stayed there and looked after Tyler and manned the radio. You should be proud of him.'

Matt's smile lit up his face—and melted my heart. 'You have a lovely boy, there,' I told his mum, who suddenly looked ten years younger. Then Matt hustled his support team off to meet Joe while I turned back to the sink.

Two minutes later, a harsh voice attacked me from behind.

'What the hell are *you* doing here?'

~

Joyce had cornered me. She stood by herself, clutching a coffee mug. The sight of that familiar glare made my skin prickle.

But I spoke calmly in my slowest country drawl. 'I could ask you the same question.'

'Do they still let you work with kids?' She was on the offensive. Always. 'I'm surprised.'

'Where's Krystal?'

'I dunno.' Seeing me frown, she added, 'As soon as we

finally found her, she pissed off again. Scared, I guess. Scared of us. Scared of being arrested. Luckily she didn't take Darren with her.'

'Wait—hang on…' I didn't understand. Was Krystal not in the picture at all? And why the aliases? I needed some facts. 'Darren? Who's Darren? I thought he was Aaron?'

Her jaw tightened. 'We had to change his name.'

'Why?'

'So she couldn't find him.' Joyce's tone was snappish and impatient, her gaze hard and bright and watchful. 'We didn't want her snatching him again. As long as she's still out there, we have to keep our heads down.' Before I could ask why, she said, 'Maybe *you* know where the bitch has gone.'

But I refused to be sidetracked . 'Aaron's sixteen. She can't take him anywhere. Why are you still worried about her?'

Joyce began to tell me there was no way of knowing what Krystal might do—she was crazy. A criminal. I wasn't really listening, though; my attention had wandered to Aaron himself, who had shuffled into the kitchen with a plate of Tim Tams.

His pale eyes glinted behind a limp curtain of hair.

'Oh! There you are.' Joyce reached out to grab his elbow. 'I was just telling Miss Ayres—it's still "miss", right?'

The question was aimed at me. I said nothing.

'Yeah. Thought so.' Her contemptuous tone lit a spark in my gut. I stopped feeling scared and started feeling angry.

'I was just telling Miss Ayres how we changed our names to make sure Krystal couldn't find us,' Joyce went on. 'And now we're used to them. You've grown up as Darren. That's who you are.'

Aaron didn't speak. His mouth was full of biscuit.

'He doesn't want Krystal tracking him down. He's got enough on his plate,' said Joyce. 'But I suppose you're going to tell her, are you? I bet you've been in touch with her all this time.' Leaning forward, her colour mounting, Joyce started to harangue me in her old, caustic way. 'You can tell her from me, Darren hates her guts. He'll shop her as soon as look at her. Won't you? Eh?' She shook his arm but didn't wait for an answer. 'That bitch is still a fugitive. She'd better not stick her head out, or we'll chop it off. You tell her that, if you talk to her. Just keep it in mind. Because if you know where she is, you've broken the law too.'

'Ms Ayres?'

It was Warren. He'd suddenly appeared in the doorway, all dramatic scars and broad shoulders. 'Everything all right?' he asked—and I realised he'd come to my rescue. He must have glanced into the kitchen and read Joyce's body language.

'I don't think everything *is* all right.' Joyce rounded on him like a pit bull. 'I'm surprised you let her near these kids. Do you know about her background? Do you know what she did?'

'It's Mrs King, isn't it?' Warren stuck out his hand. 'I recognise your voice. We spoke on the phone. I'm Warren Doyle. I used to be a sapper in the 2nd Combat Engineer Regiment, 3rd Battalion.'

Something about the way he said this silenced Joyce for a

260

moment. She shook his hand, her face working.

Aaron stood beside her, stuffing another Tim Tam into his mouth. I remembered how many times I'd seen him with Joyce in my classroom, gnawing at his hand or hanging off hers, his face shuttered, his feet twitching.

This time was different, though. I could sense something inside him: an edge. A fizz. A lit fuse. I didn't know exactly what it was, but it alarmed me.

'I hope you're proud of your son,' Warren continued, releasing Joyce's hand. 'Darren's done really well. We had a few hiccups at the beginning, but the last few days he's been stepping up with a vengeance. He got a leadership badge—did he tell you?'

'No.' Joyce turned to Aaron. 'Why didn't you tell me about your leadership badge?'

Aaron picked up another Tim Tam and bit into it. Then he began to chew, very slowly, like a cow masticating cud.

'Where's your other son?' Warren asked Joyce. 'I saw him earlier. Steve, is it?'

'Uh—yeah.' Joyce flicked me a look. 'He went off to find a signal. For his phone.'

'There isn't one,' Warren pointed out.

'I know. I told him that.' Suddenly, out of nowhere, Joyce slapped on one of her twinkly smiles—the kind that had charmed Pat and Kate and Dixie. 'Kids, eh? They never pay any attention to you, even when they grow up.' Without missing a beat, she added, 'One of the other boys broke a leg, I hear. That makes me wonder. As a parent.'

Warren returned her smile. 'It's wilderness education, Mrs King. We can't avoid the odd injury, even though we take every precaution.'

'Did *she* have anything to do with it?' Joyce cocked her thumb at me.

'No.'

'I'm surprised. She's got a history with kids.'

Seething, I opened my mouth. But Warren jumped in first.

'I know,' he said. 'Robyn was a teacher.'

'A bad one,' Joyce snapped.

'On the contrary, we've found her to be a real asset.'

'At beating up kids?' Without waiting for an answer, Joyce continued, 'Whatever she's told you is a lie. Why do you think she's hiding out here? She's ashamed of herself. I'd think very carefully about employing her if I were you—especially after this so-called accident. People will get suspicious. They'll start asking questions.' She must have tightened her grip on Aaron's arm, because he winced. 'And if Darren smokes a single joint when we get home,' she told Warren, 'I'm taking you to court. From what I can see, you haven't even improved his manners.'

All at once Shaun's amplified voice echoed across the lazaret. 'Ladies and gentlemen!' he declared. 'This is just to let you know that the ferry to Cleveland will be arriving in ten minutes. If you want to catch it, you should start moving down to the jetty.' He was out on the veranda with his mega-phone; I could see him from where I was standing. 'Those who want to stay and explore the island,' he went on, 'can catch the two o'clock Stradbroke service, or the return trip at four. Thank you very much.'

A surge of mingled voices greeted this announcement. I heard a woman say, 'Connor—toilet! Quick!' Out in the dining hall, there was a sudden rush for the food. Marcus and Sam were scooping up all the chocolate biscuits they could lay their hands on.

Joyce frowned. Was it my imagination, or did she look slightly relieved? 'If this sorry bitch was mentioned on your website,' she finished, 'I wouldn't have wasted my money.'

Warren's face turned to stone. 'Mrs King—'

'It's her fault Darren was traumatised. He's never been the same since. Don't believe a word she says—she's mentally ill.' Without even glancing in my direction, she headed for the door, still clutching Aaron's arm. But he hung back, ignoring her furious tugs. His remarkable eyes were fixed on me.

'I remember about the cockroaches,' he said. 'How they could live for a week with their heads cut off. I always thought it was cool how tough they were. It made me feel good.'

Then he stumbled out of the room, yielding to Joyce's pressure.

Warren and I both stared after them for a moment. I was feeling winded; my mouth was dry and my head was in a whirl.

At last Warren turned to me and said, 'What the fuck was all that about?'

2009

AFTER THE ROONEYS' angry visit, nothing went right. It was as if they'd put a curse on me.

At school the next morning, Phoebe gave me a note from her mother. *Dear Miss Ayres*, it said.

This is to inform you that neither myself, Pat Haas nor Dixie Whitaker can help you in the classroom from now on. We don't approve of your stance on Krystal McCall.
Yours sincerely, Kate Canning.

Later, when we were sorting different foods into 'healthy' and 'unhealthy' piles, Phoebe argued with me about a muesli bar. She also argued about counting backwards, Luke's crayons, and a reader she wanted to take home. She argued about everything, constantly. Her tone was patronising, impatient, world-weary—a perfect imitation of her mother's.

Then, just before lunch, Howard appeared in the doorway. He beckoned to me as a chorus of squeaky voices cried, 'Good morning, Mr Bradshaw!'

'Good morning, children,' he said. Next thing I knew, my kids were filing into Deb's room while Howard escorted me to the school hall, where the police wanted to see me. 'It's the only spot I can give you right now,' he explained. 'But Amy's got it booked after lunch, so keep things as brief as you can.'

I was shocked. Furious. By the time I reached the hall, I was ready to explode.

Paul Ries and Rick Waring both greeted me when I arrived. They'd arranged three plastic chairs in the huge, cavernous space but weren't using them; Ries was pacing up and down like a fenced dog. On seeing me, he pointed at one of the empty chairs. 'Thanks for this,' he said, his voice bouncing off the shiny wooden floor and lofty roof beams.

I didn't move. I didn't speak.

I waited.

'We've got a couple more questions,' he went on. I wanted to say, *And you couldn't have asked them elsewhere?* But I thought silence would be safer.

Ries glanced at Waring, then took out a mobile phone and fiddled with it for a moment before shoving it at me. 'Do you recognise this?'

'The phone?' I didn't understand.

'No. This.' Ries tapped its screen, which displayed a photo of something.

I squinted. 'That's the worksheet I wrote for Aaron.'

'It was found in Krystal McCall's car, which was found in Coffs Harbour. Do you know why she took it?'

'The worksheet?' Wasn't it obvious? 'Because it's full of

exercises for Aaron. To improve his performance at school.'

'But she was taking him away from school. Why would that matter anymore?'

I didn't answer. It was a stupid question.

'Your phone number is on the worksheet. Right here,' Ries continued. He gestured at the screen again. 'Why?'

'In case she needed help.' As he opened his mouth, I added, 'With the exercises.'

'Or with anything else?'

I said nothing, so he tried another tack.

'Have you ever been to Coffs Harbour?'

I shook my head.

'Do you have friends there?'

'No.'

'Do you have friends living anywhere on the north coast?'

'No.'

'Your dad's in Kempsey. That's only an hour from Coffs.'

I frowned. 'You think Krystal's with my dad?'

'Is she?'

I sighed and massaged the bridge of my nose. 'My dad has high blood pressure. I wouldn't let Aaron anywhere near him.'

'Have you spoken to your father lately?'

'No.' Short and sharp, like a door slamming.

'Can you tell me anything about his car? Make? Model? Registration?'

Waring had produced a notebook. Eyeing it, I took a deep breath and said, 'Look—I can see what's happening here. The Rooneys are desperate. You're desperate. So you're going to bother an old man with high blood pressure who wouldn't break the law at gunpoint.' Before Ries could respond, I held up one hand. 'You can write this down: I don't know where Krystal is and I didn't help her leave. That's all I have to say. All right?'

I thought I'd made myself perfectly clear. But Ries didn't seem to get the message. 'Were you born in Kempsey?' he asked.

I stayed silent.

'Do you keep up with any of your old friends there?'

A bell rang. I glanced out the window. 'That's lunch. I've got playground duty.'

'Ms Ayres—'

'We're finished. I'm not talking to you again without a lawyer.'

As I marched away, I wondered where I was going to find myself a decent lawyer in Otford. I knew my Sydney lawyer wouldn't have a bar of this.

~

'Hamish Staines,' Deb advised me.

'Hamish—?'

'Staines.' She spelled it out. 'He's based in Bathurst. You don't want someone from around here.'

We were walking to our cars at the end of a very long day. After my tense exchange with Sergeant Ries, I'd called Dad, whose reaction to my warning about the police made me worry about his blood pressure. Then, after lunch, Chloe had been sick all over my second-best work blouse, forcing me to change into the spare T-shirt I kept in my desk drawer. Then Caleb had wet himself, and I'd started getting a headache, and at our after-school staff meeting I'd been peppered with questions about Joyce and Krystal.

'I don't know his number, but it'll be easy enough to find,' Deb added, unlocking her car door. 'What's happening to you is outrageous. Someone needs to put a stop to it—and Hamish might be the guy. My friend Danielle swears by him.'

I thanked her. Then I climbed into my own car and drove home, feeling as if I'd been through a wringer. I had loads of work to do, I had a lawyer to call, and I had to check up on Dad in case the police had been hassling him. I also had to water my pot plants; as I pulled into my driveway, I noticed that some of them were looking a little crisp around the edges.

But when I turned on the garden tap, my hose exploded.

It didn't happen instantly. At first I wondered why nothing was coming out of the nozzle. Then I heard a hiss and turned around and saw the hose connector jump off the tap. Water sprayed everywhere, soaking my face, pants, hair, shoes, T-shirt.

After fiddling around for a while, I realised there was a blockage.

'Shit.' I couldn't clear it no matter how hard I tried; the only solution would be to cut the hose and discard one end. But I decided to do that later, because it was already past four and I wanted to ring Hamish Staines before his office shut.

Unlocking the front door, I wondered if the Rooneys had wedged something into my hose. I tried to remember when

I'd last used it. Sunday? Friday? Before or after the washing-machine incident? I was stepping into the kitchen when my feet slid out from under me.

I managed to grab the doorjamb just in time, landing on my butt instead of my back. But as I stood up again, I stepped in something sticky. There was honey all over the floor. I could smell it.

'What the...?' A lidless jar lay nearby. Someone had dumped out its contents. Someone had been in my house.

Suddenly I was on full alert. My heart began to pound like a jackhammer. I rose carefully and checked the back door. But it was locked—and the window wasn't smashed.

'Hello?' Nobody answered. I tried to ignore my panic and think. First thing: weapon. I leaned over and pulled a knife from the block. Next thing: check the house. I didn't want to tread honey into the carpet, so I kicked off my sticky shoes and sidled into the second bedroom, which contained a desk, a bunch of unpacked boxes and a built-in wardrobe. No one was hiding in the wardrobe or under the desk. The window was untouched, not a single cobweb disturbed.

Clutching my knife, I moved into the bathroom. Here the smell of urine hit me like a slap, strong and sharp and sickening. I turned on the light and advanced cautiously, holding my breath.

The tiles on the floor were dental pink. The toilet had an old black seat, and I could see darker patches on it. Dried piss? There was something on the floor as well. Lots of it. Not wet, but pungent.

I gagged. Someone had peed all over my toilet—and around it as well. No woman had done this.

I headed for the master bedroom, afraid of what I would find there. But nothing had been moved. The window was intact. The bed was neatly made. I checked the wardrobe, which covered one whole wall. No one was skulking inside. Had anything been taken? It was hard to tell.

Then my gaze dropped a little and I saw it: a fallen hem on my grey skirt. And beside that, a fallen hem on my linen dress. And my linen pants. And my red cotton blouse...

Almost every hem was down, laboriously unpicked, stray threads carefully removed. How long had this taken? At least an hour—more, probably.

Joyce, I thought.

But how had she got in? The windows and doors were all locked. It must have been done with a key. A spare key. Did Joyce know my landlord? Or had she found a spare key outside somewhere, under a stone or a brick?

Krystal's voice echoed through my head: *Scott's best friend's girlfriend used to rent your house.*

I hurried to my desk and googled locksmiths. There was only one listed nearby; he promised to come at once.

'The sooner the better,' I said, my voice tight with strain. 'Someone just broke in.'

'Oh, yeah?' He didn't sound the least bit shocked. Before I could ask him how much he charged, he hung up.

My next call was to Hamish Staines, who wasn't available. 'Can you tell him to call me back?' I asked his secretary.

'It's urgent.' I didn't want to ring the police until I'd talked to a lawyer—because really, what did this whole thing amount to? Spilled honey. A dirty toilet. Fallen hems. No sign of a break-in.

The cops would think I was trying to get even with Joyce.

I was cleaning the kitchen floor when the locksmith arrived. He was young, fair and strangely nonchalant, tossing around a lot of she'll-be-rights and not-to-worries. He exhibited no interest at all in what had happened, and I only worked out why after he'd finished.

'You can keep the old locks, but it'll cost you the same to put 'em all back in again,' he said. When I asked him why I would want to do that, he explained that half his work was generated by feuding couples changing the locks on each other. Whenever they made up, they would want the locks changed back. 'Jesus, they carry on,' he said in a tone that conveyed quite clearly how bored he was with endless tales of domestic disputes.

My phone rang just as he was leaving. Hamish Staines was at the other end of the line; he had a light tenor voice and a soothing manner. I blurted out a lot of disjointed remarks about the police, a break-in, Joyce, Scott, the locksmith and Krystal's disappearance, asking if I should get an AVO. He told me to sit down and start from the beginning.

It took me a long time to relate what had happened. When I finally finished, he thought for a moment. Then he said, 'So what do you want me to do, Robyn?'

'I don't know.' Couldn't *he* work it out? That was why I'd

called him. 'I don't want to talk to the police again without a lawyer.'

'That's wise.'

'But I need to tell them about the break-in, don't you think?'

'Absolutely. Get it on the record.'

'And after what the Rooneys did last night, I want to make sure they don't come here again.'

'Understood.' Another pause. 'You say you recorded their visit?'

'Yes. That'll help, won't it?'

'Possibly. It's illegal to record conversations in New South Wales without the permission of all parties involved, though from what I gather it wasn't strictly a conversation. I'll have to check the Surveillance Devices Act.' A brief silence followed, broken up by lots of squeaks and crackles. 'What if I swing by tomorrow?' he said at last. 'We can approach the police together and try to sort this out. Shouldn't be hard.'

'Oh, yes! Thank you!' A huge wave of relief flooded through me. I felt almost faint. 'That would be wonderful!'

'Ten o'clock?'

'Ah—could we make it after school? Four?'

'Four it is.'

I gave him my address and he said something about fees, but I wasn't really paying attention.

'What about the urine on the toilet?' I asked. 'Do you think the police will need that for DNA?'

Hamish didn't speak for a few seconds. When he finally

answered, his voice was very bland. 'No, Robyn. That's all right. You can clean your toilet.' If he was laughing at me, he did a good job of hiding it.

~

I managed to stay calm that night. After changing the locks, calling Hamish, mopping the bathroom and stitching up some hems, I even got a bit of work done. But the next morning everything fell apart.

It started with a call I made to my landlord while I was getting dressed. He was furious that I'd touched his locks without permission. 'It's the law!' he kept saying. 'I could have you evicted!' Stung, I brought up the leaky hot water system; we had a huge argument that ended only when I shoved my foot into a trainer and felt something wet.

Honey in my shoe.

I had to wear sandals to school because most of my closed footwear contained honey or tomato sauce. It was devastating. I didn't know how some of the boots would ever be resurrected. Then, just before I reached my classroom, Dad called. He told me the police had dropped by, though he insisted they'd been very decent. 'I've known Val Stavros for years—he was just going through the motions. Orders from on high, he told me. Wouldn't even search the place, though I said he could.' As I struggled to keep calm, Dad continued, 'His daughter's getting married. Remember Rachael? Maybe not. He asked after you. I told him you were doing very well, all things considered.'

But I wasn't doing well. I could feel it. During my last few weeks with Troy, I'd developed certain symptoms: a throat-clearing tic, a loss of concentration, a needling pain in my gut as if a rodent was scratching away in there. When I found myself repeatedly clearing my throat during roll call, I realised how stressed I was.

Then Phoebe started playing up.

She'd marched in that morning with a letter of complaint about the healthy food lesson I'd given the day before. According to Kate Canning, there was more sugar in fruit than in some other damn thing...I can't remember the details. Then Phoebe took it upon herself to scold Luke for wearing a shirt that wasn't officially sanctioned. When I explained that he had only one school shirt, which still hadn't dried after a hamburger accident, she became even more officious, telling the other kids where to sit, correcting their pronunciation and insisting that we should do 'more mathematics'. 'You're not challenging us,' she informed me—no doubt parroting her mother.

I dealt with it by focusing on the quieter kids. I ignored Phoebe while I was assigning leadership roles for our class activities, so she started whispering instructions to some of her classmates. They didn't appreciate it. Kayla finally pinched her.

'Kayla pinched me! She pinched me!' Phoebe cried.

'Kayla—' I began.

'Don't do that.' Phoebe shoved Kayla, who pulled Phoebe's hair.

'Girls!' I jumped up.

Enraged, Phoebe slapped Kayla. By the time I reached

them, they were locked together, squirming and screaming. When Phoebe raked her nails across Kayla's left eye, I grabbed both children and yanked them apart.

Phoebe's yell was so piercing that I immediately dropped her arm. She gazed down at the red mark I'd left on her. 'You hurt me,' she whimpered.

'No, I didn't—'

'You hurt me!' She gazed up into my face, her eyes filling with tears. 'You're not allowed to hurt me! Mum said!'

That's when I knew I was in trouble.

2019

I GLANCED THROUGH the kitchen window at the parade ground. Joyce was following a tide of visitors as they poured down the veranda steps. Her hand was clamped to Aaron's shoulder. She was muttering in his ear.

'Rob,' said Warren, 'what's going on?'

Outside, the other veterans were herding everyone down to the water. As families mobbed them, they edged towards the jetty, shouldering their packs. Colonel Creswell was leading by example; he was already halfway there, locked in an earnest conversation with Zac's father.

'Rob, are you all right?' Warren touched my arm. When I didn't reply, he said, 'I can see why you thought Darren dumped prawns on your bed. Jesus—that woman!'

'She's a liar.'

''Course she is.' His voice was gentle. 'Don't worry, mate. I'm not stupid.'

Joyce was steering Aaron down the road now, past Shaun

and Dean and the Kollios family. Dean was with the tall, balding, crumpled man from the second-last row of seats. Jake was with the male police officer. Joyce gave them both a wide berth, then passed out of sight.

Unable to see her from the window, I made for the door.

'I need to do a recce and make sure none of the kids have wandered off,' said Warren, who was hot on my heels. 'But I'll stay here and help you clear up afterwards. Shaun can't; he has to visit Tyler.'

From the veranda I had a better view of the jetty road. It was a seething mass of people. The kids were all bobbing rucksacks and boonie hats. Their families were receding into the distance at a rapid rate. If Joyce was among them, she was hiding behind a solid wall of Paratas.

I couldn't see her. Or Scott.

'Okay. I'll be back soon.' Warren brushed past and bounced down the steps. Then he made for the dormitory.

'If you find anyone who's staying on, will you tell me who they are?' I called after him.

He lifted a hand without turning his head. 'Roger that.'

I went back inside and looked around. The dining hall was a mess. There was food all over the floor. The tables were covered in smears of jam and puddles of tea. *Sponge and bucket*, I thought. I was on automatic pilot, moving sluggishly. My mind was busy with other things.

I picked up a stack of plates and carried them into the kitchen. Something wasn't right. Joyce was calling herself Aaron's mum. She was pretending that Scott was his brother.

According to her, they'd all changed their names because they were afraid of Krystal.

'Bullshit,' I said aloud, scraping plates into the compost bin. Afraid of Krystal McCall? Krystal was half Scott's size. She'd been terrified of Joyce. And if the Rooneys had managed to track her down, why hadn't the police dealt with her? How had she managed to escape?

Perhaps she hadn't escaped. Perhaps she'd gone to jail and was out again now. But no; Joyce had said Krystal was still on the run. And I couldn't imagine the Rooneys sneaking around under assumed names just because they were frightened of Krystal McCall. They wouldn't have let Krystal ruin their lives. Once they had Aaron, they would have marched triumphantly back to Otford, daring Krystal to show her face there again.

They had to be frightened of something else. Or some*one* else.

I grabbed the broom and returned to the dining hall, where I started sweeping up crushed corn chips, dropped sandwiches, squashed bits of melon. At one point I peered under a table and saw the message that had been left there for me. It was a pair of scones arranged suggestively on either side of a banana. Underneath it someone had spelled out 'F U BITCH' in toothpicks.

I was fairly sure I was looking at Jake's handiwork. Unless Joyce had been responsible? No; this felt like Jake. I dismissed the whole thing and turned my attention back to the Rooneys.

Why had they changed their names and moved to North

Queensland? Why was Joyce calling herself Aaron's mum? What had happened to his real mum?

I searched my memory as I swept up the rubbish. Krystal had disappeared on a Saturday night. She'd left everything behind except her son, her car, her phone and a load of packed suitcases. The car had been found two days later, empty except for my worksheet.

The trail had gone cold there, as far as I knew. Someone had told me that Krystal must have got rid of her phone after reaching Newcastle. Someone else had said that a slim woman driving Krystal's car had been filmed stopping for petrol on the Pacific Highway—and that there had been someone small in the car with her.

That was the last bit of news I'd heard about Krystal. Joyce had left Otford a month after the car was found in Coffs Harbour, telling everyone she would go look for Aaron herself, since the police couldn't seem to locate him. I never saw her come back; I wasn't there to see it. But what if she hadn't come back? What if she'd found Aaron, sent for Scott, moved to North Queensland, changed her name and started a new life?

Fetching the bin, I kept circling back to that question: why? The Rooneys weren't scared of Krystal. They'd never been scared of Krystal. And they couldn't have been scared of the Family Court; they must have known they'd be a shoe-in to get full custody once Krystal ran off with her son.

Unless Krystal *hadn't* run off with her son?

No, I thought. She must have. Someone had driven her car to Coffs Harbour, and it couldn't have been Joyce or Scott.

Neither of them had been the slim woman who stopped for petrol. Anyway, Mitch had seen them both in Otford on the Sunday morning.

I was dumping rubbish in the bin when I dislodged a fly, and suddenly thought about cockroaches. Somehow Joyce had persuaded Pat Haas to put roaches in Aaron's bag. She'd also persuaded my former landlord—or Scott's best friend's girl-friend—to hand over my Otford house key. If Joyce was that persuasive, could she have convinced someone to drive away with Aaron? Was Scott's best friend's girlfriend a slim woman with a driver's licence?

But if Krystal *hadn't* been the woman filmed buying petrol, where could she have gone without her car? Even if she'd borrowed someone else's car in Otford, why would she have abandoned her own? Had the Rooneys somehow stolen her car—and her son?

If they had, why hadn't she screamed blue murder?

No, I decided; she must have packed up her car and headed for Coffs Harbour. And Joyce must have finally caught up with her. And then Krystal must have been so terrified that she'd run away, leaving Aaron behind.

But once again, that begged the question: why had the Rooneys changed their names? What were they really hiding from? Not Krystal; I refused to believe that. Were they crimi-nals now? Drug dealers? Had they stolen something? Murdered someone?

Murdered Krystal?

'Shit.' I realised I was standing motionless in the middle

of the dining hall, a brush in one hand, a pan in the other. Something had roused me from my distracted state. Thinking back, I remembered three long blasts from a horn.

The ferry was leaving.

I dropped my equipment and rushed out the door, down the steps, across the parade ground. But it was too late. The ferry had gone.

I stood quite still for a moment. The creeping sense of fear welling up inside me wasn't rational. I knew that. It had been triggered by the Rooneys and it was making me paranoid. I was jumping to conclusions. There was no reason to think that Krystal had been killed. If she had, the police would have found something. People would have asked questions. Mitch would have wondered.

It occurred to me I could easily google everyone involved. Even if Krystal had changed her name, Mitch probably hadn't. I headed for my office, making a mental list; I would google Krystal, then Joyce, then Mitch, then Sue King and Steve King and Cooktown. I would work out when Sue King had replaced Joyce Rooney. I would find out when Scott had left Otford.

But on reaching my desk, I couldn't even log onto the internet. I tried again and again until I finally worked out that the phone was dead too.

When I looked outside, I discovered that the line had been severed.

'Warren?' I hurried onto the parade ground. 'Warren!'

He emerged from his hut, looking surprised. 'Rob?'

'The line's down.'

'What?'

'My line! The phone line…' I was breathless. Frantic. 'Someone cut it. On the wall.'

His forehead creased. 'Little bastards,' he growled, moving in my direction.

'No. No, not the—I don't—it might have…' I couldn't think straight. 'Did you see Scott get on the ferry?'

'Who?'

'I mean Steve. Aaron's dad. *Darren's* dad.'

'Darren's dad?'

Oh, Christ. It was all so confusing.

'I thought Steve was Darren's brother.' Warren had reached me at last. He was looking puzzled. 'Though I have to admit, it's a pretty big age gap.'

'Did Steve get on board? Did you see him?'

'I don't know. There were lots of people.'

'I think he cut the line.' Turning, I charged towards the jetty. 'We need to leave.'

'Wait! Robyn!'

I shook off his hand and kept moving. 'Something's wrong. We have to tell the police. Shit, there were coppers right here—I could have said something.'

'About what?' Warren had caught up with me.

'About Joyce. I mean Sue. Sue is really Joyce. And she's Darren's grandmother.' I fumbled for my keys. 'Steve is

Darren's father, and his name is Scott. It's weird. It doesn't make sense.' I had to slow my pace as I searched for the key to the boathouse. Ah! There it was. 'I could be wrong, but…I think there's a chance they might have murdered Darren's mum.'

'*What?*'

'I mean, I don't know for sure. But someone cut the line. What if they did it to stop me from calling the police?'

'Rob, it could have been Jake—'

'It could have been Scott.' I reached the boathouse and grabbed its padlock. 'He might have stayed behind.'

'But there's no one around. I looked.'

'He'll be hiding.' The lock clicked open. 'There's an orange fuel tank in there. Can you get it for me?' I had to check the boat locker; I was pretty sure it contained a bailer and life jackets, but I couldn't remember what I'd done with the flares or emergency beacon. 'If there's an EPIRB inside, can you bring that as well? And a yellow plastic tub? It's got flares in it.'

As I dashed down to the water, I wondered about the fuel line. Was that in the locker too? Behind me, Warren said, 'You're really taking the tinny out?'

'To Cleveland. Hurry.' I heard a familiar creak of hinges; Warren was opening the boathouse door. *Good*, I thought and grabbed the prow of my four-metre Ally Craft Indian, which had been dragged up onto the mud.

I was just about to get on board when I heard a strange noise from the boathouse—a heavy bang. Had Warren dropped something?

'Warren?'

No reply.

'Warren!'

Still nothing. I rushed back up to the boathouse, wondering if he'd pulled a box down onto his head. If he was hurt, we were in trouble. I would have to use the emergency beacon.

But the beacon was in the boathouse...

'Warren?' I couldn't see inside. Facing me was a big black square like a tunnel's mouth. I knew I'd be blinded for a moment once I passed from sunlight into shadow, so I hesitated, torn by conflicting emotions—the desire to check on Warren and a deep reluctance to pass through that door. It had been locked; Scott couldn't be in there. Yet somehow the whole set-up made my skin crawl.

'Warren?'

Nothing. I advanced a step, then withdrew again. No. I couldn't enter the gaping maw in front of me. Not without protection.

Not without a gun.

I turned tail and ran for the office, glancing back every few seconds to check that I wasn't being followed. My front door was locked. While I struggled to open it, I dropped my keys and had to retrieve them again with trembling hands.

Key. Lock. Turn. Push.

When I slammed the door shut behind me, the deadlatch engaged. No one else was going to get inside.

I had to sort through my keys again to open the gun safe, which held a rifle, a scope and a box of .223 Remington shells. It was a while since I'd cleaned the gun, but the bolt functioned smoothly as I pushed four rounds into the magazine and one into the chamber. Then I slung the rifle over my shoulder, picked up the first-aid kit and hurried outside again. I made sure to lock the door as I left.

On my way down the jetty road, I remembered the boathouse window. I couldn't see it, so I didn't know if it had been smashed. But it was big enough for Scott to crawl through.

'I've got a gun here!' I yelled. 'And it's loaded!'

There was no answer. I'd almost reached the boathouse when I spotted something that made me gasp.

Warren was floating facedown in the water.

I knew it was Warren because of his fatigues. He was bobbing gently behind my beached boat, his head not far from its stern. The incoming tide was pushing him ashore; there was hardly any water underneath him.

I couldn't see anyone else around.

'Warren!' I dropped the first-aid kit, then raced to pull him out. Splashing through the shallows, I seized his shoulders, turned him over and dragged him onto dry land. The water on his face was tinted with blood. Pale pink rivulets were running over his scars.

'Warren? Oh, shit. *Warren?*' I dumped him on the mud and bent down to slap his cheek. Was he breathing? I tried to think. Compressions. Mouth-to-mouth.

Something hit me from behind.

I was in the water before I knew it, a great weight rolling off me as I thrashed and spluttered and struggled to rise. Scott. It was Scott. I caught a flash of his bloodshot glare.

I reared up and he grabbed the rifle, trying to yank me down. But I jerked free and stumbled away, catching the wet gun as it slid off my arm. I swung the muzzle. Braced the butt. Aimed the barrel—not at him, but near him. Flipped the safety. Pulled the trigger.

Nothing happened.

Scott reached for the gun with both hands. I thrust it at him, hard. Punched him in the face with it. As he fell back into the water, he dragged the rifle with him, wrenching it from my grasp.

I turned and bolted. Flares—I still had flares. When I reached the boathouse, I spun around to slam the door and saw Scott heading straight for me. There was a gap of just a few seconds between us; I used it to snatch a yellow tub from a shelf and pull out two red parachute flares. Then I dropped the tub, jammed one flare into my pocket and pointed the other at the door.

Christ, how did they work? They were capped at each end. A memory flashed through my mind: string. There was a string. I unscrewed the bottom cap and the string fell out.

Scott burst into the boathouse just as the discarded cap hit my boot. He was waving the rifle. I tugged at the string and there was a sharp bang. Scott howled; suddenly he was flat on his back. A burning, hissing ball of light lay on the ground outside.

It was all so quick, I had trouble grasping what had happened for a moment. Then I hurled myself out the door. Scott was rolling onto his chest, holding one cheek and whining in short little grasps. His other hand was wrapped around the rifle. I was past him before he could grab me.

On my way up the jetty road I unscrewed the cap on the second flare and paused for a moment to raise it. When I yanked the string, the bang made me stagger. But instead of watching the flare as it soared overhead, I glanced back at Scott. He was already climbing to his feet again, though he looked unsteady. There was blood on his face. He was using the rifle like a crutch.

I spun around and ran for my house. The toolbox was in there. If I could just hold him off until the two o'clock ferry came...

By the time I'd unlocked my front door, Scott was halfway up the jetty road, drooling blood. The deadlatch clicked shut behind me as I staggered into the laundry and grabbed Dad's old toolbox. Hammer? Chisel? Spanner?

Nail gun.

It was a cordless finish nailer. I flicked a switch and saw there was still power in the battery.

'You bitch!' Scott's voice reached my ears, jagged and muffled. He was getting close. 'You fucking bitch!'

I finally found a belt of nails. They were pretty big—fifty millimetre. Loading them was easy; they slid into place just as Scott reached the front door. The sound of his hammering took me right back to Otford.

'Just go!' I screamed. 'Take the boat! People are coming!'

The pounding stopped. I listened, clutching my nail gun. Was he leaving? Was that the creak of the veranda steps? I crept out of the kitchen, down the hall, past the office. Two narrow panels of glass framed the front door; no silhouette was visible through them. Was he heading for the boat or lying in wait outside?

I didn't know what to do. Warren needed help and I couldn't reach him—not if Scott was down there. I tried to think. The phone was trashed. The old short-wave radio in the museum didn't work…

A bang from the kitchen made me jump. I darted back down the hall as a huge crash was followed by the tinkle of falling glass. Scott had broken a window with his rifle butt; I could see it happening through the doorway. I was about to run, then thought, *No. Wait.* I dropped to my knees and crawled into the kitchen, hugging the wall, using the table as cover.

It was dim in there and so bright outside that Scott didn't see me. His focus was on the window. More glass crunched as he chopped at the shards still caught in the frame, using the rifle butt like a hammer. By that time I'd reached the back door; I was flattening myself against it when he thrust his hand into the room and turned the window latch. Slowly, cautiously, I slid up the door, my knees straightening, my fingers still clamped to the nail gun. Scott wrenched at the lower frame of the window, trying to raise it. But the sashes were old and the wood was swollen; there was lots of grunting and squeaking and rattling.

At last the lower frame was rammed up as high as it would go. Scott used the gun to brush away some stray bits of glass. Then he planted his left palm on the windowsill.

That's when I leaned over and nailed his hand to the wood.

2009

HAMISH STAINES WAS a short, pudgy fireball of a lawyer with thinning blond hair. He came to my house on Thursday afternoon and we discussed various things: the Rooneys, the police, apprehended violence orders. Then we went to the local station, each of us driving our own car. His was a gleaming grey beemer. I wasn't surprised; we'd discussed his fee by then.

As we walked into the station, Kate Canning walked out. Her eyes flickered for a moment, but she didn't break her stride. She brushed past me as if I wasn't there.

I felt a twinge of alarm.

Rick Waring was on duty, but he didn't stand a chance against Hamish. Soon we were all huddled together in a dingy little room, discussing my statement. Hamish had advised me not to apply for an AVO through the courts because they referred all applicants to mediation 'unless you've got an axe sticking out of your head'. The last thing I wanted, he said, was to sit down and listen to Joyce trashing me for forty-five minutes. 'We'll get you a provisional AVO,' he promised, and proceeded to do so, though not without a lot of pushback. Rick Waring eventually summoned Paul Ries, who read my signed statement with a sneer on his face. But even Ries was no match for Hamish.

The lawyer treated information like ammunition. He had my plumber's bill. He had photos of my fallen hems. He pounded Ries with questions about Scott's history of violence, then asked if the two men were 'very close'. In response, Ries brought up Aaron's abduction. Was my AVO an attempt to smear the Rooneys after they'd accused me of being involved?

Hamish laughed in his face. 'You've just established their motive for harassing Ms Ayres,' he said. 'If you have one iota of proof that she had anything to do with the boy's disappearance, I'd like to see it now.' He went on to make oblique and very polite threats about false complaints and malicious prosecution.

By the time I walked out, Hamish had secured two provisional AVOs and a court date. 'Don't worry about that abduction business,' Hamish told me as he opened his car door. 'They were just trying it on. If they give you any more trouble, call me. Otherwise I'll see you on Wednesday week.'

But by Wednesday week I'd already been suspended.

~

It was Howard who did it. He called me into his office on Tuesday morning and announced that I was relieved of my duties until further notice. Allegations had been made, he said. He didn't tell me what the allegations were or who had made them. Sometimes you can wait six months before you find out.

I didn't have to wait, though. I already knew. Kate Canning had accused me of assaulting her daughter. Phoebe must have said something. Perhaps I'd left a bruise on her arm. Perhaps Kate had talked to some of the other children in the class—like George, for instance. Pat's son.

By the weekend I'd started hearing whispers in Foodworks as I waited with my trolley at the checkout. '…hurt a child…Canning…Rooney…' I would look around and see two women carefully avoiding my eye.

Deb was sympathetic. She kept phoning. Kate Canning had overreacted, she said. Joyce Rooney was coaching her. It was all part of Joyce's campaign against me. 'I hear she's taken out an AVO. Is that right?' Deb asked.

It was. On being served with my AVO, Joyce had applied for a counter order. The prospect of the court date was keeping me up at night—as were the stress and shame. Though Deb and Prue couldn't have been more supportive, I sensed behind their words of comfort a hint of what they really felt. I'd made a mistake. Not a bad mistake; not a mistake that cancelled out years of competence and dedication. But a mistake nonetheless. I should never have grabbed those girls. There were other ways I could have handled it—with threats or bribes or distractions or at least something more intelligent than physical force. If I hadn't been so tired and harried and upset,

I would have been a better teacher.

I knew what Prue and Deb thought because I agreed with them. I'd blown it. But that didn't mean the allegations were justified. Or fair. Or that I should have been arrested and charged with one count of common assault. I still have nightmares about the day Sergeant Ries arrested me. He could barely conceal his satisfaction.

I was immediately granted police bail, thanks to Hamish—who also negotiated my bail conditions. I was allowed to live with Dad before the trial, since there was no point staying in Otford. I'd been suspended from my job and I couldn't leave the house without attracting attention. Joyce seemed to have supporters everywhere. I decided Otford wasn't big enough for both of us, so I left and never went back.

As it turned out, Joyce soon did the same thing, but I didn't know that. I was in Kempsey by then, quietly falling apart.

After fifteen months, I was finally acquitted. I never returned to teaching, though, because no one wanted me. Even false allegations remain on your record when you work for the Education Department, and there were plenty of other desperate teachers out there. Why employ someone with a scandal hanging over her, even if there was no conviction?

I decided to become a builder instead. I did some TAFE courses and received a lot of training from Dad, who persuaded some of his friends to offer me casual work on construction sites. But I'd barely secured my licence before he had a stroke one day while he was fixing his neighbour's laundry door.

I nursed him for two years until a second stroke finally killed him. It was so quick that I didn't have time to say goodbye. I walked out of his bedroom to fetch his pills and when I came back, he was dead.

You don't recover from something like that in a hurry.

His house had been mortgaged to pay legal and medical bills, so I was left with nothing when I sold it. I didn't want to stay in Kempsey—not without my father. In Otford I was the woman who'd beaten up a six-year-old. In Kempsey I still felt like the girl whose mother had stepped in front of a freight train. I'd gone to Sydney in the first place because I was sick of people watching me, wondering if I was going to crack up too.

Small towns. Small bloody towns.

The job on Finch Island surfaced when I was clutching at straws; I heard about it from one of my father's friends, who turned it down because it paid peanuts. The salary wasn't an issue for me. I had the right background (carpentry, plumbing, school camps). I also had the right personality. 'Are you comfortable living an isolated life?' I was asked at the interview. I didn't admit that after everything I'd been through, I was much happier on my own. I just said something about being an introvert, and got hired.

It didn't feel like a great success. It felt like failure. It felt as if I'd lost everything all over again. My marriage, my best friend, my home, my dog—I'd been slowly recovering from those losses. But my family, my career, my foreseeable future? Without them I was a husk. A shell. And the Rooneys were the ones who'd destroyed me.

I blamed Joyce and Scott for my father's death. In a roundabout way, they'd caused it; Dad's blood pressure went through the roof during my trial and he never really recovered. His last years were less happy because of me. I was a constant worry to him.

I would lie in bed every night and rage at the Rooneys. I would mutter curses. Picture punishments. I would imagine running them down in my car—setting fire to both their houses—sabotaging Scott's SUV so it would break down in the middle of nowhere at the height of summer. Whole scenarios played out in my head. I saw Joyce's tenants destroying her rental properties. I saw Aaron becoming a famous rock musician and the Rooneys watching his rise from afar, knowing it was Krystal's achievement and being knocked back whenever they asked for money.

Sometimes I visualised even nastier acts of revenge. Food poisoning. Acid on a toilet seat. An exploding mower.

One thing I never envisaged was shooting Scott in the hand with a nail gun.

2019

SCOTT'S DEAFENING SCREAMS pursued me as I slammed through the front door and galloped towards the jetty. I was sobbing. Reeling.

I'd just nailed someone's hand to a fucking windowsill.

Would I go to jail for it? Not if I could argue self-defence. Scott had been armed, for Chrissake.

My heart skipped a beat when I caught sight of Warren down by the boat. He'd moved. He'd rolled over. Was he coughing?

'Warren!' I stumbled off the road and skidded to a halt beside him. Yes! He was alive. But he looked terrible—his eyes were glazed, his lips blue. Blood welled from a wound on his scalp.

'We're leaving,' I said. 'Just wait here a minute.' I still didn't have fuel, so I tossed my nail gun into the tinny and leaned down to check the locker, which contained two life jackets, a bailer, a fuel line and nothing else.

No emergency beacon. No flares.

The first-aid kit was still lying where I'd dropped it. I picked it up and slung it into the boat with the nail gun.

'Give me a minute,' I told Warren, who was gasping and retching, his face in the mud. I left him there and hurried towards the boathouse, plunging straight inside because I knew Scott wasn't a threat. I could hear him screaming off in the distance.

I stood for a moment while my eyes adjusted. As soon as they did, the screaming stopped. It was replaced by a thumping noise, interspersed by cries of pain.

I didn't have any trouble finding the fuel tank, which was made of orange plastic and seemed to glow in the dimness. The beacon sat beside it in a little cardboard box. I grabbed them both and rushed back to Warren, who still lay on his stomach, eyes closed, head turned to one side.

'Just a second.' I scrambled into the boat. Up at the house, Scott gave a great shriek and fell silent. There was no more thumping. Had he fainted? I shoved the beacon in the locker. Pulled out the fuel line. Attached one end to the tank. It was a fiddly job, and once it was done I still had to pump the priming bulb.

'Okay,' I said at last. 'Good to go.' Climbing back out of the boat, I wondered if I should bandage Warren's head before bundling him on board.

Then a shot rang out.

I almost pissed myself. How the fuck had that bastard got the gun working? 'Come on,' I said, sliding my hands under

Warren's armpits. I tried to lift him, but he was too heavy—all waterlogged muscle and bone. I staggered. 'Warren? Please. I need some help here.' As he moved, I lost my grip and dropped him.

I heard another shot, closer this time. *No. It couldn't be.* I looked up: Scott was heading down the jetty road. He'd freed himself somehow; one hand hung limp and dripping, still attached to a small shard of wood. Had he knocked a chunk off the windowsill with his rifle butt?

'Oh, *shit.*' It was like a horror movie. But his cheek was scorched and his hand was pierced and he was stumbling along, the rifle tucked into his armpit...He had to be at the end of his tether.

'You're going to die!' I shouted. 'Let me get help!'

His head turned. The gun moved. Its barrel rose, wavering, balanced on Scott's right arm. Surely he couldn't fire it one-handed?

There was a bang as it discharged.

I didn't hear the round hit the jetty. But I saw chips fly. *Three shots down*, I thought. *Two to go.* He paused to prop the muzzle on the ground, then worked the bolt with one hand. A cartridge popped out, clinking.

I seized a handful of Warren's uniform, but all he could do was make feeble swimming motions.

Scott pushed another shell into the chamber.

'Play dead,' I told Warren, my voice breaking. Then I dived into the nearest patch of scrub.

I didn't want to leave Warren, but I had no choice. If I'd stayed with the boat, Scott would have shot me. He wouldn't have needed a steady hand—not while I was two metres away, pulling frantically on the starter cord.

All I could do was hide. A thick belt of mangroves hugged the shore on either side of the jetty, creeping into the shallows. I knew I had to get past them quickly because of all the noise involved—splashing water, slurping mud, the crunch of pencil roots underfoot. The aerial roots were even more of a hazard, reaching out to trip me as I staggered between them. But the palisade of closely packed tree trunks and soaring root systems provided good cover. A clear shot would be hard, I told myself as I lurched along, panting, sweating, dragging my boots out of the sludge. Everything smelled pungently organic, like sewage.

I couldn't hear Scott behind me. I couldn't see him either, though I wasn't glancing back—not while I negotiated a mangrove swamp. I had to keep my eyes on the ground or risk falling. I was so scared I was like an animal, heedless of the muck clinging to me, shrinking into myself like a snail, gasping, shaking, numb with fear. There was a sense of unreality. How had it come to this?

At last I noticed a change in the light and looked up to see that the trees were thinning. I'd almost reached the track to Karboora Beach.

I stopped. Would Scott be skulking somewhere on the track, waiting for me to emerge? Probably not. He didn't know the terrain. He wouldn't realise he could trap me like that.

Then I heard the sputter of an engine. For a split second I thought someone had come to my rescue, until I realised I was listening to the sawing sound of a starter cord being pulled— once, twice, and a third time, successfully. The engine roared to life. I recognised its rumble.

Someone had started the motor on my tinny.

I knew it couldn't have been Warren; yanking the cord would have been way beyond him. Scott must have decided to cut his losses. He must have taken one look at the mangrove swamp and thought, *Nope*. For all he knew, a police launch might have been on its way, drawn by my distress flare.

The engine was moving north. It was chugging along somewhere behind me; I pictured Scott at the tiller, scanning the mangroves, my gun across his knees. He would take one last shot if he could, I felt sure. But he didn't have a hope. There was too much dense growth between me and the bay. I was safe for the time being.

As soon as I realised that, I also realised I was being sucked dry by mosquitoes. Slapping at them, I moved forward until I reached the track, then turned left and trudged back towards the jetty, sluicing mud and water, my feet squishing in my boots, my scattered thoughts gradually coalescing.

Warren. What had happened to Warren? My first-aid kit was in the boat along with the rifle and nail gun. Scott had them all, and he was heading for the mainland. But the ferry would be here soon. What time was it? I checked my watch.

It had stopped. Water in the works, probably—or mud.

'Warren?' He was lying where I'd left him. At the sound

of my voice he turned his head, raising one hand to shade his eyes.

My vision blurred. He wasn't dead. Scott hadn't killed him.

Thank God.

'It's okay.' I ran over. The tide was lapping at his waist-band, so I pulled him up, my arms clamped across his chest. Warren groaned. He was too heavy—I was going to hurt him if I dragged him all the way to the house. But I couldn't just leave him in the mud, undefended.

'Hang on,' I said. 'Just hang on.' Struggling backwards, I heaved him onto the road, past the boathouse, towards the parade ground. Then my strength failed and I had to lay him down again. The heels of his boots had left gouges in the dirt.

'Wait.' I was gasping. Trembling. Watching the sea. No vessels were on the horizon. I couldn't hear my tinny anymore.

Warren rolled over. He pushed himself up onto one elbow.

'No. You'll hurt yourself.' I bent and touched his back. 'Warren?'

He mumbled something—and at that instant I remembered the wheelbarrow.

'It's okay,' I told him. 'Wait here.' I tottered off towards the poultry shed, sweat stinging my eyes. My hands were shaking so much I could barely unlock the shed door. By the time I returned, several minutes had passed; I found Warren on his hands and knees, crawling up the road.

'For God's sake.' I trundled to a halt beside him. 'Here. Can you get in this?'

He reached up and grabbed the barrow, using it to haul himself to his feet. But instead of collapsing into it, he took one wobbly step and threw an arm around my shoulders.

'I can walk,' he rasped. 'Help me.'

I helped him. We staggered up the road, stopping occasionally as his legs buckled. The cut on his head was still oozing blood. He was a terrible colour and unsteady on his feet.

What if he'd fractured his skull?

'Can you manage this?' I asked as we reached the matron's house. It was closer than mine and there weren't as many stairs. Warren hesitated for a moment, then lifted one foot and planted it on the bottom step. 'That's the way,' I said. 'Just two more. Hups-a-daisy.'

We got to the top, but it nearly killed Warren. He was reeling when we arrived on the veranda; I had to prop him against a post while I unlocked the front door. The beds inside were all made up, except for the one I'd taken the mattress from. There weren't any towels, but everything was squeaky clean. The whole place smelled a bit stale.

I managed to haul Warren into the second bedroom, where he dropped onto the bed like a felled tree. He lay there, groaning, while I wondered what to do next. Raid my bathroom medicine cabinet?

'Hang on.' I leaned close, squeezing his shoulder. It was sodden. 'Have you got some spare clothes in your hut?'

He muttered something about his rucksack.

'Okay. I'll look.' I began to unlace his boots, but it was difficult; the knots had fused into tight little wet balls. At last

I managed to unpick them and yank his boots off. 'I'm just ducking out, okay? Don't move.'

I locked him in when I left the house; it felt safer. Then I crossed to the other side of the compound, where the huts stood in neat ranks like soldiers on parade. Warren had been assigned hut number three. I found his rucksack sitting on the polished floor beside a flawlessly made single bed. It didn't feel right, digging through his possessions, though they were mostly clothes and toiletries. I was surprised to find a biography of Charles Dickens. I would have expected a war-hero memoir.

Warren had packed spare underpants and socks, but all his other clothes were ready for the wash. They had a distinctly Warren-ish smell—a mixture of sweat, deodorant and slightly flowery soap. I picked out a white T-shirt and a pair of trousers and tucked them under my arm. On my way back to my own quarters, I tried to remember what I'd learnt about head wounds in my most recent first-aid course. Rule number one was that you shouldn't move the patient. But how could I have left Warren in the path of an incoming tide?

I felt sick and dazed, almost as if I had a head wound myself. It was an effort to think logically when I reached my bathroom and stared into the medicine cabinet. Antiseptic cream. Band-aids. Wound gauze. Paracetamol? I stuffed everything I could find into a pillowcase along with a clean sheet and a pair of scissors, then grabbed a bottle of vodka from the safe. Before leaving, I glanced at the kitchen clock. Ten past one—still fifty minutes till the Stradbroke ferry was due. And why had nobody responded to my flare?

Locking the front door took me longer than usual. At first I couldn't find the right key; then I dropped the whole bunch. When I finally arrived back at the matron's house, I had to stand on the doormat for half a minute, squinting and fumbling before I managed to push the key into the lock.

At that instant, there was a sharp bang and a pinging noise. For a split second my mind was a blank. I stared at the fresh gouge in the wall beside me and thought, *What?*

Then I turned and saw Scott Rooney.

~

He was standing on the jetty road, his left hand bandaged, his face gleaming with some kind of ointment. The orange fuel tank sat on the ground next to him. He stamped his foot in frustration as he lowered his rifle.

I didn't stay to watch him reload. Turning the key, I plunged inside and locked the door behind me, gasping, distraught, my head in a whirl. He had one shot left. One. He must have motored around to Karboora Beach. Landed there and unhooked the fuel tank. Followed the track back to the jetty.

But why take the risk? He had to be delusional. Even without witnesses, he'd never get away with murdering me. I drew the nearest blind and ran for the next one, frantically racking my brain. What could I use as a weapon? The house was practically empty; there were no brooms or hammers or cricket bats…

The scissors. Of course. I was pulling them out of my pillowcase when I heard heavy footfalls on the steps outside.

I ducked down, listening. Scott could no longer see through the front windows, and the side ones were too high to reach without a ladder. What if he tried to smash his way in again? It hadn't gone well for him last time but he might try again now that I didn't have a nail gun. *Shit*, I thought, *he's got everything.* Rifle, nail gun, first-aid kit. He must have used the first-aid kit to dress his wounds.

What if he managed to get the spare shells out of the gun safe?

At that instant I smelled petrol: fumes seeping under the door. I heard a splashing sound and realised what Scott up to; he was trying to smoke me out. Or burn me to death.

I ran for the extinguisher. It was attached to the kitchen wall and as I wrenched it off its bracket, I wondered fleetingly why I hadn't thought of it before. Then fear swamped my speculation. Rushing back to the living room, I heard Warren mutter something, but I couldn't stop. By this time the stink of petrol was so strong I had to hold my breath.

I peeked between the straps of the nearest vertical blind. Scott was standing on the front steps, the rifle slung over his shoulder, a cigarette in his mouth. He must have tossed the fuel tank away. He was fiddling with a plastic lighter. *Of course he bloody smokes.*

I yanked out the extinguisher's pin and thrust it into my pocket. Then my hand crept towards the deadlatch. If I could burst through the door and cover Scott with foam, I might be able to hit him before he could shoot me. He was lighting the cigarette now. I pulled away from the window and turned the latch just as a strange *whump* reached my ears.

I opened the door.

Scott was screeching. Burning. His legs were on fire and so was the veranda. I reeled back, then grabbed my nozzle and aimed it, squeezing the handles and releasing a white jet of foam that cascaded onto the flames. There was a loud hiss and a billowing cloud. I moved the nozzle back and forth, back and forth, as if I was watering a flower bed. Then, coughing and teary-eyed, I pointed it at Scott.

He stumbled backwards, screaming, and fell to the ground under a layer of white foam. I sprayed the veranda again while behind me Warren called, 'Robyn?'

I ignored him; I was too busy smothering the fire. When the boards were covered with foam, I released my grip on the two handles and hurried forward, wading through the lather until I reached Scott.

He was making horrible noises, but the fire was out. I wondered if I should hose him down. The rifle strap was still looped over his arm; as I reached for it a voice cried, 'Don't move! Don't touch that!'

I raised my head. There was a policeman coming up the road.

It was the cop from the parade: Bill Khatri. With him were Jodie Morris and Shaun Steiger. From where I was standing I couldn't see Jodie's police launch. I assumed it was moored at the jetty.

Shaun took one look at me and stopped in his tracks. 'Robyn?' he said. 'What the hell…?'

I dropped the extinguisher and raised my hands. 'He tried to shoot us. He set fire to the house.'

'It's true.' Warren spoke from the doorway, his voice cracked and feeble. 'That fucker nearly brained me.'

Bill and Jodie had already reached Scott, who was gasping and twitching on the grass. A horrible scorched smell filled the air.

'What do you think?' Bill asked Jodie, grabbing the rifle. 'Back to the boat?'

She shook her head. 'Medical evacuation.' She unhooked her radio.

Shaun came up and laid a hand on my shoulder. 'You okay, Robyn?'

'Yeah…'

'Are you sure?' He glanced at my arm. There was blood on it. Warren's blood? No—I'd scratched myself. When had I done that?

'It's nothing,' I said. 'But Warren's hurt. He needs a doctor.'

'Right.' Shaun's gaze moved to the veranda, which was still smoking. Trapped behind a carpet of white foam, Warren looked ashen and bloody. 'Lie down,' Shaun told him. 'The medics are coming.'

'It wasn't her fault,' Warren rasped. 'That crazy bastard went for us.'

'I know what happened. Don't worry. Just go and lie down. That's an order.'

'She deserves a medal,' Warren finished, before disappearing into the house.

Shaun turned back to me and asked, 'What's that? Petrol?' He jerked his chin at the fuel tank.

'Yeah. Scott poured it all over the place.' Suddenly I felt bone tired. I wanted to lie down and never get up. 'He set himself alight. It wasn't me.'

Shaun nodded. 'Happens all the time. It's the vapour that's flammable. People don't realise. They ignite a plume.'

'And the gun's mine, but I only got it out after Warren was hurt—'

'Save it.' Shaun lifted a hand. 'Really. The police will want to know, but I don't. I'm on your side.'

'Steve's real name is Scott—'

'Scott Rooney. Yeah. Darren told us.'

'*Darren?*'

'Why do you think we're here?'

I frowned. 'Because of my distress flare?'

'What distress flare?'

I glanced over at the two police officers. Jodie was still hurling orders into her radio. Bill was checking the gun, his dark face tense.

'On the ferry,' Shaun continued, 'Darren and that woman he says isn't really his mother—'

'Joyce.'

'Right. Apparently, they had some kind of argument. I

missed that. Then Darren went straight over and told Bill to turn the ferry around. Said his father had probably killed his mother and was going to kill you.' As I blinked, Shaun offered me a crooked smile. 'You can imagine what Bill thought. Especially after Joyce told him Darren's just a crazy kid who smokes weed all the time—'

'—and you can't believe a word he says.' I'd heard the same thing before from Joyce. Over and over again.

'The thing is, Darren's one of my lads,' Shaun went on. 'I know him. I've seen him in action. And I haven't heard him lie. Not once.' Shaun's gaze drifted towards Scott. 'I thought he might be mistaken at first, but the longer he talked…well, I remembered what you'd told me about his name being Aaron. And I realised we had to do something.'

Another police officer was running up the jetty road with a first-aid kit. I recognised him; he'd once dropped in to ask me to keep an eye out for a stolen boat. When he reached us, he flung himself onto his knees and tucked a silver blanket around Scott, who was starting to shiver.

'We'd almost reached Cleveland by that time,' Shaun went on. 'There was a lot of mucking around, but me and Bill—we managed to get hold of the local force. That was after we couldn't reach you by phone. No answering machine, so we knew something must be wrong.' As the three police officers huddled around Scott, elevating his legs and checking his pulse, Shaun explained that Joyce was currently back in Cleveland, being questioned. Her grandson had been left in Joe's care. 'Darren was always told that his mum tried to steal him because she was worried about losing the custody case,' Shaun said, 'and that's why he was sent off to live with Joyce's cousin, way up north. He didn't know anything about his mum disappearing, or people thinking she'd taken him—not until he talked to you. He blamed her for not even trying to come after him.' Shaun was watching me closely, weighing, measuring, assessing. 'He says he remembers an argument. And being told to wait in the car. He says he was sleeping a lot, so he doesn't recall who drove him to Queensland. Some lady, he says. He'd met her at his dad's house a couple of times.'

I could barely absorb all this. I was feeling light-headed. Shaun must have noticed because he took my arm. 'Come and sit down.'

'But what about Warren?'

'I'll take care of Warren. The medics will be here soon.'

He steered me to the front steps and left me there, returning briefly after a minute or so to drape a blanket over my shoulders. I barely noticed; I was still trying to make sense of what I'd just been told.

Scott had killed Krystal. And it must have happened that Saturday night—in Krystal's new apartment, perhaps—because she hadn't been seen since. Then someone had driven Aaron away forever, ensuring that Krystal would be blamed. And Aaron had been lied to. He'd been told that Krystal was about to snatch him. Hide him. Keep him to herself.

I tried to work out what had happened next. Joyce had left Otford a month after Aaron's disappearance—or so I'd been told. She must have moved in with her cousin and pretended Aaron was her son. Changed her name somehow; it can't have been too hard, out in the boondocks of Far North Queensland. If there was no internet, hardly any police force and a shifting, marginal populace…well, that would have worked in her favour.

Scott must have followed her. Maybe he'd quit before his superiors could sack him. The Rooneys had kept their heads down. Cut all ties with Otford. Started a new life in a place where no one was going to ask awkward questions. Where they weren't the only ones toting fake IDs.

And then I'd shown up. And they'd panicked. And Scott had tried to stop me from airing my suspicions.

And Aaron had rescued me.

I'd failed him all those years ago, but he hadn't hesitated. As soon as he'd worked it all out, he'd gone straight to the police. To warn them. To stop his dad. To save my life by wrecking his own.

At that moment I heard the pulse of chopper blades. I looked up and saw the rescue helicopter beating its way towards us. Soon it was hovering over the parade ground, churning the air and forcing me to bow my head, eyes screwed shut. Then it slowly descended from the vast blue sky, like an act of divine grace.

NOW

WE ROLLED INTO Otford on an overcast Sunday morning. Dead leaves skittered across the main road. Most of the shops were shut and some were vacant. The second butcher was gone; so were the Commonwealth Bank, Cool Beans Café and the corner florist. Roadside plantings were full of discarded soft-drink cans.

I flinched as we passed Foodworks.

'Seen better days,' Warren remarked beside me.

'Mmm.' The footpaths were almost deserted, though here and there a lone pedestrian trudged along, grim-faced, holding a takeaway coffee or towing a dog. I didn't recognise anyone.

'So where do we turn?' asked Warren, on reaching the end of the retail strip.

'Keep going.'

We passed the RSL. A nursing home. The Sunburnt Country Motel. I was pleased to see how shabby the motel looked, with its cracked concrete carpark and spindly box hedges. We'd stayed in Bathurst the previous night because I'd refused to spend a single unnecessary minute in Otford—and one glance at that motel told me I'd made the right decision.

'Here,' I said. 'Next left.'

We turned into Hamilton Street and I braced myself. I knew the school was coming up. I saw the familiar zebra crossing. The big claret ash, leafless now. The chainlink fence.

Warren must have sensed me stiffening. 'What?'

'That's where I used to work.' Two of the demountables were new. I didn't recognise one of the murals.

'You okay?' Warren asked.

'Yeah.'

'Sure?'

'Next right.'

I spotted the fibro place with the green shutters. It had once been rigidly neat, its hedges clipped, its lawn a master-piece. Now it was ringed by broken toys and car parts. The little white weatherboard next to it had sprouted a big glass extension like a tumour. Trees had been cut down. An old garage had collapsed.

Mitch McCall's brick box had completely lost its quirky charm. Most of the garden statuary was either gone or smashed. Empty bottles were piled on the front porch. Weeds flourished. Firewood had been dumped along the fence.

'There.' I pointed. 'Stop.'

Warren pulled over. 'Shit,' he said, but left it at that. We already knew Mitch had died. His niece Angela had moved into the old McCall house with her partner Nick, her son

Blaine, Blaine's girlfriend, and Aaron Rooney.

Aaron had told us all about it.

'Is that him?' There was someone sitting on the front steps.

'That's him.' Warren killed the engine and climbed out of the car. I followed his example. My back felt stiff, but not from sitting. I was very tense.

Aaron stood up, a cigarette tucked between his fingers. He'd filled out a little and his hair was shaved close to his head, but otherwise he looked the same. He was still restless. Fidgety. Loose-limbed.

He dropped the cigarette and ground it into the earth with the toe of his trainer. Then he shrugged on a bulging rucksack.

'Well, that's not happening,' Warren muttered behind me. I figured he was talking about the cigarette.

Aaron stooped to pick up a plastic milk crate full of bits and pieces. I couldn't see anything else on the porch that might count as luggage, though there was a lot of junk scattered around: a turntable, a mangy broom, a lamp, a baseball cap, a battered bar fridge.

'Is that all you've got?' I raised my voice as I fiddled with the front gate.

'Yup.' Aaron wedged the milk crate under his arm and headed straight for me. We were about a metre apart when he stopped. His clothes needed washing. There was an angry pimple on his chin.

'Hi,' he said. Then his gaze shifted to Warren. 'Hi.'

Warren held out his hand. 'Cigarettes.'

Aaron blinked.

'You're quitting. Right now. It's non-negotiable,' Warren announced.

Aaron's mouth tightened. But he reached into his cargo pants and pulled out a small box plastered with health warnings. 'You haven't changed,' he said, tossing the packet at Warren.

I disagreed. Warren had changed. He'd lost confidence. Gained insight. Learnt to relax his grip a little.

He'd also grown out his hair, to cover the scar on the back of his head.

'So where will I stick all this stuff?' Aaron jiggled his milk crate. 'In the boot?'

I frowned. 'What about your aunt?'

'What about her?' said Aaron.

'Is she in there?'

He glanced back at the house. 'Yeah. She's in there. Off her tits.'

Warren and I exchanged a look. We'd heard about Angela. According to Aaron she was a thief, a slob, a liar and an addict, emotionally unstable, selfish, deluded and completely untrustworthy. Even if half of what he'd told us was true, she didn't sound like a responsible adult.

'I still think we should have a word,' I said.

'She'll just make a scene.' Aaron pushed forward, using the bulk of his rucksack to nudge me aside. 'Come on. Let's go. We need to get out of this fucking dump before Blaine hits you up for slab money.'

Aaron had been based in Otford since leaving Finch Island. With Joyce and Scott on remand, the poor kid had needed a new home—and Angela McCall had offered him one. I don't think Aaron would have moved back in with the Rooneys even if they'd been granted bail. He'd washed his hands of them, and Angela was his next closest relative.

I knew all this because I'd kept in touch. After the incident on the island, I made a point of thanking Aaron for what he'd done. Scott was still in hospital at that point, and Joyce was in a lock-up. Shaun had agreed to house Aaron for a few days while everyone waited for Blaine McCall to drive up from Otford. It was a strange, unnerving time; I was shuttling between Brisbane and the lazaret, answering endless questions and trying to pull myself together. Warren was recuperating at home. Shaun was constantly out and about, visiting people: me, Warren, Tyler, the police.

I met Aaron in a McDonald's not far from Shaun's place. I'd already decided to quit my job by then, so I was a little distracted. But when Aaron arrived, looking wary, I bought him an enormous lunch and asked him how he was. He immediately started complaining about Shaun's family—how they had a lot of 'stupid rules' about beds and bathrooms and eating and phones. How they didn't really want him there, even though Shaun said they did. I listened for a while, wishing he would keep all four of his chair legs planted firmly on the ground. Then I told him I was grateful for what he'd done, and we talked about his mother.

He had some fairly strong memories of Krystal—and of Mitch. I was able to add a few details, though we agreed that his Otford relatives would be a better source of information. We already knew Mitch was dead. 'I never got a chance to thank him,' Aaron quavered. He hardly mentioned the Rooneys, though from one or two of his throwaway comments I deduced that life on the fringes of Cooktown had been tough, tense and secretive. 'Dad's a fucking alki. And a psycho,' he said. 'I hope he gets raped in jail.'

I tried to steer him away from the past and focus on the future. We discussed the $15,000 recognition payment he would be receiving as the dependent victim of a homicide. He wanted to buy a car; I urged him to think about using the money to fund some kind of tertiary education. 'There's no guarantee the McCalls will be able to help you launch yourself,' I said.

'Nah, they'll do what's right. They want to. They told me.' He leaned back in his chair and burped, the wreckage of a family-sized meal spread out before him. 'Blaine's got a motorbike. It's gunna be great in Otford.'

But it wasn't great in Otford. Almost as soon as Aaron arrived there, he began to complain. I'd given him my email address, with the promise that if he ever needed help or advice, I owed him. I didn't think he would actually want my help, since I was a middle-aged drifter who'd failed him once before. I figured he would find someone else to lean on: an uncle, perhaps. A teacher. A social worker.

Instead I started to receive long, rambling messages

about empty fridges, police harassment, school bullies, false accusations, weekend binges, pub fights and Angela's junkie boyfriend. None of it sounded good. I asked him what he liked doing, and he said he enjoyed tinkering with all the broken equipment strewn around Angela's house. After emailing back and forth for a while, we decided he might consider getting a Certificate III in air-conditioning and refrigeration. There was a course available at Bathurst TAFE.

But Angela's house wasn't conducive to hard work. Blaine had bought a dog that was shitting everywhere, and no one cleaned up the mess. The electricity had been cut off for a couple of days. Aaron was turfed out of his room at one point because a friend had moved in. His school results had been woeful; his TAFE results weren't likely to be much better. Not if he stayed in that house.

'Can't I come and live with you?' Aaron begged me. 'I can do the same course at Newcastle TAFE and it won't be such a hassle to get there.' The bus trips to Bathurst were a drag, he wrote. No one in town wanted to hire him as an apprentice because everyone hated the McCalls. He could use some of his leftover money to pay me a modest rent.

If he had to stay in Otford he would end up a dropkick 'just like the rest of them'.

I realised it was time I talked to Warren.

~

Warren and I were living on the outskirts of Newcastle by then. After leaving Finch Island, I was troubled by nightmares, insomnia, panic attacks; Warren invited me to join his PTSD support group, and things developed from there. I quit Parks and Wildlife. Found casual work in Newcastle with a builder who'd once worked for Dad. Rented a granny flat from the same builder and spent my evenings on the phone to Warren, cautiously opening up. Then the pandemic torpedoed Vetnet, and Warren moved in with me just before the borders closed.

He already had a logistics job. It was flexible and had never interfered with his Vetnet duties, but the change was very difficult for him. He had migraines. A touch of vertigo. He had to cope with gym closures and cancelled support groups. We were lucky that rents dropped—it meant we could afford a bigger place where we weren't bumping into each other all the time. It was a three-bedroom house out on the fringes, near a zipline adventure park where Warren eventually picked up the odd shift. He found some online counselling; I tracked down a good local therapist. Bit by bit, we were knitting together a life. Going for bushwalks. Making each other cups of tea. Discovering a shared interest in high-tech thrillers.

Then Aaron reached out and I was torn. He was a kid with issues. He wouldn't be easy to live with. If I took him in, I would risk everything that Warren and I were creating.

On the other hand, I owed Aaron a debt. And if I managed to help him, I would finally be able to shrug off the load of guilt I'd been carrying around for more than ten years.

Warren understood this better than anyone. 'Don't worry about me,' he said. 'I can handle him—you know I can. Shit, it'll be good for me to keep my hand in.'

Three weeks later we were driving through Otford, with Aaron slumped in the back seat. It had been relatively easy to communicate via email, but now that we were face to face, I felt awkward. I didn't know what to say. Neither did Warren.

'So have you heard anything about court dates?' I finally asked, because Scott Rooney still hadn't been tried for murder. He'd been convicted of assaulting Warren, after a brief trial that had played havoc with my mental health. But he hadn't yet faced court for killing Krystal.

'Nope.' Aaron was never keen to talk about the Rooneys. 'Hey, can we make one more stop before we go? I have to say goodbye to Mum.'

'Sure.' I directed Warren towards the cemetery, which lay at the very edge of town. On our way there, I watched Aaron in the rearview mirror. He was gnawing at his nails as he stared out the window.

I wondered if a small part of him was sorry to leave.

'We can't stay long,' Warren said. 'It's a hell of a drive back.'

Aaron grunted. Soon we were bumping through the cemetery gate and pulling into a parking lot beside two other cars. Around us the landscape was dry, rough and scrubby— the kind of place you have to mow with a whipper snipper. Apart from the graves themselves, I could see only concrete paths, a few scattered trees and a toilet block. Here and there a bright floral tribute added a touch of colour.

Aaron was out of the car before I could ask if he wanted company. He headed towards the top of the hill, where raw mounds and gleaming headstones marked some of the more recent burials. Not knowing whether to follow or not, I went for a hesitant kind of stroll, keeping my eye on Aaron without intruding on him. Warren joined me. 'How long has it been?' he asked.

I knew what he was talking about. 'Fourteen months,' I said. After a massive search, Krystal's remains had been found in one of the old mine shafts that dotted the hills around Otford. Aaron had described the funeral: the turnout hadn't been great because Blaine and Angela had burnt so many bridges in the local community. One of Aaron's high school teachers had made an appearance. So had Prue Wilmott, now retired. Aaron didn't remember her, but she'd marched straight up and apologised for not doing more to help his mother.

Deb hadn't come. She'd moved to Wagga after her father died. Last I'd heard, she was an acting deputy principal with a post-graduate degree in early childhood learning.

'I think he wants you,' Warren remarked. I'd been distracted by two distant figures—a couple of women tidying a plot—but when I turned my head, I saw Aaron looking at me.

As soon as I reached him, he said, 'When I get a job, I'm gunna pay for a proper stone.' He flapped a hand at the wooden cross that marked his mother's grave. I nodded, then asked if he wanted to clean up the dead flowers.

'Can I?'

'Of course you can.' I began to collect them. 'Are they yours?'

'Some. Some are Mrs Wilmott's.'

'That doesn't mean you can't throw them away.' I beckoned to Warren, and we all cleared the grave of shrivelled brown sticks. Then Aaron replaced them with a cheap little porcelain statue of a unicorn—the kind of thing you'd buy at a dollar store.

'Mum loved unicorns,' he said.

'Did she?' I wondered who had told him that.

'She chose my name too.' He sounded almost defiant. 'That's why I'm Aaron now. Not fucking Darren.'

I nodded. Warren didn't speak. He was hovering respectfully in the background, though I saw him glance at his watch.

After a long pause, Aaron said, 'I feel bad about leaving her.' There was a catch in his voice.

'She wouldn't mind. She'd be pleased. She'd be proud of you for doing the right thing.'

'I guess.'

'We'll meet you back at the car, okay? You take as long as you want.'

'Nah. I'm finished here. Let's go.'

Together we returned to where Warren had parked. There was now only one other vehicle in sight—a white SUV with an open hatch. The two women from the grave were loading buckets and secateurs into it.

As I drew closer, I recognised the older woman. Kate Canning. The younger one must be Phoebe—or perhaps Sarah. They'd both had red hair.

When I caught her eye, Kate turned on her heel and slammed the hatch shut.

'Hey, Feeble,' said Aaron, his voice harsh and flat. 'I'm fucking off now, so you won't have me to blame for your boyfriend's skunk anymore. Just so you know.'

Phoebe reddened. She'd blossomed into a beautiful girl, tall and willowy.

'Get in,' Kate told her, then turned to Aaron. 'I'll have you charged with intimidation, you little shit.'

'Oh, no, you won't.' I spoke before I could stop myself. One look at Kate had triggered all the old feelings of fear and anger and betrayal. 'You'll leave him the hell alone.'

Kate's lip curled. 'I wondered when you were going to sneak into town,' she said. 'Someone told me you were poking your nose in. Trying to feel like a teacher again, are you?'

'No. Just acting like a human being.' I'd last seen Kate on the steps of the Bathurst courthouse, and the memory still rankled. She'd spat at my feet after losing her case against me. 'But you wouldn't know anything about that. I mean, your best friend was a lying, murderous bitch—I guess birds of a feather flock together, right? She probably told you all about what she did.'

Kate's eyes flashed. 'That's not true!' she spluttered.

'True or not, you still owe me an apology.' Feeling Warren's hand on my arm, I took a deep, calming breath and continued in more even tones, 'You helped Joyce destroy my reputation.'

'Because you *assaulted my daughter*!'

'Bullshit.' I was conscious of the two kids, who were

staring at me in astonishment. 'You knew it was bullshit and you went after me anyway—thanks to your good pal Joyce. But you know what? I can do without your apology. I'm fine. Better than you, I'm guessing. Now that everyone knows you enabled a killer, things must be pretty tough around here, eh?'

I hadn't laid eyes on Joyce since that day on Finch Island; I'd had no desire to visit her in jail. But for a long, long time I'd been wanting to tell her exactly what I thought of her—and venting at one of her gang was the next best thing.

'I hope you stay here and rot. Just like Krystal. I hope they wheel you out of that shitheap nursing home down there one day and drop you in a hole next to her. Aaron deserves better than this, but you don't. You belong here.'

When I finally finished, there was a short, stunned silence. Then Phoebe shouted, 'Fuck you!'

By that time, however, I was already climbing into Warren's car.

'Well—that was unexpected,' he said as we drove away.

'It was awesome.' Aaron was wearing a broad grin; I could see it in the rear-view mirror. 'You're a legend, Rob.'

'Not really.' I felt ashamed for attacking Kate in front of her daughter. 'I should have had more self-control.'

'It was her fault,' Aaron pointed out. 'She was the one who threatened me.'

'Yeah, but you were the one who put her back up in the first place,' said Warren.

'So? I was telling the truth. Phoebe pulled some crap and got me in a lot of trouble.' Aaron's smile suddenly dissolved into a familiar scowl. 'I had nothing to do with that fucking stash, but everyone thinks I did.'

'Everyone in Otford, maybe. But who cares?' I turned in my seat to reassure him. 'It doesn't matter because we're leaving Otford.'

'Not if we go this way, we're not,' Aaron said.

He was right. We were heading back into town. I told Warren to make a U-turn and soon we were on the road to Bathurst, arguing about music. *Thanks for visiting Otford,* the sign said. *Please come again.*

Aaron gave it the finger as we sped past.

ACKNOWLEDGMENTS

The author would like to thank Louise Dungate, Justine Jinks, Janine Bellamy, Margaret Connolly and Mandy Brett for their help with this book.